DECODED DOG

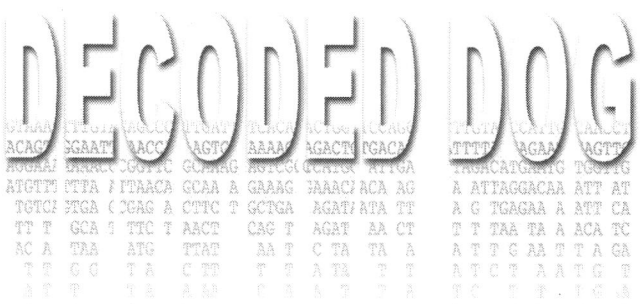

Dianne N. Janczewski

Quo Vadis
Publishing

Decoded Dog

eBook: ISBN 978-0-578-44028-6

Print: ISBN 978-0-578-41765-3

Library of Congress Control Number: 2019900370

Quo Vadis Publishing 1914991

DEDICATION

This book is dedicated to my family.

To my parents who inspired me to be ethical, hardworking, and empathetic, and my siblings who challenge me to be as productive as they are.

To my daughters, Roxanne and Andrea, who provided insight on the thoughts and speak of the new generation, and who keep me focused on what's important.

To my husband Wayne, who encouraged me to continue to work on this book, despite long gaps in motivation; who always made me feel like it was of course going to get finished; and who shares my days, my nights, and my dreams. Thank you for learning to love poodles, and for loving me always.

And to the dogs in my life, past, present, and future, for they complete my family.

PROLOGUE: A PERFECT MOMENT

The softness of her paws on the hardwood floors ruffles the silence of the night. I know it's her by the distinct sound of her gait, and because for thirteen years, this magnificent creature has been my constant companion, my heart-dog. Ania stops at the end of the hall and lifts her head, scanning the living-room for me, then continues her journey. She gently places her front feet on the couch. I lean forward and offer my cheek. She snuffles, content, and climbs up next to me, collecting her legs around her, morphing into a warm, fuzzy ball. But before she tucks in her muzzle like a snow goose in a winter storm, she looks back at me and asks with her big brown eyes, "You okay?" I rest my hand on her, absorbing the calm she radiates. She sighs, curls in, and falls sleep.

I exhale and settle into this perfect moment.

I close my eyes. A kaleidoscope of thoughts spin around in my head creating fleeting patterns, but leaving unanswered questions. None of them seem the right fit. Where is this coming from and how can it be stopped?

Dogs are dying. By the thousands. And no one has figured out why.

FIRST TO FALL

SIX MONTHS AGO.

Like those first few leaves that floated to the ground unnoticed when the season quietly phased into the next, the first dogs fell in late summer. A Pekingese—it was suspected she overheated on the return trip from a local dog show. All attempts to rehydrate her failed. Two weeks later, several hundred miles up the coast, an Irish setter collapsed a few days after earning her final major points at a show sponsored by the Hunt Club. She wasn't even two years old. A leaf here, a leaf there, so many still brilliantly green clinging to the trees. Each one that fell an isolated death of no collective consequence.

The late August air was still hot and thick. Ania and Sofie told me that my homecoming was an occasion to be celebrated, as they showered me with soggy, stuffed-animal gifts. They reminded me to value the return of a pack member.

I passed by the family room and set the groceries on the kitchen counter.

"How was your day?" My hopeful voice added to the noise of the television.

One week until school started. Relief from the boredom and swelter of summer was imminent. Somewhere along the timeline of growing up, a moment slipped by when my children stopped greeting me with the enthusiasm of the dogs.

From the amorphous pile on the couch that resembled my sixteen-year-old daughter Tess, words emerged. "Mama, did you see that story on the news?"

"About the dogs? Yes, I heard it on the radio. Really sad. You're watching the news?"

"Just for a minute. They were showing a picture of a cute dog so I stopped to see it."

"Well, that's a start for becoming worldly. What are they saying now, about the dogs?"

"They said that nine dogs that were at the Balistar Dog Show in New York this weekend died and another two are sick and since they were all at the same dog show they think that someone poisoned them."

"That's not surprising."

"Mom! That's mean."

"I'm not being mean, it's just an unfortunate reality. There have been incidents like that at other dog shows, though I don't think it has ever involved this many dogs all at once."

"Really?"

"Yeah. There's a pretty well-known case of poisoning of an Akita and another dog—I can't remember the breed—at a benched show like Balistar. We went to one like that. Remember? Where all the dogs have to stay in the holding area until the end of the day?"

"Uh-huh, it was kinda cool to see all the dogs up close, especially those giant mastiffs. Their heads were bigger than a basketball."

"I know, and those naked Chinese crested dogs that needed sweaters! But since all those dogs are right there within everyone's reach, I suppose it would be possible for someone to easily slip one a poisoned treat."

"Who would do that?"

"Unfortunately, there are a lot of people who are against the world of dog breeding and showing, who think that animals shouldn't be bred for our entertainment and comfort, and are willing to sacrifice a few to spotlight how bad that world can be for dogs. Or maybe it was someone who didn't want their dog to lose."

"That's so wrong."

"Yes, it is."

"They said that they're bringing in the FBI. They said that some of the dogs are worth a hundred thousand dollars!"

"I guess the FBI has to get involved when there's that much money at stake. I think they also get involved when a crime crosses state lines. If the dogs are traveling for the shows, that would be the case. Balistar is a huge show, so they come in from all over the world."

"How can a dog be worth that much? Is that a lot of money?"

"Yes, dear, it is. One *hundred* dollars is a lot of money. The fact that you don't seem to register that when we're at the mall confirms my failure as a mother. So, I guess it doesn't surprise me that you don't know if a hundred thousand dollars is a lot. But it is. You could buy several cars, fill a house with furniture, or maybe buy a cabin in the woods with that."

"Or a very expensive dog."

"Well, I don't think many people would sell theirs when they reach that level. Champions can bring in a lot of money and make a name for their owners, so owners and even sponsors will invest a lot in their champions for professional handlers, advertisements in the major dog world magazines, stuff like that."

"Every show dog's dream. To be on the cover of a magazine," she crooned as she surfed the channels.

"Sounds kinda silly I guess, but it's important to have your dog seen if you want it to win. By the time a dog makes it to a show like Balistar or Westminster, they've been on the cover of a lot of magazines, and seen by so many of the judges. They're so well-known that there's a huge buzz about them at the show, and they're already favored to win."

"So it's rigged."

"No, not rigged, just an example of good marketing. At the big shows, judges see hundreds of dogs. It helps to know which ones to concentrate on since they have consistently been placed at the top. But even with all the money invested, a dark horse will occasionally win." I chuckled. I thought I was witty.

"Stop, please."

"Thank you. Besides, not every breeder aims for those shows. Most just love their breed and want to produce beautiful examples of it, so they participate in local and regional shows –" And she was texting. "I've lost you, haven't I?"

"Yup."

I couldn't shake the unsettling feeling that there might be some new dog disease on the rise. I researched dog diseases, so I knew the complexities of trying to trace the origins and find a cure. In a lot of ways it would be easier to track some crazy person targeting dog shows. And the truth of the matter is, there were a lot of people who disdained dog shows—and dog breeding in general —so poisoning was a possibility.

We have men's pride to thank for creating the modern dog show in the mid-1800s; men who bred for the best hunting dogs, designed to serve with webbed feet, strong chests, muscular legs, and even coats of hair instead of fur. I could picture them standing on a foggy hill in England's countryside, guns at rest, barking dogs at the ready to chase a terrified fox. "That's a fine hound you've got there, is that from Sir Edmund's sire?" asked one English chap of another. "She is at that. Yours too is rather impressive. What say we have a bit of friendly competition to see whose is the top dog?" Not many years later, fog replaced by billows of cigar smoke in the Westminster Hotel in New York, the Westminster Dog Show was conceived. It continues today, having the distinction of being the second longest running sporting event in the U.S., beat out by only a year by the Kentucky Derby. No different than tennis or NASCAR, dog showing and breeding is a sport, a hobby, a love, with a thriving industry of clubs and events to occupy the enthusiast and captivate the spectator—and draw the ire of detractors.

"What about cats?" Tess spoke again, engaging in a rare, two-part conversation.

"What about cats?" Hope rose in my voice but I stifled it. Teenagers can smell enthusiasm and they reject it as vehemently as any attempt to wave goodbye in front of the school.

"They must have shows too."

"Oh dear Lord, have you ever seen one?"

"Obviously not, if I just asked you if they have them."

"You are merciless. Yes, they have them, but I've only seen a few on TV, and from what I have seen, they are hysterical! They fluff up the cats, then pick them up over their heads and parade them around the room, hoping that the cat won't decide it's had enough and take off! In one show I saw, they had to chase an escapee all over the building. It was quite a spectacle, particularly with the long-haired cats that are fluffed up so much you can't even see their faces."

"Mom, really? As someone who owns poodles, don't you think it ironic that you're making fun?"

"Ah, sarcasm and irony being your best skills, I guess you recognize that." She confirmed my statement with another of her well-honed talents, the teenaged eye roll. "Okay, you have a good point. The parade of poofed out Poodles, Pekingese, and Pyrenees probably proves your point!"

"Oh God, Mom, please stop."

I stared at the bags on the counter dreading the eminent D-word, dinner. I used to love to create an elaborate meal, like conducting a fun science experiment you could eat, but dinner became a chore. I wondered what happened to the Claire who used to be mildly amusing, but now parented by sarcasm. I used to be spontaneous, now I was over-scheduled and harried. I used to love to *feel.* I read poetry and was never without music playing in the background to nourish my soul. My emotions were exposed, on the surface. But somewhere along the way I traded poetry for newspaper headlines, and melody for TV chatter. It became easier to keep all of the adult balls in the air if they were smoothed down with no raw edges.

"You just don't understand!" was a common retort of my children. To them I was decisive, responsible, dogmatic, and unemotional. I was the mom who knew where every missing object was and dutifully cycled laundry, meals, and other acts of love. To others I was the lab director who orchestrated novel research and shaped a new generation of scientists, and to Chris, a wife, a solid partner in a marriage.

But that is not how I saw myself. I saw myself as adapted. I was still passionate, loving, and vulnerable, maybe even more empathetic than when I was younger, but it was all encased in a hard outer shell.

"Settle down," I've told my daughters many times. "It's not such a big deal." "Why do you let that bother you?" Each time those words came out of my mouth, I knew I was shaping the same contained future for them.

I was glued to the news for the next few days, watching as reports came in, hoping that the dog deaths were isolated to the Balistar show. Each story tore a bigger hole in my heart and made me afraid that this was only the beginning. The first was a Labrador named Champion Sterling Heathcliff, aka "Boingo," from Texas. His owner, a big burly guy everyone called Chuck, said he raised him from a pup and gave him the call name Boingo because he looked like he had springs in his feet when he jumped over obstacles in agility trials. Chuck sat on a dock, feet hanging over the side, talking to the reporter. "His favorite thing to do was dock diving," his eyes began to well. "Man, that dog could fly. I've had a lot of dogs in my life, but this one, Boingo . . . he was . . ." He could barely continue. "He was somethin' special." His pain was all too familiar to me, having lost special ones, and knowing that someday Ania would leave me too.

A day later, Boingo's story was followed by one from Kelsie, a teenaged girl who competed as a junior handler from Ohio, with her Schipperke. "I was so excited to make the cut for Balistar," clearly trying to remain stoic. "Phoenix was the first dog my parents let me raise and show completely by myself." Video clips rolled of the two of them from competitions leading up to Balistar, winning title after title, girl and dog moving as one. Kelsie's mom continued, "Phoenix began vomiting on the trip home from the show in New York, and within hours of getting him to our vet, he died in Kelsie's arms." Her daughter buried her face in her mother's shoulder, sobbing. I don't know what was more awful, the loss of their dog, or making the kid sit for the interview.

As the stories continued to surface each day, the mainstream media and even the late-night talk show hosts didn't dare make light of the situation for fear of reprisal from millions of dog owners. But there are always detractors, and online blogs, Twitter, and less diplomatic "news" venues tried to implicate the show dog world, focusing on lavish lifestyles that support the luxury of breeding one hundred thousand-dollar dogs. They had a field day with a beautiful brindle-colored Scottish terrier named Sebastian, whose owner Evelyn raised her dogs on a sprawling New Hampshire estate. While the national media reports angled toward sympathy for her loss, stories posted to Facebook and other social media turned on her. Lead-in footage on her story showed rolling landscapes of bright green, neatly framed in white board fencing that complemented the Dearborn estate house like Mikimoto pearls adorning a plunging neckline. But once the cameras entered her home they mocked her, focusing on the thick mascara running down her face, as she sat on the sofa, surrounded by her remaining dogs perched on fringed pillows. "He was one of my most successful studs" she blubbered, as she stroked a prized female with aged shaky hands weighted by excessive jewelry.

"Well, I can see why it's hard for her to find a good stud!" the commentator snickered.

"Ah but she must be able to find one in that expensive stable of hers!" the other pseudo-reporter responded.

"That's so wrong," my younger daughter Diana said as we sat together at my computer looking for the latest on the dogs, though I wasn't sure if she grasped the double meaning.

"Yes, pretty cruel," trying to scroll past the other sensationalized reports, "I'm sure a lot of people found that funny, but she lost a dog she obviously adored." That was enough for me to reach for the Kleenex and pass the box. "How about we look at a more reputable site for information?"

It was in our search that we stumbled on the details of the Pekingese that died two weeks earlier than the Balistar dogs. "He was like one of those trendy furry balls that girls hang from their purse," his owner Lisa described him, with a faint, melancholy smile, "a round ball of fluff with a cute nose."

Her eight-year-old son jumped in, "And Oscar helped keep the house clean too! He collected anything around the house that wasn't put away and hid it under Mom's bed. If you were missing a sock or a pair of shorts, all you had to do was look in his pile." Now in tears, Lisa wrapped her arms around her son. "There's an emptiness in our house now."

"And a mess," her son added.

Oscar's death would not have even made the news, except that he was a celebrity at The Grinder coffee shop. But the description of how he died seemed to me to be too similar to the others to be a coincidence. He was from the same town as Phoenix.

By the end of the week, twelve more dogs that had attended Balistar had died upon returning home. Each brought a story of careful breeding, excitement, triumph, and utter despair punctuated with a final framed picture of a lost love.

Beyond the sadness of the loss, I was focused on the cause. Was it something toxic in the dog food? Owners are very particular about what they feed their dogs, and there didn't seem to be any consistency in diet based on stories in the news.

Was it poisoning? Since it happened in New York, the New York City Police were joined by the FBI and Balistar's governing body, the American Kennel Club, to figure out if a crime had been committed. In the following weeks, dog shows became circuses of fear.

"It's worse than an airport," one handler complained when asked about the tightening of security at shows. "Handlers, owners, and even the dogs are plastered in barcodes and badges. It took forever just to get in the building 'cause they had to clear our equipment—hair dryers, combs, scissors, all the metal objects they claimed had to be checked by hand, even though those dogs didn't die from a metal object. Just stupid. They should be looking for the person who did this!"

And spectators also complained. "The handlers are so suspicious of everyone." "They used to be so friendly and were happy to tell you all about their dogs and the breeds. Now they practically bite your hand off if you get anywhere near their dogs!"

"We've had so many smaller shows cancelled because they can't afford the extra security," lamented one breeder on the local news.

Intentional act maybe, but my fear was that it was some new disease. Was there a connection to the two earlier deaths? Obviously this was the same concern of the American Veterinary Medicine Association—the AVMA—as they moved to collect medical information from anyone who thought their dogs had died of the same thing. I knew how fast a disease could surge, how some could take forever to fully understand—human AIDS came to mind—while others were relatively fast to address. In the 1970s, parvovirus was a relatively new disease, and when it hit, it rapidly killed off large numbers of dogs, particularly puppies. But barely ten years later, local vets had a vaccine to offer pet owners. It was impressive how quickly the cause was found and a vaccine was developed, but not before thousands of animals were lost.

But the weeks went on, investigations into the Balistar show deaths were inconclusive, and no more cases were reported. I breathed easier, thinking that it might be an isolated incident, and refocused my daily scanning of news and science publications on things related to my own research. A last, short-lived current of warmer days washed over the East Coast, staving off thoughts of the coming cold and torrent of falling leaves. The media lost interest and the story faded in fickle, short-attention-span America.

DOG DAYS

ANIA PRANCED up the hill, grinning as she led the way. Sofie charged from behind to take the lead. Feet momentarily lighting on the ground, they jointly sprang forward in a rhythmic gallop. Sofie would have smiled too if it weren't for the tennis ball in her mouth. I watched from the front window as the human love of my life, Chris, brought up the rear, paper in hand, completing the ritual that each morning bonds him and his shadows, as he calls them. The dog beat him to the house, as usual, bouncing trampoline dogs on their powerful standard poodle legs.

Chris drew his arm overhead ready to throw as Sofie bolted halfway back down the hill in her impatience, abruptly stopped, and frantically searched back and forth, while Ania stood rigid as she tracked the ball's trajectory before vaulting towards its predicted landing. Ania trotted back with her prize raised triumphantly, dropping it at Chris' feet. Again, she watched him intently, as Sofie barreled down the hill, turning when she heard the ball thump in the underbrush. They both dove in, only their wagging tails visible in the tall grass.

I envisioned minuscule particles of gooey tennis ball happily floating in the air until they were sucked into the dog's nostrils, and tumbled into the labyrinth of three hundred million smell receptors in the dog's astounding olfactory system. The exquisitely evolved scrollwork pattern on the front of their noses allowed them to draw in new particles through the center orifice, while pushing the outgoing air through the side slits, thus avoiding disruption of previously inhaled particles dancing around the receptors, and adding new data with each rapid sniff. Each nostril wiggled independently, speaking to a separate part of the brain telling which side smelled stronger, which smell was newer—clues to determine which direction the smell was heading. Both dogs knew the world through their noses. And found balls. Ania emerged triumphant once again.

The house came alive when they entered. Eight paws, two feet, like raindrops randomly spattering on the kitchen floor. The dogs' bodies were in full-on greeting mode, squirming against my legs, snorting, presenting their muzzles to be kissed and rubbed. They panted loudly around their mouthful of toys. They filled the space and my world with life.

"Morning Claire!" Chris mimicked their wiggle and tousled my hair, "Are you going with a matching your dog's look?"

My shoulder-length, unruly spirals of mutt-brown hair was typically collected and secured with a clip, comb, stick, scrunchie, or hair tie – depending on my ever-changing connection to a particular decade. I often woke with the finger-in-the-light-socket look, this morning having made no attempt to tame the beast, I especially resembled an unkempt poodle.

"Good morning." I half grinned, momentarily connecting when I saw his smile and felt his warmth. "I find even this do a challenge without coffee."

"Ah." He embraced me and I lost myself in the comforting smell of his slept-in tee shirt. There is a strength he exudes, from his slender, tall build, but more from his quiet, circumspect demeanor —I found solace until the day's demands tugged at me. Accepting the fleeting connection, Chris and his shadows retreated to the study.

The girls off to school, Chris pulled into his work on the computer, I stood in the bathroom subjected to the cruelty of a row of bright lights and three-quarter length mirror glaring at me. Slender lines had started to invade the contours of my face, and the shifting dimensions of my frame were a consequence of serving as a human incubator, twice. But I grinned, slightly, comfortable with my evolving self.

Despite the battles with my hair when I was younger, I'd grown to like it. It went well with my hazel eyes and olive skin. My Spanish conquistador look, Chris observed, as I stood firmly on the bow of his boat a lifetime ago.

I opted for my dress jeans and untucked, button down shirt instead of a casual summer dress. There's an unpretentiousness about working in a university lab, constrained not by business norms, but by lab safety requirements, which mostly limited my choice of shoes to the practical, not fashionable. Or, as my daughter so lovingly put it, 'fatigue-chic'.

So, not trendy or fashionable. Except for my glasses. Having been burdened with them since the sixth grade, I've embraced their presence, turning my collection of frame colors and styles into an expression of my mood and attitude. Feeling positive and hopeful, today was a fun turquoise cat-eye I found on a vintage frames store online.

As I biked in I thought of the poor owners of the dogs that died after the dog show a few weeks ago. If it had been one of my dogs I would have been devastated, frantic not knowing what happened, and afraid my other dog might die too. I felt their broken hearts.

While my personal time is spent in the company of dogs and my hobby is the careful breeding of dogs, my career time is spent looking at their genes and trying to figure out what might cause a seemingly normal dog to develop Addison's disease. My company in the lab, Megan and Jamie, are my graduate students, whose lives revolve around an intensified, concentrated effort towards their own distinctive research discoveries in dog disease-related genes. We are well matched in our collective quest.

"Hey, how are the cells growing?" I asked Megan.

"Slow, painfully slow. But growing."

"Well at least that's in the right direction. I guess the extra serum did the trick." I dumped my computer bag and lunch on a chair, countertops being restricted to research activities. Megan's area was as neatly organized as an Ikea catalog. "I always find it amazing that every species' cells need something a little different. You would think that all mammals would grow in the same media, but I guess since they need different temperatures, they can be picky about what we feed them too." Megan stood up, silent, so I could peer into the microscope at the spider-like cells in their flask.

"When I was in graduate school we had a devil of a time trying to get exotic cat cells to grow," I adjusted the focus. "We found that they liked horse serum over bovine—"

And there they went. Out of the corner of my eye I could see Jamie scrolling on his computer, and Megan looking over her notes; my reluctant audience tried to look busy. I was lecturing again. They'd probably heard this one already and were hoping desperately that I'd lose interest if I didn't get any feedback. Grad students were worse than my family. They didn't even love me, just tolerated me because I kept them employed and bought them an occasional beer.

"Where's Kate?" I asked.

"She called, said she would be late. She had to wait for her boyfriend to get home from the gym to take their dog to the vet. I fed the cells for her." Megan's competitive nature prompted her to note the extra work she did, though it wasn't necessary, she was kick-ass talented and dedicated.

"Oh geez, is the dog okay?"

"Apparently not. The dog started throwing up last night, and won't stop," Megan explained.

"It's too small to have bloat, isn't it?"

Jamie jumped in. "Yeah, it's a scrappy-looking mixed breed. Looks like a yappy little creature. It's the one in the picture taped to the hood." He gestured with his head over his shoulder. "Wouldn't have the chest capacity to allow the stomach to twist and flip."

Jamie was always unsympathetic to our research subjects. He wasn't into the organism as a whole, but he was a master at the bench and he knew every disease and ailment in the domestic dog, so I couldn't ask for much more. He was in it purely for the science. He had no pets.

"Maybe Kate's dog has the same thing that the dogs got at the Balistar show and it'll be put out of its misery soon," Jamie's widened his eyes. "We could use it to study whatever is killing them." I wasn't sure he was joking.

"Okay, now you're just being ugly. Unless the dog was in New York that weekend, I doubt it. And besides, you said it was a mixed breed. Hardly the kind that Balistar allows. And there haven't been any more cases that we know of. I wouldn't be surprised if some nut job poisoned them to accomplish some twisted agenda."

"Damn, nothing cool to research with that." Jamie feigned disappointment.

"You really have a one-track mind don't you?" Megan piped up. "And it is not of the typical male grad student kind."

"Oh, I have that too, Megan. I can multi-task just like you

women claim to be so good at. Science and sex share equal importance in my thoughts and activities."

"Well, at least I'm better at English! And I'm well aware of your little late-night side interests in the lab with that biochem grad student. Certainly demonstrates your priorities." Megan quickly lifted her hands off the lab bench. "Ew."

"Out of the gutter please," I interrupted. "Can we get back to the task at hand? What did you guys find out with regard to the sequence variants that we saw last week in the Addison's dog families?"

"I'm still looking at the SNPs, as there are a fair number of these small sequence differences, but I haven't worked through all of them to see if the correlate." Jamie pulled his attention from his computer. "But the microsatellite sequences are a dead end, I think. Turns out that they show up in DNA in a bunch of other related, but unaffected groups. But hey, maybe we'll help decipher the convoluted pile of genes and alleles that make up all the poodle colors."

"Not a chance," I turned away from his work area. "And since our grants are for studying Addison's, let's stick to that." I turned to Megan, "Please tell Kate I'm fine with her staying with the dog all day."

I headed into my office to go over my lecture notes for my Genetics and Endocrinology course. The semester had started, and after the first couple of lectures on endocrinology when a number of students who were not impressed with the subject matter—or me—dropped the class, I gave a more interesting lecture on the relevance of the field to real-life problems. Of course, since Addison's disease is an example of how the beautiful orchestration of communication between cells can go awry, the captive students were subjected to a lecture on the target of my research.

I started with an overview on the hypothalamic–pituitary–

adrenal, or HPA, system, more commonly referred to as the fight-or-flight response. When our brain perceives a danger or a threat, in a split second it chemically and electrically communicates with the adrenal glands, which respond by releasing over thirty different hormones, including adrenaline, causing the whole body to spring into action.

Then I gave them the fun facts. If all goes right, these hormones cause different changes in different cells. The heart starts to pound to process more oxygen and increase the metabolism for more energy. Goosebumps pop up due to skin surface muscles tensing as the rest the body's muscles prepare to bolt. That feeling when everything seems to be moving in slow motion in a stressful situation like a car accident? It's due to increased blood flow to the brain that intensifies concentration. Even the shiver down the spine that accompanies fear is due to an adrenal hormone that results in constriction of skin surface arteries to push blood to where it is needed more. Like a flash of lightning, the whole system is set ablaze.

Those with Addison's disease, both humans and dogs, have at least one dysfunctional or non-functional adrenal gland, resulting in an inability to react properly to stress. Without the adrenal gland, they suffer from fatigue, muscle weakness, and countless other debilitating symptoms. Often called the "great pretender", these symptoms often come and go, in different combinations, presenting as a myriad of other possible diseases until an Addison's *crisis* results in complete collapse, which can quickly become fatal. It's treatable if caught in time, but so far no genetic marker has been found, and there is no cure. I walked the students through our research and how we search for genetic factors by comparing DNA from families of dogs with affected and unaffected individuals.

I didn't need my notes, this was in my blood.

I quickly glanced at the news feed on my computer. More dogs lost at shows in New England, and a theory circulating that it was a new form of Lyme disease caused by a mutated bacterium.

I joined Jamie to look at results of DNA sequencing. "I'm not convinced this is anything important," he folded his arms. The power of statistical significance loomed over our hopeful first-blush observations.

Jamie's forté was data analysis. He was a stickler for strict interpretation of the data and didn't get excited over a potential lead until he'd gnawed on it like a dog with a bone. He'd been with me for two years, coming off a few years of seeing the world after finishing his undergraduate degree. I was still floored by his ability to know when the data meant nothing or when a subtle observation would turn into a major finding. I'd learned not to question his silence or seeming lack of participation in meetings and to take notice when, after everyone else was out of ideas and he leaned forward offering, "Y'know, if we just …" He had a killer instinct when it came to knowing what was worth pursuing.

Twenty-five and uber-smart, Jamie chose the scruffy scientist look over the together metrosexual nerd, but he was anything but laid back and aloof. First impressions can be burdensome. "Are you going to the Department picnic?" I had asked him at the beginning of his first semester with me.

"No. Not my thing," he answered. "Not a fan of people's party personalities." I learned quickly what he meant. No matter how he played it, he was dealt a full hand that made many desire him, while others envious.

"Is Mr. Jamie here?" The co-eds would start calling like clockwork once the semester started. As my Teaching Assistant, he was required to keep office hours for student questions. Little did they know he saw the tweets.

When the new hot guy turns out to be my TA! OMFG!!!

TA's big brown eyes, curly brown hair, and sexy crooked smile... think I need some tutoring!!!

He was uncomfortable with all the female adulation, and he was often outwardly unsettled when they peeked their heads into the lab "just to say hi." The few women I met whom he dated seemed to be more interested in their work than him, a mutual non-commitment that seemed to suit him fine. I gathered that his respect for women came from having three sisters and a close relationship with his mom.

"Do you happen to know where's the best place to order flowers?" he asked me one day. "My little sister broke up with her boyfriend and she's a mess," he offered to my inquiring look.

I felt affection for him as the son I'd never had. I was old enough to be his mother—barely, mind you—and while his groan-inducing double entendre and sharp wit were so nuanced it kept me on my intellectual toes, I got why he was tucked behind his carefully crafted persona.

Curiously, he and Megan's banter had an undertone of sexual innuendo that reminded me of my graduate school days with Neil.

My cell phone buzzed, I headed to my office to answer it, and everyone scurried off to their bench areas, staked out by arrangements of reagents, supplies and equipment. Anna, my research collaborator and best friend, wanted to do lunch. She was convinced that we should apply for more funding based on our latest cohort of samples.

Anna and I met in college.

Her room was at the end of our hall. She was smart and engaging, with carefully chosen words that left you wanting to hear more. And she was stunning. Perfect, creamy skin, with auburn hair, sparkling green eyes, and a sprinkling of freckles. Long legs contributed to her five-foot nine inch arresting stature, towering over my five-foot five average everything. I was drawn to her, wanted to be in her circle. She was breezy and friendly, and entranced students buzzed around her like bees to honey. I held back to avoid getting stung.

It wasn't until we had a semester under our belts that we connected.

The first day back from break, Sunday, it snowed in the morning, blanketing the campus in white glimmering speckles that smiled in the afternoon sun. Sidewalks were hidden, the bushes made soft lumps under the covers, and conversations were muffled as we settled in to start the next term. Roommates huddled in their rooms sharing vacation stories and modeling Christmas presents.

The first day of class was dreary and overcast; the snow had turned to gray slush that lay dying on the streets. Each academic building greeted us with a wet, dirty entrance; sloppy footprints left by oversized winter boots trailed down the halls. "Welcome back," the doors cragged as they slammed shut behind us.

But the dreary quickly brightened as I entered my biology class. Anna sat front and center, with one empty seat beside her. Mine to claim. I slid in. "How was your vacation?" I asked.

"Great, mostly family stuff. We spent a week skiing in Vermont. But it was so hard to leave. My dog is old and I don't think she'll be there the next time I go home." I could see the pain in her eyes, but she brightened and asked me about my break.

"It was great. I have dogs too, three of them. My mom breeds poodles and the puppies are always fun—well, at least until they get teeth. I'm bummed though. I'll be here when the next litter is born. And this will be Abby's last litter."

"Oh, that *is* a bummer. Puppies, how sweet, I'd love to see pictures!" No cell phones back then, so we stopped by my room after class to go through my box of puppy photos I kept on hand for down moments. She told me she liked my glasses. "Are they new?" she asked. They were, and she had noticed.

Two weeks later she stood in the doorway of my room, barely able to speak, her face red and wet with tears. "My mom called. She had to put Penny down." We walked for hours in the cold, cried together, and laid the foundation to be best friends. The dog bond is strong, even when it's person to person.

It took time, but I came to know Anna well. Though it seemed as if she knew everyone and everyone knew her, it was all an illusion brought on by everyone's wish to know her. In reality, she was confident, looked you in the eyes and said hello, but she was very private. She kept everyone at bay, engaging in and eliciting small talk by asking about their lives. Distracted by self-absorption, they never noticed she revealed little about herself.

We roomed together over the next three years. Both majoring in Biology, we planned classes together and scheduled a rotation of days off when the other one would take notes. We spent summers together, fell in love with the wrong men, comforted each other with potato chips, sappy movies, and bitch sessions, and held on tight as the world around us spun. We listened to Little Feat, watched Mork and Mindy, and covered for each other—bad dates, meddling parents, nosy students, lecherous professors—we had each other's back. When Anna was accepted to vet school I felt like a parent: so excited for her, and proud to have been part of her success. We drove down to Virginia Tech a month before school started to find her a place to live. We hiked the Blue Ridge, went tubing on the New River, and said goodbye knowing it would never be the same.

"I can't imagine not spending every day with you," I felt

weighed down by the reality. "Who's gonna actually think I'm funny?"

"I know! I keep thinking, who's going to let me have the last scoop of ice cream in the box? And will I just be eating the whole carton myself? Am I going to get fat because you're gone?" She looked startled with the realization.

We both laughed as we acknowledged that we had, as usual, both had the same thought.

It would never be the same with Anna and me, but in many ways it became better as we grew into our careers and ourselves. She finished vet school, moved to a small town in Virginia, and went to work for a small animal vet who was willing to mentor her. When he retired, as luck would have it—okay, maybe that's not the right way to put it—but at just about the same time, her grandmother passed away and she bought the practice from him with her small inheritance. I fell a few years behind her trying to get a job with a BS in Biology; a tough road for even those who are really bright, unlike I. Finally I settled into graduate school.

It was an exciting time when breakthrough technologies in genetics were just being invented. PCR amplification—the ability to rapidly duplicate small pieces of DNA in a test tube—opened the door for a slew of new analyses. Within ten years the stage would be set for determining the entire sequence of DNA for an individual species—the genome—hundreds of thousands to billions of bases long. The promise of a DNA blueprint would significantly aid in discovering the genetic causes of diseases and revolutionize the field of medicine, making it even harder for me to decide what I wanted to be some day.

So I thought I'd start with what I loved, dogs, and managed to make my way to a lab where the study of canine evolution was booming. Unfortunately, once I got there I found out that other, more senior graduate students and postdocs had dibs on all the dog work. So I was assigned research to determine the evolutionary relationships between the thirty-seven species in the Felidae family. I couldn't imagine it going anywhere, but tried to find an interest in cats. After all, DNA all looked the same, whether a glob of goo on the end of a glass rod or on the computer screen as a string of As, Cs, Ts, and Gs. But the mere mention outside of the lab about my work invariably brought out anecdotal stories of pet cats. "You work on cats? Oh my Jasper is so funny, he always wakes me by smacking my face!" I grinned politely, and tried to appreciate what cats gave to their owners. I had never owned a cat and was admittedly ignorant of their value, and often wondered if I was missing out on something. I did get to trek through the jungle to help collect field samples with some of the exotic cat researchers, and their dedication shed light on the wonders of the cat family. But was a dog person.

To survive graduate school, the long laboratory research hours, the coursework, and the demands of my major professor and committee members, I got my first standard poodle, Izzy. Having grown up with a miniature, I knew I needed the intellect of a poodle, but I wanted something more substantial to wrap my arms around. When Izzy was around two years old my temporary roommate sought comfort at the animal shelter in the form of a big, sweet mutt. Izzy was not happy, but more than that, she began to slip away. Ever so slightly at first, she became more snuggly, more sensitive, less interested in food. Within a week she crashed, barely able to lift her head, and I was lucky enough to have a vet who instantly knew what was wrong when I described the symptoms and she looked at the breed. Addison's had been slowly destroying her adrenal gland, and the stress of a new dog accelerated full onset.

The diagnosis of Addison's involved injecting the brain chemical, ACTH, that stimulates the adrenal glands, and measuring the production of adrenaline in response. Within a week of treatment she was back to normal, but she would need monthly injections of replacement hormones to substitute for cortisol, and a daily dose of prednisone to help balance blood potassium and sodium for the rest of her life. Maintaining the required low-stress lifestyle was the easy part, as she had a gentle personality that enticed everyone to open a spot on the couch for her.

As I neared the end of graduate school, Izzy's disease gave me purpose. "I'm thinking about going into Addison's research," I told Anna.

"I'm in! I'll get samples from my patients, and get my colleagues to do the same, and we can apply for grants!"

I eventually established my independence at the university with a grant for a postdoc from a veterinary pharmaceutical company that makes Addison's treatment drugs. Anna and I were named as co-principal investigators.

Anna was my best friend, the first one I told my secrets to. The first one I told about Chris.

Landing in Los Angeles from Malaysia, I had a six-hour layover until my morning flight home. Anna would not forget to pick me up, but I had to call her anyway, had to tell her.

"Anna, pick up the phone! Are you there?" Her answering machine patiently recorded my frantic message. "Anna, I have to. ."

"Of course I'm here, it's the middle of the night. Are you okay?"

"Oh yeah, hi, just wanted to make sure you'll be there to meet me, and I have to tell you … Uh, sorry, how are you?"

"I was asleep. Nice try, yes, I'll be there, and you have to tell me what?" Maybe I should have called Neil instead, I thought. He was a night owl.

"That I have met the most amazing man, on an island in the middle of the ocean . . ."

"Um, okay. I must be dreaming—or you are. That couldn't wait a few hours? Should I pour myself some coffee?"

Obviously I hadn't thought this through. I had to tell her the moment I got home, and for me that meant the moment my feet were back in the States. I didn't factor in the West Coast layover, the time difference, and the hours left still to travel. It would have cost way too much to explain it all on the phone, and I didn't have that much change, but now she was awake and not likely to go back to sleep.

"Guess I just wanted to share."

"Uh-huh. "

Trying to justify myself, "if I were there I would have been knocking on your door right now."

"And you would have gotten the same sleepy response."

"Okay, so go back to sleep."

"How about you just set the scene for me and tell me the rest on the long ride home."

And there she was, standing at the back of the crowd as I came through security, holding what used to be a big sunflower, its dead eye hanging towards the floor surrounded by limp dark yellow eyelashes.

"For me?!" I smiled brightly. "How beautiful and thoughtful."

"Yes, I brought it to reflect my enthusiasm for your homecoming." She handed it to me as it flopped over.

For the next two hours I talked and she listened. She always knew when to validate, when to offer fixes, and when to stop the crazy. She was silent mostly, asking a question here and there. Then she turned on me.

"So let me get this straight. You met the perfect guy half way around the world who lives on the East Coast, somewhere in Virginia, but he never gave you his contact information, nor did you give him yours. He claims to have spent the last year sailing around the world, meeting all kinds of people, including, he modestly admitted, many women who he managed to not have sex with until he met you, conveniently at the end of his year-long boondoggle. And now, you think that it would be a good idea to pay this guy a visit, uninvited, to see if you can recreate the unimaginable fantasy of your romantic four-day tryst on a tropical island. And somehow this new romance will fit right in with your finishing your graduate degree."

"You are a dream crusher."

"And you are an unrealistic hopeless dreamer, but I love you anyway."

"You too."

We went silent, me not wanting to admit that she was right, she having said enough.

"Geez," Anna finally said in an I'm-rolling-my-eyes-at-you tone. "Why can't you just accept that it was a wonderful experience that you'll always remember fondly? Why does it have to be something more?"

"I don't know, Catholic guilt?" I suggested.

"You're not a practicing Catholic anymore"

"Yes, but it's like being an alcoholic, you never leave it behind completely. So I'm a recovering Catholic." As I acquiesced to her truth my shoulders dropped slightly. "I guess I just want to continue believing in spontaneous generation of love."

"Pasteur disproved that long ago. There is nothing there. It was a wonderful, fleeting moment. Move on."

"Pasteur's research only applied to maggots. And you, have you taken your own advice? You've been rather silent this whole way about your escapades while I was gone. What's the status with Greg?"

"I have been silent because you haven't stopped talking," gently reminding me of my bad habit of taking advantage of her polite silences. "Done, gone, moved on. At least he has. Saw him the other day at Morgan's sharing a dessert with his latest."

"Really? Do you know her? Did he see you? Did it bother you?"

"I don't care. Really. It actually didn't bother me like I thought it would. Surprised me, but didn't bother me."

Anna was destined to be single. I often wondered how it was that we could be so close; she let me know everything she was thinking, told it like it was, but she could never do the same with men. She suffered from having an aloof father, whom she always tried to please, and managed to find and fall for men of the same type. Men who liked the idea of a relationship, particularly at the beginning when she was there to please, but the backpedaling always seemed to start when she showed the slightest sign of needing them, rare as that was. She would finally open the door a crack and invite them in, and they would wonder what happened to the woman who needed nothing from them, as they bolted for the door. A man who wanted an equal partner in both intellect and need would be perfect, but those never seemed to find a way into her life.

I would eventually marry, have two beautiful daughters, and live the family life. Anna did marry, briefly, then found solace in her practice.

Together we would take on a killer disease, or two.

I sat quietly in my office waiting for my daughter Tess. Jamie and Megan were entranced in their work, and I perused the internet looking for any news of more cases of dog show-related deaths. Nothing since the initial reports three weeks ago.

Having successfully indoctrinated at least one of our daughters into considering a career in science, it was a proud mom moment last spring when she came bounding into the kitchen with an Eppendorf vial containing a white glob of her DNA floating in alcohol hanging on a yarn necklace. "Look at me!" she announced, holding it up.

But her high school couldn't afford to take them much beyond the basics in molecular biology, so being the pushy mom that I am, I connected her to a lab at the university willing to help her come up with a project for this year's science fair. Since the beginning of August, she had donned a lab coat once a week and become a university researcher, creating a new bond between us.

Like a refreshing gust of wind she blew through the lab entry. "Mom! Look what I made!" she announced as she excitedly shoved a picture at me—a close up, 4x6 color photo of a beautiful *Drosophila melanogaster* head. Her creation, a red-eyed, straight-winged, fruit fly with legs growing out of its head where its antennae should be.

"Ah, learning to play God are you?"

"Mom, staaahp, this is so cool. Did you know that *Drosophila* have these cassettes of genes called homeoboxes? They're kind of like train cars that each make up a different segment of the fly, and you can turn them off and on, and rearrange them to make antennae grow out of their heads, or double sets of wings, or . . ."

"Not to be a mutant crusher my love, but you know that that is not the intended purpose of genetic research, right?"

"Yeah, I get that it's kind of icky, but it's so cool how you can see the how the promoter region of the gene acts like a switch, and just by blocking it at the right time, the segment gets messed up! There're so many genes and promoter switches. So many places where things can get screwed up. It's amazing that anything ever comes out normal!"

I gave her language a pass since she was parroting her mother. I could see Megan and Jamie eavesdropping through spaces between reagent bottles.

"So I guess you'll never see those little buggers flying around our bananas the same way again."

"I know! They've been studied for over 100 years and they're the best understood animal model and research on them has shown how genes are organized and inherited and expressed! They've been used to study development, neurology, immunology ..."

"And they're the only animal model you're allowed to work on for the science fair."

"Actually, I could have done Planaria but who wants to sit and watch a flatworm grow a new butt? *Drosophila* are so perfect. Short lifespan, easy to raise, simple inheritance."

"Speaking of promoters, did you learn about the TATA box?"

"You mean the DNA sequence at the beginning of most promoters?"

I nodded.

"I did, but you know homeoboxes don't have those, right?" Tess sounded appalled at my potential ignorance.

"Yeah, so I'm surprised you learned about them, but glad. They're fairly common."

"I think Mathew, the creepy graduate student I told you about, just wanted to say TATA in front of me. But I just listened and didn't give him the satisfaction of reacting." She looked me straight on and genuinely hugged me. "Thanks, Mom."

As we walked to the car, Tess chatted non-stop, alternating between a budding scientist and teenaged whack-a-mole. I contemplated the emerging young woman beside me, as I moved in slow motion to register this milestone.

"So Mom, I know that *Drosophila* are a lot simpler than a dog, but why is it so difficult to find the gene for Addison's if you have so many samples of dogs with it?"

"For starters, dogs have fifteen times the number of bases in their DNA—two and a half billion, and close to twenty thousand protein coding genes—nearly double the number in *Drosophila*."

"Yeah, but still there are so many laboratory techniques and computer algorithms," spoken as a scientist.

"And, Addison's is likely either be multi-genic, meaning caused by interaction of multiple genes—"

"I know what that is, Mom," spoken as a teenager.

"Or it could result from mutations that occur at a number of sites along a gene, so it's not caused by the same thing in every animal. Or both multi-genic and multi-site. Not to mention that in higher animals like the dog, there's a larger proportion of DNA that doesn't directly code for a protein, but instead controls expression, or may just maintain order in the DNA so everything can interact directly. There's a lot more, as in millions of bases, for your generation to still figure out."

"Higher animals, Mom?"

I smiled at her attempt to express her liberal, anti-Classist foundation. It was refreshing in its raw form.

TUMBLING SLOWLY

ANIA AND SOFIE sat, side-by-side at the top of the hill. Alert, ears twitching, adjusting to pinpoint each sound. Silently they watched the day flow by, the wind and birds teasing with sporadic flutters. Only the occasional herd of deer in the early evening was worth a bark, and even then, they rarely bolted for the chase. Creatures of habit, their daily routine varied only to match the season. Cooler days shifted their duty to watching squirrels plant future generations of trees. Dog TV. Their view was flowing, as the hill rolled down to the open field, falling off at the creek, and climbing back up from the other bank until it crested above their line of sight. A lone sycamore tree down in the field of green grass gone blonde prepared to mute its leaves to the color of butterscotch. They sat, the two of them side-by-side, lording over their territory, until they were drawn by a human voice.

Mid-September, just as complacency set in, seventeen more dogs died after two dog shows in Maryland and Pennsylvania, and the dog world perked its ears again. As the warm days dissipated and the nights chilled, bold colors emerged. Shades of amber, yellow and red painted the landscape so vibrant that everyone stopped, everyone noticed, and each of us felt the emerging chill and the closing in of the shortened days. As if on cue, the crescendo of the fall palette suddenly shifted to ugly; leaves shriveled and tumbled to the ground en masse. The wind grabbed and swirled them up, tossed them aside where they lay dead and scattered on the ground, composting to dust. The dog leaves too began to fall in droves, stripping the warmth from the hearts of those bonded to their special brand of love. It was cold and bare without them.

The first week of October, on opposite coasts, new incidents at nine more shows loomed ominously. News media called it the "show-dog syndrome," eager to invent a ratings-grabber headline that was punctuated by tacky graphics; much like they did in the early part of the AIDS epidemic, referring to it as the homosexual-Haitian-hemophiliac disease. The AVMA preferred a symptom-based naming system, flooding the airwaves with Canine Rapid Fading Syndrome—CRFS—which finally won out. As with AIDS, the word "syndrome" was used because it involved a variety of possible symptoms, and it was still not known whether this was caused by an external factor such as a bacterium or virus, or an internal factor like an autoimmune response, or whether it even fit the loose definition of a disease—an abnormal condition of the body or part thereof.

All eyes were on the purebred dog world. Headlines splashed "Only purebred dogs fall victim to CRFS!" and "Genetic defects finally take down purebred dogs."

One of the quasi-news outlets featured an "expert" who declared, "Well, we've been saying this all along. Mutts on average live much longer than purebred dogs. I had one that lived to be seventeen!" Another grabbed her fifteen minutes of fame by declaring, "Those purebreds are so highly inbred, they have all kinds of problems. It's no surprise to me that they're getting knocked out by some new disease. Thank goodness we have mixed breeds."

Though no actual data or studies were ever cited, verification of facts no longer seemed to be the standard for reporting. Meanwhile breed organizations and the scientific community countered in vain that there was no consensus of scientific studies that supported claims of genetic inferiority or susceptibility of purebred dogs. It was moot though—without a known cause, the show dog world was uneasy and under a public microscope.

Conspiracy advocates theorized that terrorists were killing dogs to target the hearts of Americans. That they developed a new virus or agent just for canines. If that was true, they were more cunning than our government could ever imagine. With more than seventy-five million dogs in the US alone, and over 35% of households having a dog, the devastating impact of an attack on our inter-species soul mates would be unimaginable, and brilliant.

Blustery fall days spun leaves in a cyclone of brown. Gray branches and scantily clad trees stood bracing for the winter as the air turned cold. Eighty-six more dogs died. Dog leaves lay in dead piles.

I was in early. So was everyone else.

Walking into the lab, one was blinded by the bright, ceiling-to-bench windows on the opposite wall, and it took a moment to adjust and focus on the two rows of black granite lab benches running perpendicular to the window, each with open shelves stacked with supplies. The tissue culture and chemical hoods lined the right-side entry wall, the left housed bright chrome wire shelves of clean and sterile glassware, and loosely arranged boxes of pipettes, beakers, well plates, and bags of microtubes. My office was carved out of the far-left windowed corner.

I headed to my space, dumped my bag and walked back into the lab to the giant whiteboard on the wall next to the door. Megan, Jamie, and Kate all stopped what they were doing and waited for me to speak. Normally exuding confidence and a sense of invincibility, they looked more like hopeful but worried dogs watching the ritual of their human packing the car.

"I guess you've all been listening to last night's news," I picked up and uncapped a marker. "We need to do some major brainstorming."

"You think we can get some funding to work on this?" Kate asked. Though she wasn't a graduate student, she knew that even a technician's position required successive funding through "soft" grant money.

"I don't know. I don't even know if we even want to work—"

"We have to work on this!" Megan interrupted.

Jamie and Kate jumped in "Yeah!" "We can't ignore this!" "This is going to be very big, and cool!"

"Okay folks, then anyone got any ideas on what angle we might explore? One that won't take away from our Addison's work? There's a lot of competition for the samples from the dogs, and limited funding, and not very many clues on what needs to be researched." I cleared the scribbles from the whiteboard that filled the wall by the door. "Let's start with what we know."

"It affects only purebred dogs." Jamie remarked blandly.

"Oh dear Lord, really?" giving him my best incredulous teenage act. "What anti-purebred group have you joined? You want to rephrase that?"

It was a pet peeve of mine when someone jumped to a conclusion based on simple association. We called it the pantyhose-cancer connection. Since most people who get breast cancer wear pantyhose, then it must mean that pantyhose cause breast cancer, right? No. There's a huge difference between association, correlation, and cause.

Jamie cringed. "Sorry. So far, only purebred dogs have been affected and—"

"Only dogs at dog shows have been affected, thus only purebred dogs at dog shows have been exposed," Megan interjected, rocketing to the front of her class.

"Or so we think," Jamie stood. "We don't know if there are isolated cases here and there that aren't noticed because they don't have an obvious connection."

Good point. I drew a big circle labeled dog shows, and a smaller inner circle, purebreds. "What else?"

Kate joined in. "They haven't found signs of poison, have they?"

I drew a line down the center of the board. "I haven't seen any reports, but I'm not sure they've ruled out anything." Megan and Jamie shook their heads in agreement. "Okay, we'll put that over here in the possible, but out of our bailiwick column. But that brings up a good point. Since our research is geared towards genetic research, what's a plausible explanation for why we think the cause might be caused by something live—a bacteria, virus, or fungi."

Crickets.

"Come on guys, think about the three possible transmission routes—inhalation, injection, or ingestion."

"Well if it was injection, wouldn't there have been some evidence?" Kate asked.

"I don't mean injection with a needle. Bloodborne diseases like HIV can be transmitted by coming in contact with the blood stream through open cuts or sores, which is considered *injection*. But I think you're right, someone would have seen evidence of injection as show dogs are so carefully groomed." I sat down on a stool. "Look, it's likely that a lot of proposals will involve looking for a DNA or protein signature from the causative agent, which is also what we will do. But what might set us apart is if we can demonstrate some due diligence by suggesting possible sources and thus routes of infection that would support looking for telltale signs of a foreign organism." I could see them bracing for my lecture. "Back in the 70s when the first known outbreak of Legionnaires disease occurred it took almost six months to identify a bacterium as the causative agent. That was after chasing all kinds other potential causes—including toxins and viruses—from a myriad of sources until it was found in the air conditioning system. They didn't know what they were looking and the shotgun approach didn't help quell the panic. We have an advantage here in that there were multiple venues and we can look for commonalities of potential sources and routes." They still didn't look convinced. 'So if this is a live agent, what are the potential sources? Think about where the incidents took place."

"We already have dog shows," Jamie pointed to the board.

"*Where* these took place," I prompted.

"You mean the convention center," Megan stood.

"Yes. What are some variables connected with each venue?"

"Environmental factors!" Kate shouted. Jamie's hand shot up for a high five.

"Right, such as . . ."

"Air, water," Jamie said. "Inhalation and ingestion."

"Ventilation systems, like with Legionella." Megan added. "But I guess I just don't see how this is helpful. Both viruses and bacteria can be inhaled. Anthrax, the flu. So what does it matter if we think it was harbored in the ventilation systems and inhaled as an airborne particle? Besides, this is way out of our line of research. What could these possibly have to do with dog genetics and Addison's?"

"You're right, it's a huge leap, and out of our area of expertise." I was starting to agree with the futility of perusing this line of thinking. "I was just hoping that if we could suggest a plausible route of transmission, we could better justify asking for funding to research to screen DNA, as opposed to doing more toxicology screenings. If we found out something like . . . like they used the same manufacturer's substrate in their dog relief area at the shows, like shredded mulch, we might be able suggest that it is more likely a bacterium or a virus. We could then offer to include screening our Addison's samples as a large pool of non-CRFS controls thus cover some of the cost of processing our samples that can be used for other purposes. Kill lots of little birdies with one big boulder."

"Or dogs with one," Jamie added.

We all shot him a look.

Advancing technologies like *shotgun sequencing* allow scientists to rapidly sort through sequence data from short pieces of DNA, which is made up of four compounds—adenine (A), guanine (G), cytosine (C), and thymine (T)—and use computer algorithms to match those with a known sequence of interest, such as the dog genome, which consists of over two billion base pairs. The trouble is, for diseases such as Addison's, it's likely that the genetic change that causes it is very small, and different forms of the disease may be due to mutations at several different locations, as with cystic fibrosis. We knew we were looking for a very small change because the dogs survive, often functioning normally for the first few years of their life. If it were a more dramatic change, they would have never survived after birth. Such a small change is similar to natural variation in many genes, and thus there is a lot of noise in the analysis.

Since Addison's is likely inherited, we needed to look at DNA from a lot of related animals, affected and not, as well as unrelated animals, to observe a pattern of tiny changes, and match these to pedigree of related animals that are being studied to determine the disease inheritance. The world of breeders and owners with Addison's dogs had rallied to the cause, and we slowly worked through the freezers full of samples from them. As we knew this would likely take years of research, it was daunting to think how far we had yet to go with CRFS.

We spent the next two hours brainstorming and Internet searching. The venues didn't seem to have any matching characteristics—several shows were held at county fairgrounds in dusty indoor arenas on grounds used for everything from 4H shows with chickens, horses, and other barnyard animals, to Irish and Polish festivals, to monster truck rallies. One was at a retired elementary school that was rented out for art shows, kids' day, and dog and cat and even rabbit shows to keep the venue alive. And then there was the Balistar show held at the Gardens, as in Madison Square, sharing the venue with rock concerts, sports competitions, and kids' extravaganzas. No common thread between them except the dog show.

We researched each of the cases, the breeds, the other scarce information available on pathology reports, and the disease progression. Some of it had to be pulled from news reports, but much of it was available through websites established by the AKC, the AVMA, US Department of Agriculture, and the Centers for Disease Control, or CDC, who were now involved over growing concern that CRFS might make the jump to humans. Each had a different focus, each with a different dataset.

Throughout the day, in between spinning DNA, loading gels, and combing through computer readouts of combinations of ATGCs, we filled the board with more circles, lines, and x's, zeroing in on any connections we might follow. The most important observations, like so much in science, were the negatives.

Jamie came to me after lunch. "So I looked at the transmission rates. It doesn't appear to be highly contagious. There are a hundred and fifteen suspected cases, with over four thousand dogs attending the shows with the dead dogs."

"Can we maybe call them the victims or something less gut-punching, please?" Megan joined us.

Jamie shook his head, but seemed to acquiesce. "There also don't seem to be any reported cases of dogs returning home to pass on CRFS to other dogs in their homes and kennels."

Since breeders tend to have a number of dogs at one time, often including puppies—very expensive puppies—I knew this would be a major source of relief in the community.

"So if they didn't get it through direct contact with a sick dog, maybe it was airborne," Megan suggested.

I thought about that a moment. "That would make sense. Dogs' noses are like vacuum cleaners. Something could easily be sucked up. I doubt it was by ingestion since handlers are fairly vigilant about not letting their dogs eat off the floor. So, yes, I'd guess inhalation too. One thing, though—we can't say anything about its virulence."

"Why is that?" Kate asked. "Virulence is the strength of a pathogen to cause a disease, right?" I nodded. "So since we know that the dogs died really fast, wouldn't it be considered highly virulent?"

"Possibly," I understood her dilemma. "But what we don't know is whether the dogs that died were the only ones exposed. If that were the case, I agree that CRFS would be highly virulent. But what if lots of dogs were exposed, but only a few got it? That could certainly be the case at a big show like Balistar."

Megan moved her stool closer. "So how about we see if we can look at a larger population of dogs that attended the shows, get samples from some that died, and some that were fine, and as controls, from others that were nowhere near the show? If it is a virus or bacteria, we might find a genetic trail, or an odd protein that doesn't belong."

"Good idea," she was heading in the right direction, "but we still need to focus in on what we're looking for. Since we already have a bunch of Addison's and control groups that we've run genetic variants and pathway analysis on we can use some of those and the same screening tools on any dog show samples we can get. Adding our data to Balistar's would show that we're sharing the costs."

"You think that's an issue?" Jamie asked.

"Added value is always the catchphrase. If anyone comes close to proposing the same thing, at least we'll have that," though I hated even the concept of competing science based on price.

By seven, we had fleshed out an idea for a proposal. Even Kate stayed beyond her normal working hours, caught up in the intrigue of chasing clues. I sent her home, and the others finished up their lab work while I went to my computer to search for funding opportunities. Two hours later Jamie's big puppy-dog eyes woke me from my electronic trance.

"You want me to stay and help?"

"No, I'm good. Megan still here?"

He motioned over his shoulder. "She's packing up. Probably pissed that she didn't beat me to offering you help," he whispered.

"Stop. Don't poke the bear, Jamie."

"Yes boss, but it's so fun to razz her." Jamie pushed aside my computer bag clearing a small space for him to sit on my only guest chair. "I really do want to help," looking to Megan. "We both do." He smiled. "You know it's after nine. You sure I can't help you at least do some searches?"

"Actually, I found some grant opportunities. They're pretty straightforward. The awardees will have access to samples collected from a large number of victims as well as other dogs from shows whose owners donated samples in the hope it would help. I'm going to go through their application requirements a few more times and head home. But thanks."

"Okay. Good night."

"See you tomorrow," I waved and he hoisted his backpack and turned.

"Bye, see you bright and early tomorrow!" Megan called out, joining him.

Jamie really needed to give her a break. Megan had an amazing talent for making things work at the bench. She could isolate the smallest unique sequence of DNA and duplicate any technique in the literature. If she couldn't duplicate it, then the author had omitted a critical step. Jamie teased her like a relentless brother, telling her that she was so good at the bench because women were so good at domestic work, like cooking. He wasn't a chauvinist by any means, but instead was always trying to get her to lighten up and self-promote her awesome talent.

I suspect she had to also battle stereotypic first impressions. She is tall and striking, with long jet-black hair and blue eyes. It's a look I've always found stunning and unnerving at the same time. But I had rarely seen her with her hair in anything but a sloppy bun, wearing heavy black-framed glasses, purposefully camouflaging her allure and communicating a don't-mess-with-me persona. Sometimes I wanted to sit her down and tell her she didn't have to carry the burden of women in science on her shoulders by being so serious and always one step ahead of her male counterparts. I'd seen this too often in young, talented women, maybe even recognized some of this in my younger self. Neil helped me to navigate my transformation during graduate school, though my hard edge could always use some softening. If only Megan would let Jamie be her Neil. I frequently coaxed her to come have a beer with us. And on the rare occasion when she did, chemically modified by alcohol, she let her guard down and even sometimes her hair, and offered insight on the world of science that was dead on. I was in awe of her killer instinct.

And then there was her sneaky sense of humor. "Shhhhh," she'd whispered the evening that I found her at Jamie's bench, secretly rearranging his equipment to mess with his obsessive organization. The next morning, back in her serious costume, she reminded me of Sofie when I found her lying next to a pile of food wrappings from the trash: Whoa, how'd that happen?

They had flipped off the main lights in the lab; a blue glow laminated the room, backlighting the bottles on the shelves into a modern art bar graph. Cells silently grew in the incubator, DNA strands microscopically peeled off bases tallied by the automated sequencer, quiet clicks and ticks, and tiny colored lights whispered like night creatures of the lab.

I stood up, stretched, and looked out across the campus at bundled-up students scurrying along pathways and darkened buildings dotted by illuminated rectangles. Science majors were still shackled to the lab bench, history majors gone home to their computers. A little longer in my quiet space and I would head home.

The house was still, my daughters were asleep, and Chris was sitting at his computer reading the newspaper. Odd that I still thought of it as "paper." Ania and Sofie wiggled quietly at my arrival. I knelt down, taking comfort in the everyday reminder of their devotion. They trotted behind me to the study.

"You're up late."

"You're home late."

Silence.

"You get all my texts?" I asked, pulling up a chair beside him.

"I think so. Tess was picked up and delivered to Max's, Diana was picked up, delivered, and picked up again from piano, and Tess has an orthodontist appointment tomorrow at 10 that I have to take her to," there was a flatness to his voice.

"You okay?" I asked.

"Sure."

"No you're not. You're pissed."

He turned his head toward me, looking over his reading glasses, and gave me his I don't get pissed at the little stuff look.

"Okay, peeved. I'm sorry I'm so late. Sorry I missed the evening."

"Diana is upset about something, but I can't get her to talk."

"She's fourteen."

He shook his head.

"I'll talk to her."

"We had cereal for dinner."

"That works." He knew my growing disdain for cooking dinner, and that I did it because we had agreed to split the duties. I got dinner, he got the bills. I didn't know who got the better deal, but I didn't keep my part of the bargain tonight.

"I would have made something if I had more notice," that was fair.

"Cereal is fine."

"Dogs are fed too."

I left the study and wandered through to the kitchen/family room. Standing in front of the sink, I poured a glass of water and stared out the window, but only saw a tired me staring back. Chris followed me in a few moments and wrapped his arms around my waist from behind. I settled into his embrace. He was the best at keeping us moving forward together.

"Anything you want to talk about?" he asked.

"No. Well yes, but not tonight. I'm exhausted." I turned to face him as he leaned down and kissed me gently.

"Then I'm off to bed," he walked a few paces and turned. "You coming?"

"Not yet. Need to decompress a bit. And read through some info I bookmarked."

"That's not decompressing, that's working," adding emphasis to his turn. "'Night." He headed down the hall, Sofie bouncing behind him, leaving Ania laying on the floor, watching in anticipation of my next move.

"Hey, thanks for holding down the fort," I called after him.

"You got it, partner," echoed down the hall.

That he is.

The morning was rushed. The girls jockeyed for position in front of the mirror, endlessly checking and rechecking their wardrobe selection and makeup application. Lunches tossed in their stylish lunch bags, we hurried out the door to meet the bus at the insane hour of 6:15. Our four-minute walk left us little time to talk. Diana was fine.

"My biology teacher snapped at me and embarrassed me, but all I was doing was trying to fix something. If she only would have given me a chance to explain, but she's a butthead and thinks we're stupid and can't imagine that any of us would be talking because we were actually trying to help another student understand."

"She's human. Let it go," though I knew she couldn't. "You can't let something that small set your whole mood. And how about we not call someone a butthead, especially a teacher?"

But she is fourteen, the mysterious age at which girls' brains seem to misfire and make it impossible for them to modulate feelings, behavior, communication, life. You would think that teachers, witness to this phenomenon every year, would keep that is mind. Thank God it is only one year and then the magic switch at fifteen smoothed them out a bit. The difference in maturity between my fourteen- and sixteen-year-olds was astounding. I waved off the bus, grateful that the girls are still okay with me taking them to the bus stop, ignoring the fact that it's only because when it gets cold, they knew I would cave and take them in the warm car. They led the privileged life we created for them, embracing the latest technology, trends, and lingo with the energy only teenagers had. I struggled to find ways to infuse some reality, a greater purpose, a sense of social responsibility. Summer camps to help the needy seemed to only confirm their entitlement as we wrote the check for the experience they would post to social media.

Chris was standing in the kitchen, leaning against the counter, coffee cupped in two hands, obviously not having looked at himself in the mirror yet.

"Nice hair," I teased. We are a perfect match even in coiffure.

"Thank you, I came up with it in my sleep." Puffing up his chest, he posed proudly. I find if I give him credit, it only encourages him. He refilled my cup as I set it on the counter. "So want to tell me what's up?" He headed our big comfy chair, motioning me to come sit beside him.

"Well, we decided that we can't ignore what's going on with CRFS, so we spent most of yesterday coming up with some ideas and investigating funding sources."

"Really? You're going to jump in on this? What's your angle? And how in the hell are you going to go about getting samples from any of the dogs involved?"

Putting the milk back in the refrigerator, I headed toward him. "Why not? We do have a lot of dog DNA laying around the lab."

"And the house," he pointed out.

"So that's what I was doing for the last few hours last night," trying to slip in my excuses. I folded up my legs and sat cross-legged facing him. "Interestingly, two pharmaceutical companies are offering grants to investigate CRFS, and the AKC has a roster of all the dogs who attended the shows and 'is coordinating with AVMA and its member vets to obtain samples from as many dogs as possible.' Their intent is to split the samples between the two companies under the agreement that they will give out grants for work on CRFS."

"No doubt the deep pockets are eager to find the cause so they can capitalize on any prevention or treatment that results."

"No doubt. You and I know the potential for profit is a big motivating factor for them." I looked at him and shrugged. "We're both guilty of taking big pharma money at some point in our careers, so we're all in cahoots anyway."

"True. So who are the magnanimous supporters this time?"

"Well BeneVivite is one."

"Ah, 'Living Well,' the giant mega-pharma, and let me guess. The other is Regnum."

"Yup."

"And you just happen to know the Chief Scientific Officer at Regnum."

"Yup."

He nodded, affirming the connection.

"You don't have a problem with that do you?" I asked.

"With Neil? No, I never have. I just don't want you to set yourself up for disappointment."

"How so?"

"Well, I can't imagine that he can be anything but unbiased, but as long as you accept that . . ."

"Of course I do. I think my work stands for itself. I can hold my o—"

"Hold on there, cowgirl, I wasn't disparaging your work. If you honestly have no expectation of him elevating your proposal, then it's all good."

"You don't sound like it is." I was a bit defensive. "Neil and I are good friends, *were* good friends, I should say. Seeing him barely once or twice a year I don't think really constitutes good friends anymore."

He smirked at me. "You were much more than that."

"How many times do we have to have this discussion, Neil and I nev—"

"Never slept together. I know that. I know and believe that every time you remind me. But you loved him, and there was—will always be—something special, and a strong bond between you two."

"I think you're—"

"Methinks thou doth protest too much." He put his arm across my lap. "I'm okay with it, I've told you that a thousand times. Just don't ignore your feelings or you may get hurt. And don't expect anything from him that he can't give. You're the one who keeps bringing it up."

"Um, I think you did this time with your snarky lemme guess comment."

"I was just kidding."

"Bad joke." We both paused to close that chapter and open a new one.

"So okay," he proposed, to start fresh. "Tell me your plans."

I told him how we wanted to look at any of the dogs that were potentially exposed, particularly those that were housed at the shows near the affected dogs. We were going to look for signs of a receptor—a protein or level of some expressed gene—which would indicate a potential causative agent. We wanted to keep our investigation simple; the less dependent on a succession of positive findings, the more likely that we would contribute at least something.

"Regnum's offering grants of up to $350,000 for innovative research related to CRFS."

"Geez, that's big in our world!"

"Huge. To them, peanuts. The main catch is that instead of the usual six or so months to work on the proposal, we have just four weeks to submit the application. They want to make the award in forty-five days."

"Wow, that's tight. They're that eager to get moving on this?"

"I would guess that the urgency is due more to the upcoming veterinary medicine conference in late November, rather than the immediate need to save dogs." Regnum was known for hosting a lavish evening session at the annual conference where they announced the year's grant recipients, but only after two hours of corporate propaganda. The event was always packed.

"We'll have to scramble," I grabbed a pen and paper and made a note to call my Department Director. "Once we get the proposal fleshed out, the university still has to approve it, after they tack on their huge fee, of course."

Chris rolled his eyes in agreement. Our building, our lab, the accounting department—it all cost money. I got that. But it was still painful to watch close to 40% of the grant money disappear into the school's coffers before I saw my first check.

We wanted to submit applications to both companies, but each had indicated that the proposal needed to be exclusive.

"Why not just group the dogs by AKC group since they are

each housed together at shows? Aren't there CRFS dogs in each?" Chris asked.

"I'm not sure they are always together, depends on the venue, but I think CRFS has hit all groups. I've seen at least one in terrier, sporting and non, working, and toy, but I don't know about herding or hound groups. I'll have to search that today. I did see that there have been cases in a number of the breeds prone to Addison's – a Great Dane, two Rottweilers, and a Porti, but so far no standard poodles. So if we go with your idea and ask for samples from the groups they are in, we could capitalize on the data for our Addison's research." His perspective added to our study design, which we hoped would give the widest application of the data.

"I'm going to have to put in a lot of long hours in the next two weeks if I'm going to get this to the university in time. You okay with being a single dad for the duration."

"You need to let the girls know though."

"Okay, but I don't know when." I felt my abandoning them already starting, "I'll try to call them this evening." Tag team parenting wasn't the way to raise children, but they are good kids and a few weeks of an absentee mom weren't going to push them into therapy yet. I was a text away, or heaven forbid, a phone call, if they could bring themselves to use that old-fashioned method of communication. I packed up and left him in his home office. Darn it, I thought as I shut the door. I'd forgotten to ask how his day went yesterday.

As I biked to work feeling much colder than I had anticipated, my thoughts turned to the summer I met Neil.

I had been in the lab for six months and was finishing my last semester of classes for my Ph.D., to be followed by three more years of full-time, bench research. Neil had been in the lab two summers before as an undergraduate and was now returning to do his graduate research.

I had been told that he was good-looking, charming, and brilliant. Clearly there was something alluring about him, as all the female technicians and secretaries went wispy whenever talking about him. Even the guys were in awe. He had charisma.

We were to share low status as that year's crop of graduate students. I braced myself for the comparison between our obviously polar opposite personas. I would never be described as having charisma.

Heading out to the hallway to grab a beaker from the glassware shelves, I turned and smacked right into him and yelped.

"Oh! Geez, sorry!" he reached out to steady me.

"Sorry!" I gasped. "I startle easily." And I shoved my glasses back up in place.

"I'll have to remember that. Hi," he was way too cheery, "I'm Neil. You must be Claire. I understand we're a team!" Glancing at my gloved hands he pulled back from offering a handshake and instead offered a broad smile full of perfect teeth. I knew I was going to hate him.

He became my best friend. Long hours in the lab, late-night Fridays with nothing to do but chip in and rent a movie together, hundreds of carry-out meals scarfed down between sample runs, and infrequent road trips to loud clubs—we built a relationship to rival any of those I shared with my girlfriends. With Anna finishing up vet school and starting her new career, it was good to have someone to talk to. Neil arrived attached, briefly living with a co-worker he met while temporarily joining the working world, but that relationship ended as soon as he escaped to his own apartment closer to our lab. We spent the next three years alternating through a series of "what was I thinking?" relationships with other people, that we pulled each other through and over. We met each other's families, celebrated holidays together, held each other through pain, loss, and occasional triumph. We dreamed up schemes for the demise of our major adviser: lacing his coffee with acrylamide, beta-mercaptoethanol, or just plain old potassium chloride, but the taste of that would be hard to hide.

We had a deep love, a deep trust, and an unspoken freedom between us. Nothing was off limits. Sharing our most intimate selves, we unburdened our consciences of secrets of unfulfilled dreams and mistakes, and behaviors straddling the boundary of morality. He was so like Anna, strategically placing people in his life like a master chess player. Though her game was to keep them at a distance, his was to get what he wanted from each person. He was also more deliberate than Anna, but the effect was the same. I watched as he hypnotized people into thinking that they were close to him, simply by showing interest in their lives. He knew everything about everyone, he asked about their kids and their parties, they confessed infidelities and twelve-step programs. They all thought he was their best friend. No one realized that they actually knew virtually nothing about him. They were too busy talking about themselves.

Somewhere along the way we came to an unspoken agreement that our relationship was best as it was. The value of what we had was not worth the risk of shifting to a romantic or even sexual relationship. We were brutally honest with each other, and our support and advice was unencumbered by physical entanglements. That's not to say we weren't attracted to one another. Neil was perfectly built, his body sculpted by his Mediterarian heritage mixed with his ancestral Ethiopian regal cheekbones and bronze skin that accented his disturbingly intense brown eyes. It was not easy to keep from drooling. Back then I was slender and fit, and my long hair was an asset. We flirted and talked graphically about our latest sexual adventures and fantasies, baiting each other to make the first move.

Maybe it was when we shared a room at the conference in Ithaca because our adviser was too cheap to spring for two. Maybe it was when he got snowed in at my apartment and slept next to me in my bed in his underwear. At each pivotal moment, we moved close, felt the challenge, and retreated back to the path we were on. By the time I met Chris, we were both in our final semester of school, making it easy to go our own ways—or so I thought. I ended up remaining in the lab through the summer, and the moment Neil left for a postdoc in California in late May, unexpected sadness and loss engulfed me. I felt abandoned and lost. Chris understood, probably better than I, the depth of Neil's role in my life. Newly in love, Chris was willing to gently take my hand and lead me away. I tried not to look back.

By the time I arrived at the lab from my bike ride down memory lane, I decided to call Neil when our time zones meshed, and just give him a heads-up. Though Chris suggested against this as it might put Neil in an awkward position, I thought it would help not to blindside him, and it couldn't hurt. His assistant answered the phone. She was her usual overly bubbly self. Recognizing my name, she said he was about to head off to a meeting, but would see if he could take my call.

"Hello, Dr. Winthrop."

"Hi, honey. I see Perky is still with you."

"Yes she is. Some people like her."

"I'm sure the men do."

"You are too harsh on other women. And as you know, this is a man's world."

He was right. I ignored him. "Hey, I just wanted to give you a heads-up."

"That you're submitting a grant proposal?"

"Ah, so I am not the first friend giving you a call."

"I'd say you are the only friend. The rest just think they are."

"I love you too." I smiled. "I thought it best that you knew before it hit your desk."

"Sure you did," his tone oozing sarcasm.

"Stop it."

"It's okay. We learned from the master to capitalize on any connection that might give us an advantage, didn't we?"

"Guilty, but I refuse to accept that I've turned into our dick-head adviser."

"Never. So go ahead and send it directly to Donna and she'll—"

"Donna?"

"Perky. She does have a real name."

"Oh, my bad," I was glad he couldn't see my chagrined face.

"I'll tell her to look out for it."

"Won't that flag your direct involvement?"

"It is what it is. When the reviews are done, I might have to recuse myself on the decision anyway, but not before I give my opinion," he acknowledged. "You think you have a good angle?"

"I think so. We had several ideas, but this one seems to provide the best chance of finding some link. And we can add our own data. How's Regnum handling this new opportunity?"

"Jury's still out. The Board has been watching this since the first dog deaths—always business smart—and made sure we were poised to jump in there in the event that a pattern emerged."

"I was surprised to see grant offerings from both Regnum and BeneVivite happen so fast."

"We had it pretty well fleshed-out and ready to go. It simply required an emergency board meeting when the first reports of the

October dog deaths came in. Within forty-eight hours of the decision our web developers were posting the application page. I think the bodies were still warm."

"I could tell. There're a few typos on the page."

"Geez-us, you would think a multi-billion-dollar company could hire a proofreader."

"I'm available—if I don't get any new funding," I chided. "How are you?"

"Okay I guess. Like I said, it's frustrating that this is taking all my attention. I feel it's at the expense of all the long-term projects. We have a separate committee for this, but they still want me heavily involved. Frankly, I don't think that this is going to lead to anything."

"You don't?" I was taken aback. He was and is brilliant and I had always trusted his instincts, especially when it came to science.

"I think a lot more dogs have to die before we have anything to research, but my Board wants to be the first one out of the blocks. I think it's going to cost us dearly."

"So I assume you had a hand in getting CDC and AVMA to work together?"

"Did you like that? Money talks, and with our profit margins, we have a lot to talk with. Let's just leave it at that in case my phone is bugged."

I couldn't tell if he was kidding. "But if you're right . . ."

"It's a bad investment. Between you, me, and the lamppost, I'm not happy with the gamble, but then I'm only one vote."

It sunk in that he was always right and I was likely wasting my time.

"Does Perky have a last name?"

"Don't take a sip of your coffee or you will spray it all over the place. Peebles, Donna Peebles."

"Oh my God, Perky Peebles?!"

"Send her the proposal. Gotta run. Love you."

"Bye," I mumbled.

The day steamrolled along as I filled out forms, conducted more background research, and wrote, rewrote, and wrote some more. Purpose, technical approach, sample plan, data analysis plan, every sentence carefully crafted. Preliminary data would be a plus, and we could include the summaries of our cohorts of DNA, from a variety of breeds and mixed dogs. With only fifteen pages to convince the reviewers to give us several hundred thousand dollars and a share of the coveted samples, every word was critical. Even more so the budget. Over the next two days my team would have to think and rethink how we would divide, process, and analyze each precious sample to get the most out of it; more than likely, something would be reveled in the course of our research that would lead to more questions and more possible paths to explore. Maximizing the amount of DNA was paramount. Being able to grow and preserve live cells from samples would be even better, but as of yet, no one had started collecting those from dying dogs.

Anna and I met to discuss some new Addison's patients she had, but more importantly, her thoughts on how we might piggy-back Addison's research on anything I did on CRFS. Though it's a common practice in the research community to overlap projects, I wanted to be very careful on paper to separate the work proposed for the grant from on-going work in the lab, yet ensure that we had all our bases covered so we could peek over the shoulder of the CRFS research to see if there was anything Addison's-related.

A stack of messages awaited me when I returned from lunch. The university grants office was none too pleased with my request that morning to accelerate their approval process. They said they would do it, of course, but that I "must understand that this was not the normal process." Their need for acknowledgement of their self-importance was duly noted. Messages from sales reps, recycled; message from students, I'd start on this evening.

"You got a call from someone at Xlar. A Dr. Kendal Kovak?" Kate sounded hopeful to help with a connection.

"Oh, reeeeally," my skepticism evident. "What did she want?"

"Something about whether you kept any of your cell lines from domestic cats. Are those the ones marked FCA in the freezer?"

"Yup. *Felis catus.* I hung on to a few just in case I ever had nostalgia for the good old days." I searched for and opened a file on my computer. "I don't even know if they can still be revived, but would you pull a vial of FCA3, and see if you can get some to grow? Did Dr. Kovak say she wanted to talk to me?"

"No, but I have her number."

"That's okay. You can call her back and arrange a shipment with her. She isn't one of my closer friends, so I'm happy to let you handle it."

Kate headed out into the wide hall, opening the -135°C freezer, where live cells are suspended in tiny vials of solutions that prevent them from cracking open as they wait for someone to restart their life. Cold smoke billowed as she pulled a rack of small boxes that was immersed in the liquid nitrogen. No respectable graduate student hadn't learned the hard way to hold their breath as they leaned into the freezer. The lungs immediately informed you that there was nothing usable in vapor.

"Who is she? Dr. Kovak?" Kate asked, returning and putting the vial in the benchtop water bath to warm up the suspended cells.

"She was a postdoc in my lab, a few years ahead of me. Very smart, somewhat talented, but not warm and fuzzy." She'd had a crisp, carefully-crafted look about her that tried to say she was headed to bigger and better things than the rest of us. "We were essentially colleagues."

What I wanted to say is that she was a, well, not a nice person. She was a major source amusement during my days as a graduate student, but also irritation. She was insecure, and insecurity can be dangerous. imagined her as the kid who was a tattletale in order to gain the teacher's attention, a behavior she carried into adulthood with greater consequences. Everyone screwed up, splattered solutions across the bench, poked, sliced, cut, and bruised themselves in the quest for data. Lab work is physical; everyone wasted materials forgetting a critical step and ruining a run, bubbling over solutions onto the stir plate, and forgetting to account for a reagent or two. The lab was full of "Oh, shit!" moments, and these were late-night fodder for the inside jokes between grad students and postdocs. Kendal made it her job to report these mishaps to our main adviser, particularly those of anyone who made her feel the slightest bit threatened.

For some unknown reason, I was one of them. As far as I could tell, my only egregious offense was that I was younger. She branded me with a target on my back for the duration of our overlap in the lab. Her attacks ran from laughable commentary on the correct way to do things, to the ultimate insult to a scientist, accusing me of making up data, which caused me to have to endure extra sessions with our adviser to scrutinize the raw outputs of my experiments—the autorads, the sequence alignments, all my notes. Scientific integrity is paramount and assumed until evidence to the contrary, and it took all my strength not to pay her back for casting a shadow over my work. I was convinced she would have finished her work a year earlier if she hadn't spent so much time spying on the rest of us. But I suppose I would have been less prepared for the real world without her training in mind games.

Anyone with a Ph.D. would tell you that getting one was not a matter of brains, but a matter of tenacity. When I started, my father, who obtained his from Georgetown, gave me one piece of advice, and it became my mantra—"Don't let the bastards get you down." Pure and simple, it was the adviser's and committee's job to toss in the obstacles and spin you around until you either crashed and burned and were out, or until the ride stopped and you were still hanging on, albeit a bit befuddled. It wasn't so much a matter of doing great research, though that was the hope from the student's perspective. It was a matter of becoming one of the club who had survived the long, arduous, tedious, and painful journey. One who stood in the face of those bastards and smiled, and answered yet another question about the evolutionary theories of Richard Lewontin and EO Wilson, and drew B and Z DNA on the board, and spent an obscene number of late nights in the lab. Mine had a special brand of torture that involved pitchers of cheap beer in smoky college town bars, listening to my adviser pontificate, words increasingly slurred and demeanor increasingly belligerent, as his alcohol consumption accelerated—and being stuck with the bill on a graduate student's paltry salary.

I survived by the comradery of my fellow students. Kendal survived by being a suck-up. One of our adviser's warped benchmarks was to make most graduate students cry. He was an equal-opportunity bully who found this an effective way to assert his dominance over those who would someday be a competitor, and to humiliate subpar performers, driving them from the program. To her credit, Kendal managed to turn this benchmark in her favor. She excelled at tears, making him so uncomfortable that he learned to leave her to her work.

While she was seemingly successful at manipulating our adviser, she was not very astute on the coming realities of the scientific community. She left the lab with few friends, few who would trust and collaborate with her, which was critical in the science world. To my surprise I learned that our adviser was not actually blind to her manipulative tears and tattletale antics, but since the project she had worked on was important to the lab's foundation, he took the path of least resistance. That revelation was worth at least that night's contribution to the beer purchases.

I could have said all this to Kate, but instead, I verified with her at the end of the day that the cells were viable, and the sample had been sent. I needed to grow up myself and let it go.

Four weeks flew by, and our proposal came together; it was well-designed, intriguing, and solid. After it was approved by the university, I sent it off to Perky. I made my hotel and plane reservations for the conference and allowed myself thirty seconds to envision the moment I heard our lab announced as one of the Regnum grant recipients.

With our proposal in, two weeks remained to finish up some work, plan for the conference, and get to know my family again. Home is found in the mundane—grocery shopping, laundry, even making dinner. My family was grateful that the house elf was back and tending to their daily needs.

Surrendering control of my schedule to wait in the parent taxi line rewarded me with an infusion of commentary on events critical to the new generation. "Ugh! This annoying girl in my biology class always has to interject her own story to top yours even if it's made up, which it often is! My teacher is supposed to be teaching government but can't help but spout his personal beliefs on how religion should be the underlying principle of laws and he doesn't even believe in climate change!"

"Can we go shopping this weekend for new dance shoes?" asked Diana.

"Why? I thought–" I started.

"Last year's are the wrong color and besides are too small and so are my winter boots and can you chaperone dress rehearsal?"

"Don't forget you said you would volunteer at the science fair next week!" Tess having lost faith in my ability to stick to my schedule.

"Yup. Science fair is on my calendar. How's your project coming along? Are you going to at least do a run-through for your dad and me since we aren't allowed to judge your grade?" She said she was counting on our input, and I caught my breath at her adult-like recognition.

Reconnected to my daughters, a strange transforming frenzied calm set in. Captives in my car, they occasionally forgot that I was there and chattered between themselves, unveiling a closely-guarded side.

But two weeks wasn't enough time to reestablish connections in all directions. Kids come first, dogs wiggle in between, and there wasn't enough time to become content and to fall back in love with the amazing guy who shares my bed.

Enough time though for three more dog shows, and twenty-three more dead dogs. Two were breed-specific or "specialty" shows, one for two types of collies (rough coat or smooth) held at a rec center in southern California, the other a specialty for dachshunds of two sizes, standard and miniature, and three coat varieties, smooth, wirehaired, and longhaired, held at an equestrian center in Middleburg, Virginia. The third show, at another recreation center in Texas, was a Group show that involved all breeds in the AKC Herding Group. Twelve dogs were lost there including shelties, border collies, corgis, Briards, German shepherds, an old English sheep dog, and an Australian cattle dog. This was the first-time multiple animals of the same breed were stricken at the same show, and though reporters pounced on this as a new revelation, the scientific community was not impressed. Two does not a pattern make. But it was startling to see several shows hit at the same time.

There was also a fermenting belief that there were non-show dog deaths resulting from CRFS. Dogs die every day from unknown causes. Often they eat or drink something toxic, but more often a dog dies of a long-term ailment—cancer, organ failure—unnoticed until it is too late. We love our dogs because they bear the weight of our needs, rarely asking for reciprocal support, keeping silent until it is too late. When a dog dies quickly, grieving owners rarely have the emotional capacity to ask for a necropsy to determine the cause.

Anna called me while I sat at the airport. "Just off the phone with Dana, remember her? She was in the class after me in vet school. The bohemian one who was a great cook. She works as a traveling vet between a number of shelters and rescue centers. She swears they are seeing cases of CRFS with large numbers dying right and left. They thought it was a new strain of parvo, but the pattern of infection doesn't follow the same progression."

"Why hasn't there been anything on the news about it?"

"Think about it. No one wants to say anything. They are afraid that if word gets out, adoptions will come to a screeching halt, and you know what that means—more dogs euthanized. Dana called me to see if I have had any deaths that I think are related."

I hadn't even bothered to ask in the past few weeks, as I figured she would tell me. "Well, do you?"

Silence answered my question.

MONEY AND FAME

I LEFT my car at the airport. Chris wanted to drive me but I didn't want to have to depend on him to get a ride back, he had enough on his plate being a single dad for the next five days. Disappointed, he was still engaged and loving, reminding me that I had other great research to do, that this was not the center of my life's work. He is always pragmatic, and I knew he meant it to help me focus on what was important, but that didn't take the sting out of the implication that he wanted me to be prepared in case we didn't receive a grant award.

Chicago in November. I would have preferred to see the city in the summer, as I've heard it's great, but I had only been here in the winter for meetings, confined to inside venues. The scientific research community is not a wealthy bunch, living from grant to grant, and it's common for us to get our kicks from the free, great outdoors. Hosting meetings at expensive, lavish locations is not typically reflective of our ilk, though we are known to host conferences in the winter at ski resorts. Big pharma on the other hand, will grace us with their presence, but only as a break from their usual over the top locations like Las Vegas.

Having avoided any contact with Neil the past few weeks, I texted him and asked if he wanted to get together while we were both here.

Sorry no time, he texted back. *I'll be in Virginia in two weeks though. Lunch then?*

Sure, but hope to have good reason to talk to you sooner.

That was odd. Wouldn't he meet with all the grant recipients here after the award ceremony?

Drifting from session to session, I couldn't concentrate on the presentations of new genes identified, new lab equipment invented, and new treatments, preventatives, and cures on the horizon. Not until the end of the four-day meeting did Regnum host their event; it was always on the evening of the closing day to keep participants from bolting early.

It was a rare, slightly formal event for my typically casual colleagues, but I found it fun to play dress-up for the night. Donning a long skirt and flowy blouse, I had carefully pinned up part of my hair, with select tendrils looking as if they just casually cascaded along my face, when in fact it took several tries to get that carefree look—I kept reminding myself that the perfect is the enemy of the good, to no avail. I added simple costume jewelry and gold metal frames. I actually felt confident and ready to be on for the night.

The evening proved interminable. Regnum hosted a lengthy cocktail hour for all of us scientists to stand around in unfamiliar business attire amongst strategically placed sales reps espousing their latest product. Luckily they tend to stay clear of the run of the mill university scientist, i.e., me, and congregate around the potential decision makers from veterinary schools or private industry that do their best to stay on the cutting edge of technology. The wine was helpful though. It took the edge off and allowed me to engage in exchanges with colleagues and competitors, and hear a bevy of theories on CRFS. Neil was nowhere to be seen.

Finally we were seated at large round tables, and several hundred scientists sat politely, quietly, as Regnum executives thanked collaborators, recognized innovators, and I don't know what else. It all blended into one long presentation punctuated with occasional forced applause. The minutes ticked by slowly. Neil sat on stage at the head table, his face a familiar, pleasant mask. He suffered with the rest of us who would prefer to have been on the barren tundra with a herd of caribou, than to be stage right. He was a master of the façade.

Dinner, dessert, coffee (decaf as I was already wired). There were to be five awards. Regnum had received thirty-two applications, a fair amount given the narrow time frame. It was all boilerplate: Thank you to all who took up the challenge, thank you to all who are as devastated by this syndrome as we at Regnum are and who want to find the source and cure as much as we do. We encourage all who do not receive an award this time to reapply if there is another round, though truthfully we hope for the sake of our canine companions that the mystery of CRFS will be solved quickly.

And oh dear God, would they just make the announcements?

The first three awards went to well-known researchers in domestic animal infectious diseases. All three proposals sought to look for the causative agent, but in different ways, using DNA-, antibody-, and blood-sourced biomarker-based techniques. The fourth went to a small private company for a novel idea to look at blood chemistry on a small group of victims for which a succession of samples had been taken as they died. Understanding the moment-by-moment changes that occurred as the poor dogs died might reveal clues on how the causative agent worked, and thus reveal the culprit. Intriguing. Gentle applause encouraged the cautious recipient to the stage to receive his check. The fifth and final award had everyone on the edge of their seats. It went to the Xlar team led by Dr. Kendal Kovak, for research on SNP comparisons in breed cohorts. The applause grew, if not for the recipient, at least for the end of the announcements.

Something was wrong. That was our proposal, but with the wrong name. Had they screwed up the award? I looked at Neil, blank-faced, staring directly at me, and mouthed, "Did they mess up the name?" He blinked long, briefly locking eyes with me, then he turned his attention to applaud Kendal as she took the stage.

Everything moved in slow motion. The few colleagues at my table who knew about our proposed approach were leaning in, whispering questions. "Wasn't that your proposal? Did the committee screw up?" Kendal floated across the stage, shaking all of the executives' hands, giving Neil a hug. He smiled; was it genuine? The president of Regnum took center stage to thank everyone for coming, as a cacophony of chatter rose in the room. People were rising, chairs were shifting. Kendal's table mates were shrieking as she rejoined them, drawing attention. I looked back at the stage to find Neil chatting with some unknowns. Look up, look up! I willed him. For a fleeting moment he met my eyes, then turned away without communicating his thoughts.

The remainder of the event was a tornado of faces flying by and hands reaching out in goodbyes spinning me towards the exit. I crashed through the conference center doors, and headed up the block, frantically searching my phone for the airline's number to get a flight out that night. I stumbled as I dodged around a gray stranger, only to look up as the lamppost glared down at me. I retreated back into my little screen. The tips of my fingers were barely warm enough to elicit a response from my iPhone, by the time the agent searched all the remaining flights with no luck, the cold announced itself on my hands and face with brutal pain.

I darted quickly into a convenience store to pick up a questionably drinkable bottle of wine. My pace quickened as I stormed to my hotel, which was beyond a comfortable walking distance. My stupid room cardkey flashed red several times before I slowed down and slid it in the slot the right way. I tore off my clothes and threw on my sweat pants, ordered cheesecake and chocolate mousse from room service, and searched for the night's schedule of B movies knowing sleep would keep its distance, taunting me. I would not allow myself to think. Chris called and texted me twice, the final one reminding me why he was my rock.

I take it by your silence that you need to be alone. I'm sorry. I'm here when you need me.

You were right, need some time, love you, I texted back.

I turned on the t.v. as I was getting ready to leave. The local news aired coverage of last night's events, highlighting the hope of the grant awards. But they also showed scenes from outside the conference, focusing on a growing group calling themselves the Canine Crusaders, who were picketing outside the center. The commentator said something about how they believed that the pet industry is being used to further the agenda of an as-yet-to-be-named hate group, reminding the public of other post market product tampering cases of Tylenol, Jello, and even Girl Scout cookies. Though they didn't say how or through what mechanism or what this supposed group hated. I angrily switched it off.

Friday morning, I engaged in every distraction—the paper, in-flight magazine, a downloaded movie on my iPad. My plane landed, mid-day. I couldn't go home. Tired, angry, and disappointed, I had to shake it off before I faced Chris. He was right, I should have repeated his suggested mantra, that it was only one of many grant applications. It was not personal. Chris was smart and insightful, and knew my vulnerabilities. He would never rub it in my face, but even so it takes me a while to eat crow. I needed to pay more attention to him, in a lot of ways, just not yet.

The lab was quiet, though everyone was there. Each of them said a quiet hello, then returned to being busy. No one made eye contact, no one mentioned what happened, but obviously everyone knew we didn't get an award. Jamie broke the silence as I stood there frozen in the doorway.

"Other than that Mrs. Lincoln, how was the play?" Jamie's look was sincerely empathetic.

Megan rolled her eyes.

"The conference was very interesting. There are some new immunotherapy cancer drugs coming out, in particular one for canine osteosarcoma that shows promise, and Regnum has developed a rapid detection kit for parvovirus that should be on the market by the fall."

Megan not only opening the wound, but getting out the salt shaker. "What happened? Did someone really get an award for the same thing we proposed?" She was defiant. "Is there anything we can do to protest?"

"Guess our idea was solid, just someone else got there first."

"Who?" Kate asked.

I cut off Megan's response. "I'd prefer if we all just concentrate on the work we do have funding for. There will be other opportunities, and we should be grateful for what we do have."

Kate remained the only unemotional one, "Is there anything we can do?"

"No. Thanks. It's not the first time, nor will it be the last that we do not get a proposal funded." My demeanor shifted as I accepted the truth, and I smiled for real. "It's all part of our world." I parked my suitcase, dumped my computer backpack on the bench, and shifted my attitude. "So, how are we doing on matching pedigrees to genetic markers?"

Jamie slid over and spread a computer-generated pedigree out in front of me.

"I'll print out the spreadsheet," Megan clicked on her computer. "We also got a whole new set of samples from Dr. Anna. She said this is a new family group of Addison's carriers."

Anna. Shoot, I'd forgotten to call her. I had been planning to while I waited for my plane. She would have already looked at Regnum's website for the announcement of awards and was probably giving me some space.

Jamie and Megan crowded in on either side of me and started showing me the data. Competitors in some ways, they did make a good team, she excelling at bench work manipulating samples to extract the smallest detail, he best at bioinformatics identifying the results using computer statistics, algorithms, and databases containing billions of sequences identified and submitted by the scientific community. Exciting possibilities were emerging in my own lab, patterns of DNA showing up in affected dogs and potential carriers that hinted of an Addison's-related gene in one breed, in one family. Setting up our next set of experiments to test against other pedigrees and other breeds cleared my mind, and pulled me back onto my path. This was where I belonged.

I sent everyone home early, and closed up the lab for the weekend. I told the grad students that they didn't need to put in any time over the weekend; a rarity in their world. I knew they would still show up for at least a few hours, as hanging in the lab was what they'd become accustomed to doing in their free time. If they only knew how valuable and rare free time would become.

I picked up Anna's call "So what happened?" she asked.

"I don't know yet! I was so angry I couldn't even think straight. I guess I could pick up the phone and call Neil, but I got the distinct impression he won't tell me anything. Maybe I've been wrong about our relationship staying strong all these years. What's the saying? Nostalgia is the memory of the past that never really was."

"You're taking this rather personally. It's just a grant, and not even in your field of work," blunt Anna grounded me once again.

"I know, you're right. I need to figure out why I'm so angry. For a second I caught Neil's eye and there was a message there that I have never seen before. Like—I don't know—'Don't question me'? It sent me into a tailspin."

"Pick up the phone and call him. What did Chris say?"

"Nothing. He's been careful to stay back, like you, but he's been texting the grocery list. Guess it's his way of emphasizing what's important. He warned me this might happen and tried to prepare me. I haven't actually been home yet, but called him when I landed. We didn't even mention it. Talked about kids and dogs and life."

"Real life. Pay attention to that. Don't let this consume you. And don't hold it against him that he was right," That was Anna, ever my conscience. "Or against Neil for doing business as business people do."

"Yeah, whatever that means. I'd never make it in the business world." I leaned back in my chair. The disarray in my office, in the lab, would never cut it at Regnum. I shook it off. "That's why I'm still at the lab. I need to pull myself together so he doesn't get the brunt of it."

"Neil?"

"No, Chris," silently acknowledging that sometimes their roles were similar.

"Isn't that what husbands are for?" she chided. "Though what do I know?"

"Beats me, I'm still reading the manual. So, tell me what is going on with CRFS in your world."

"You sure you want to know? You're still in an emotional state and you aren't in the position to do anything about it."

"I'm not in that fragile a mood. My love of dogs trumps all."

"It's going to get bad, really bad. All the other vets I've talked to swear they have been seeing cases of it. And yes, that includes me."

"You kept samples, right?"

"Ahh, the truth revealed. Science trumps all, not love of dogs."

"Um, I . . ."

"You are such an easy target when you're wounded!" She laughed. "Yes, of course I have. I wouldn't have sacrificed my life if I wasn't in it for the science too."

"Hey, about that, what have you been doing for fun these days? We need to meet for dinner."

"Sure, but nothing actually. I've been pretty busy with emergency cases."

"Of CRFS," I said, not asked.

"Of CRFS," she confirmed. "It is steadily escalating. I don't imagine I'm going to see much fun in the coming months."

I didn't feel right asking about details of her cases. It had to be hard losing patients. And as our research was always interdependent, I was sure she took the grant award, or lack thereof, as a blow too. We agreed to get together sometime during the week. But I had a feeling she was going to cancel our date.

I called home to engage in what really mattered. Chris tried to comfort me but was rebuffed. It wasn't nice of me, but I couldn't bear to admit that he had been so right. Would I have taken this so personally if it hadn't been Neil? I've applied for numerous grants that I didn't get. Most scientists do, and this one was not even for work directly in my area of research. But this was personal and raw. "I'm on my way. I miss you guys."

They had a surprise for me, he whispered.

I was greeted at the door, not just by two wagging dog bodies, but two teenagers with genuine smiles and hugs of gratitude for my coming home.

Chris stood in the kitchen stirring a pot. "Hi! Welcome home!" He met my embrace and held me for longer than a hello. "I'm sorry." I held on a little longer, melting in the security of his arms.

I pulled away, and we kissed briefly. "Thank you." I felt myself recalibrating.

Dinner was cooked, mostly by the girls, laundry was done, the house was picked up. Even their bedrooms revealed expanses of the carpet rarely glimpsed under the clothes strewn in a frantic search for just the right ensemble. With barely enough time to take off my coat, I was whisked into the dining room, which was set with plates and silverware and glasses, just the way their Polish Babcia had taught them. A bottle of wine was breathing, snuggled in its cool clay container. Food was in serving dishes I didn't know we owned, and everyone managed to be seated around the table at nearly the same time. Not a cell phone in sight.

"Come sit, Mom. You get to relax while we serve you." And that they did. Salad, spaghetti, veggies, all cooked to perfection.

We talked about their friends, their teachers, and about taking a trip to the Eastern Shore over Thanksgiving break, our favorite place during the off season. Maybe we would drive down the DelMarVa Peninsula to Assateague Island and bike through the Chincoteague wildlife refuge, taking in the mosaic of landscapes of dark brown and puffed white spent cattails that peek out from swaths of amber marsh grasses, around the dense dark green and brown loblolly pine that huddle close, making pockets of forest, to the white sandy beaches that stretch out and frolic with the Atlantic Ocean.

Assateague island forms a thin barrier between the Atlantic Ocean and the Virginia/Maryland coasts. It's topography and brackish waters insulate the island, keeping it mild both in the summer and winter months. Hoodies and jeans are all that is needed in November, as the temperatures are still in the fifties. And maybe earplugs; definitely earplugs, since thousands of birds migrating along the great Atlantic Flyway create a discordant cacophony of honks and quacks and chirps. A symphony warming up, but never playing a singular tune.

The Chesapeake Bay area waterways rarely freeze over, offering year-round feeding grounds that attract avian travelers from both northern and southern migrations, who come to the barrier islands to rest or take up temporary residence. A field of white grows as tundra swans with their graceful long necks tipped in contrasting black bills arrive on outstretched six-foot wings. They are joined by the more compact snow geese whose bills wear a distinctive "grin patch." Smaller brant sea geese wearing a scarf of white plumage dot the marshlands. Brown-headed pintail ducks, their tail feathers extended in black pen strokes, make their way from Canada and dominate the view and soundscape.

Closer focus reveals the smaller black-capped gray catbirds, petite striped-winged flycatchers, and an assortment of other song-birds that are passing through. The tiny dusty-blue northern parula warbler with splashes of yellow on its throat, chest, and shoulders offers both resident and migrating populations. And deep in the pine forests, the diminutive northern saw-whet owl with its giant yellow eyes makes its winter home.

Most will have traveled on by the end of the year, leaving the resident herons, osprey, egrets, and eagles to soar across a quiet winter sky. Throughout the seasons, the resident white-tailed and smaller sika deer, red foxes, and the famous rotund wild ponies go about their days, meandering across the shores, marshes, and forests, while doing their best to ignore the tourists.

The best part of a winter visit? The absence of the bird-sized mosquitoes. Really, you needed an extra-large fly swatter to kill them.

"They drink DEET for lunch." "No, a tennis racket, Mom!" "Hit one of them with your car," Chris mimicked the impact, "and you can't see out the windshield anymore!"

It was good to be home.

"Dad told us what happened," Diana's laughter quieted. "He said we could say we were sad for you, but to not dwell on it."

"Your dad is a wise man. You should listen to him often."

Chris and I cracked smiles at each other, knowing we were both thinking "So should I."

"So do you think that they can find a cure for CRFS without you?," my eldest asked.

"We're not supposed to talk about it!" Diana glared at her sister.

"I can at least ask!" Tess snapped.

It was so nice to be home, really. I'd missed the energy.

"Girls, it's okay. There are lots of really smart people working on it. I'm sure they'll figure it out. And there will probably be other opportunities to join in the hunt."

"But didn't someone steal your idea?" Diana asked.

I looked at Chris. It was sweet that he'd explained it that way.

"Someone had the same idea as we did. I don't know where she got it. But that's not what's important. It only shows that several people were thinking along the same lines, so maybe that means that we were on the right track."

"What did Neil say?" Chris slid in his question.

"Nothing." I met Chris' eyes. "I didn't get a chance to ask him. It was pretty crowded and he was rather tied up with all the official Regnum stuff."

Still locking eyes, both of us expressionless, Chris asked, "So you haven't talked to him on the phone or by email since?"

"No, and I don't plan to. I think this is better left alone. I need to get back to concentrating on Addison's work."

Chris gave me a slight nod in support of my painful release. He knew I was trying to convince myself. "So girls, what's on the agenda for this weekend? Where are we going to find ourselves driving you to this time?"

Two weeks later, nearing lunch, Kate poked her head in my office. "You have a visitor."

I looked up and frowned. It had to be a salesperson hoping to sell the latest innovation in pipettes. Anyone who knew me would have simply walked into my office. "Who is it?"

"Neil Franklin. He's very . . ." She seemed flustered.

Everyone was hiding in their work. I glimpsed him through the spaces in the shelves, my heart pounding, anger welling. I stood, steeled myself, and walked towards the lab's entry.

"Hi," Neil dared not hug me. "I was wondering if you would have lunch with me." Had he really come all the way to my lab to humiliate me in front of my team? "I suspected you wouldn't take my call so I took a chance . . . I know you are probably—"

I brushed past him drawing him into the hall and away from our audience.

"Pissed? Correct. How did it happen?" I was seething.

"Can we go to lunch? I can't tell you about our decision process. But I wanted to—"

"Isn't that convenient? I don't give a shit about the process. I want to know how she got my idea. No one had seen or heard anything about it until the meeting, so how did she just happen to have exactly the same idea, and even supposedly have preliminary results in advance of mine? She doesn't even work on dogs!"

"Are you accusing me of leaking the information to her?"

"Not you, but one of your staff. Perhaps Perky wants a vacation with her boyfriend to the Bahamas but didn't have the money. Then suddenly, just after I submitted my proposal, she happened to take leave."

"She's a lesbian."

"I'm not in the mood for your—" My face was shrinking in like a prune. "Maybe Kendal got to a reviewer who fell for her bullshit seduction. I don't know. You tell me."

"There would not have been enough time for that. Believe me, I've been trying to find out quietly ever since I saw her proposal," his condescending, calm voice, was disquieting.

"And?"

"And I can't say anything for sure."

"Can't or won't."

"Both." He glanced over my shoulder at my team, who were pretending to not be straining to hear. "Can we step outside or go to lunch to talk about this, please?" He caught my gaze, and his big brown eyes sucked me in.

He let me keep venting as I stormed down the hall. "So wait, you knew she submitted a proposal similar to mine early on? And you never even bothered to warn me?" What a dick. "Because I would have what, said something? Done something?"

"Actually yes, then I wouldn't have been able to sit on the review committee and wouldn't have—"

"In other words, your ass or mine. Guess self-preservation trumps friendship." I crashed through the building doors, hurting my hand. I slammed on my brakes and spun around. Neil almost ran into me. "How could they have voted to support her? How did she fully develop it in such a short period of time? How did she get to them and move to the top of the list?" I glared at him and tears welled. "How could you have not warned me?" He simply stared at me, expressionless. "Did you approve it?" I demanded.

"My board approved it. I'm only one vote."

"That is such crap. They never approve anything if you don't at least support it."

"I thought you said you had other ideas if this one didn't pan out."

"None were as promising or fully formed, and there aren't any more opportunities for funding or access to the samples at this point. But you already know that because you and Regnum have control over them. All I can do is limp along until more dogs die and open up more opportunities, and that's not an option I would ever hope for." I paused. "Or, I can just give up."

"You? Give up? You're the most tenacious and creative person I know. I'm sure you have other ideas you can pursue, probably better ones."

"Don't patronize me. She stole my work, she has the attention of the world now, and . . ."

"I thought you weren't interested in fame."

"You know what I mean. Attention means funding. I don't give a shit about fame." I spat out the words. "Tell me what happened, or what you think happened." I could feel rage building, as I leaned in, physically challenging him.

He looked down and shifted away from me. "You don't need to know."

"How can you say that? I have to know. You betray our friendship, and all the respect I have from the canine research community."

"So now this is about your standing?" he asked, raising one eyebrow.

Dear God, I thought, was he actually being smug?

"To hell with you. We used to have the same goal—making a difference. I was so excited that I had the opportunity to maybe make a contribution to saving these animals."

Taking both my hands, he forced me to focus. "You still can." He looked so sure, so confident.

I steeled my jaw. "Why am I even wasting my breath?" I stomped on. "I don't want to talk about it anymore."

"Your choice," he looked ahead.

We walked silently to the noise-filled student union. We could have gone off campus to a quiet restaurant, but I embraced the distraction which forced us to talk about anything but failed grant proposals and dying dogs.

We parted with a stiff goodbye; he was clearly trying to help me accept that it was just business, and I was struggling to figure out why I couldn't. I watched him disappear around the corner. The silence was deafening.

A flurry of thoughts and emotions spun faster until they reached a pinnacle and I stood in the lab doorway and time stopped. Slowly, quietly, in the background, the sound increased — bubbling water, thermostats clicking on and off, incubators hissing as they aerated growing cells. People were suspended in motion.

Three sets of eyes were locked on me. They had never heard me get that angry, never heard me spit obscenities.

"Is Kendal that one woman who called here for some cat cells a few weeks ago?" Kate asked tentatively, peeking around the shelves on the workbench.

"Yes, and I suspect that she was really fishing around for some information. I don't believe it was a coincidence that she called."

Megan got up and stood before me, putting her hand on my arm. "Can we do anything for you? Do you want to have another brainstorming session? Want a beaker to throw against the wall?"

I looked at each of them and managed a grateful nod. "No, we have work to do on Addison's. But thank you." I squeezed her hand as I walked past her, and shut my office door behind me.

LIFE IS SHORT, PLAY WITH YOUR DOG

I SAT on the porch, encased in my hoddie and blanket. My coffee cup and I sharing our warmth. Having said good morning with a wagging tail and body slides along my legs, Ania laid quietly warming my feet. Sofie bopped out the dog door to dance in the cold, then back again to make sure she didn't miss anything. I drifted into thoughts about why these creatures are so special.

The energy changes when a dog is in the room. Whether they lie quietly by your side, nudge you to elicit a stroke along their back, or stare intently to tell you it's dinner time, you can feel the power of their presence. They are transformative. The weight of the world is released when nose meets hand. Their rhythmic breathing can slow your pace, calm your spirit, and extract your stress. Their state of being is infectious. Paws pitter-pattering raise your heartbeat and draw you to the door, unleashing an explosion of frenzied anticipation. The promise of a lifetime together, renewed, as you share in the delight of a walk.

Dogs live in the moment. The past is done, the future unknown. There are no grudges, no guilt, no burdened history.

Even those rescued from the worst of circumstances and rehabilitated, embrace life to the fullest, with only the occasional resurfacing of a painful memory and that resurfaces a reactionary behavior. Each day brings new possibilities.

Ania's world is simple. She delights in good meal; a hug, a treat, an invitation to join me on the couch. A ride in the car is ecstasy. When a new ball is bounced and bounced, her entire body is giddy. Pack members returning home are celebrated with the dog waggle dance. But take out a suitcase, and she becomes anxious at the sight of it laying open on the bed, uncertain if this trip will include her. She follows me from room to room, ears flat, head lowered; she is crestfallen. Her tail and her spirit drop when I open the front door and say, "I'll be back."

Our alliance is the foundation of her well-being. I give her the context in which she is content, translating human love into social nourishment. She thrives on attention. She gives respect and loyalty to all members of her pack. As the alpha dog I am not better. It just works. There is social order; knowing your place settles disagreements before they surface. She will defend, comfort, acquiesce, or dominate as defined by her place in the hierarchy. She is fulfilled with a sense of belonging.

Her communication is often subtle but always consistent. I simply have to pay attention to the movement of her tail, position of her ears, or tilt of her head, and I will know the tenor of her mood. She rumbles soft and low warnings, and barks loud alarms. She keeps Sofie in line with a not-so-subtle show of teeth. She does not overexaggerate or understate. She says what she means. I speak to her as a child, a partner, a student, a friend. She understands a diversity of words. The inflection of my voice is like a symphony to her well-trained ears. She recognizes my smile and feels my stress. She can laugh when I rub her belly. She can pout when I tell her no more. She can love. Yes. Love.

Dogs are good at keeping secrets. Ania and Sofie will stare me blankly in the face, sitting next to the overturned trash can, not revealing even a hint of which one is guilty. Both will cower if I scold, both will be elated if I ignore the mess. Some would say they don't have the type of memory that connects them to these incidents, but I have lived with dogs long enough to know they know. They keep my secrets too. I can be in the best or worst of moods, reflected back at me by their exuberance or quiet, but the moment Chris or the girls walk into the house, they reveal nothing, greeting them as if all is right with the world. They are stoic and unflinching as part of my covenant with them.

Some of dogs' behavior is learned, some is innate. Dogs have an instinct to respond when something is amiss, but learn to temper their response when satisfied they have been heard. Despite the repeated positive daily reinforcement of the mailman's retreat, Ania learned that he does not need to be reminded that this is her territory. He comes and leaves quickly. She no longer needs to tell him to.

They are keenly aware of where I am in the house. Sofie, still a pup, is always underfoot. The length of the kitchen must be traversed together. Clean laundry is escorted from room to room. I have no privacy in the shower. But she will learn, like Ania has, when to follow and when to stay put, because *I will be right back.* Lying by my side, Ania pays close attention, listens, and interprets my movements, looking for signs. She springs to life at the sound of the leash or garbage bag being tied up. She knows these mean she will accompany me to familiar places.

Our relationship with dogs is believed to have begun 30,000 years ago, when we first began to domesticate them from wolves. Domestication is a twist on the theory of natural selection, with selection done by man, not nature. Random mutations accumulate naturally in a species, as long as the organism can survive with the mutation. With natural selection, if the mutation confers an advantage, or is at least neutral in its effect, it can be retained in successive generations. Domestication, on the other hand, occurs when man chooses to retain the mutation, expressed as a physical trait (phenotype) that we see as beneficial or desirable. Both natural selection and domestication ultimately result in evolution of the species. But domestication can result in retaining genes that help us, yet harming the species we are creating.

As for dogs, the latest belief is that humans and dogs coevolved. Capitalizing on the hunting strategies of wolves, humans mimicked them to track and hunt prey, while wolves benefited from scavenging among the humans' discards. Canines who were sly enough to befriend the humans benefited most from the humans' curiosity about the world around them. Those dogs relinquished their territories to track with the humans. Slowly we became each other's guardians, co-hunters, and eventually companions. While definitive evidence would be hard to find, it is reasonable to assume that early humans assisted by dogs would have a higher chance of success.

Once domesticated, humans became a necessity for the dog's survival. Though today's dog can adapt to becoming feral, no domestic dogs do well in the wild. Stories abound of how even the most street-wise dogs express their domesticated genes, and find a spot on the bed when offered a chance at the good life. This is not the same for their wild relatives. An Australian dingo, a coyote, or a wolf can be tamed, but not domesticated. From the start, wolf puppies will not make eye contact with humans. Unlike dog pups, they are not interested in what we have to offer. A wounded coyote will not show appreciation or adaptive behavior to the rehabilitation we offer, but will bolt for freedom the moment the cage door is opened. They are wild animals.

So are foxes, distant relatives in Family Canidae. They are

exceptionally skittish, and rarely tamable. They want nothing to do with us. However, in a fascinating fifty-year long study, a group of Russian scientists chose and bred less aggressive foxes through successive generations, resulting in docile animals that were somewhat interested in their human captors. This isn't too surprising, as this is the typical process for domestication, though it will take several hundred generations to solidify traits that are predictably conferred to the next generation.

But the most surprising result was that the docile foxes were cuter. Their ears were a bit floppy and their muzzles were more rounded. These friendlier adult foxes looked more like cute baby foxes, or kits.

There are two prevailing theories on how this may have happened. One suggests that the genes that are commonly expressed when immature, for both cuteness and less defensive behavior, are physically linked with one another on the same chromosome and are thus inherited together. The other theory is that it could be a single gene that influences a bunch of others, controlling the expression of sets of genes at different times in development. A similar gene has also been found in humans in which a particular mutation confers Williams-Beuren syndrome, which is characterized by elfin features, a shortened nose bridge, and exceptional gregariousness.

It's theorized that having a baby-like appearance allows the young to be recognized across the animal kingdom, providing either a basis to recognize and protect the young across species, or signaling dinner. As for the foxes, it will take many more generations to prove the linkage—and unfortunately a lot of discarded animals—but the study of canine domestication is too intriguing for us to ignore. However it happened, our selection of more engaging animals pulled along the genes that laid the foundation for the myriad of dog breeds with characteristics we adore.

But why so many dog breeds? For better, and unfortunately sometimes for worse, humans are solely responsible for the creation of more than 400 dog breeds; created through artificial selection to serve every imaginable purpose, from the working retrievers and herders, to therapy and guide dogs, to those that provide comfort and companionship. Similarities to some of the oldest domestic dog breeds—pharaoh hounds and Ibizan hounds—appear in Egyptian tomb drawings dating back to 2000 BCE. Bas-reliefs from 150 BCE in China show a hunting dog similar to the chow chow, and the greyhound is believed to be mentioned in the Bible. Modern dog breeds begin to appear in the thirteenth through fifteenth centuries: the poodle in drawings from Germany, the Portuguese water dog in writings of Portuguese monks, and a variety of spaniels in Spanish paintings.

No other animal connects with us as does the dog. You can't lie on the couch watching TV with a bunny, or go for a three-day hiking trip with your ferret. And cats? While I haven't had the pleasure of sharing my life with one, some of my cat-people friends will admit that a cat's goal in life is not to be there for us. We are here for them.

But a dog: a dog's sole purpose is to be by our side. They will wait indefinitely for us and forgive us for the length of our absence. They sleep contentedly at our feet, and they have a way of knowing, especially as they age, how to be exactly what we need at precisely the right moment.

Their main shortcoming, their only shortcoming, is that they don't live long enough. But even that might be a mixed blessing as we would not have a succession of wonderful companions if their lifespan equaled ours. Perhaps we should be grateful that they force us to renew our relationship with them every fifteen or so years, if we are lucky.

I try not to remember those final moments, frantic hours,

flashing days, or agonizing weeks when my dogs may have been dying, and that look in their eyes that told me to let go. They are stoic even when in pain, and they will conceal any weakness from the alpha. They will not let you know until it is too late. I try to trust my instincts when I feel that something is off, but sometimes denial is easier to accept when instinct tells you it's bad, and too often it costs the ultimate price. It is the greatest responsibility in our covenant with a dog. It is also an unparalleled privilege to have to make the decision to let them go

I remember better the stilled silence. Coming home to an empty house where before I was greeted with love. Seeing an empty spot on the couch, feeling cold against my feet on the bed. No dog there when I needed one the most. The loss leaving me wandering an empty house.

If only the dogs could tell us when this whole CRFS thing started, their situation may not have gotten so bad. Maybe we could follow the trail better if we knew the moment they felt something amiss, and maybe we could save them—and so many of their caretakers—from broken hearts.

MYSTERY SOLVED

Dear Dr. Winthrop,

This is my resignation as your technician. I am so very sorry for telling Dr. Kovak about your proposal. I thought she was a friend of yours and when she asked what was new and exciting in the lab, it never occurred to me that she was trying to get inside information.

I have enjoyed working for you, and I will miss everyone in the lab and miss the important work that I had the privilege to do. Thank you for everything you have taught me.

I was able to get a job in the Chemistry Department, even after I explained the reason for my leaving your lab. If you need me to help train a new technician or cover my work until you find someone new, please let me know. I can be reached in Dr. Newman's lab.

Again, I am so, so sorry. I hope that someday you can forgive me.

Kate

It hadn't been Perky, or anyone else at Regnum. Kate. I wished she would have come to talk to me. I would have understood; it was an innocent mistake and given how cunning I know Kendal can be, I wouldn't have put the blame on Kate. Still, one of my own—that stung. I called Kate's cell phone; she didn't pick up, though I'm sure she saw my call since she was never without her phone. It was such a shame, I really liked her; I would have let her stay. I left a message on her voice mail. I was sorry too, that she hadn't come to talk to me, that she had probably been manipulated by Kendal. We could have worked something out. I wished her the best, and told her that if she ever needed a recommendation to let me know. The work she did in the lab would not be overshadowed by this one misstep. She didn't call back. Neil should have told me it wasn't one of his team; but did he know?

It took three weeks to hire Haley. Megan got her settled into the routine of feeding the cell lines, and showed her the layout of the lab. Haley came from a family of scientists, so she had been playing with lab equipment since she was a kid. Friendly and inquisitive, Haley was an undergraduate in her second year, majoring in zoology. She came highly recommended by one of my colleagues down the hall who was leaving in the spring to take a tenure track position at another university, and wanted to make sure Haley had a place to finish out her year of work-study. I was happy to help as I'm sure it beats working in the dining hall.

"So Dr. Winthrop, we were just talking in my molecular biology class about evolutionary studies and I was reading up on your work. Why did you start out studying cats and not dogs?"

Megan shook her head and cracked a grin, not looking up.

"Well, I am a dog person—stop rolling your eyes, Jamie—but by a series of right place, wrong time I got handed cats as my project since all the dog work was taken. But it was actually pretty interesting. Besides, I was there to learn how to analyze DNA, not interact with the whole animal."

"They all look the same on a gel," Jamie added.

"And cats are a great model for the study of human disease. They have surprisingly similar order to their genes, more so than a lot of other animal groups except primates, and they have a lot of parallel diseases. Like Sandhoff disease; it's a disease that causes progressive degeneration in nerve cells. Humans and domestic cats both suffer from it."

"But how does that relate to studying cat evolution?"

"Well, there's also the need to understand how genes evolve in natural and subsequently domesticated environments, and cats have some pretty interesting evolutionary quirks."

"Oh yeah, I've heard how all cheetahs in the world have the same genes."

"Pretty much. They have so little diversity in their alleles that in a study done in U.S. zoos and in Africa, the different cheetahs didn't even reject skin grafts between each other."

"Skin grafts?"

"Yes, the group of genes that normally make an organism reject something that is not self, were so similar in the cheetahs that they didn't recognize small areas of skin that were grafted from one animal to another."

"Wow."

"It was a pretty remarkable study. It was done back in the 1980s; they couldn't get away with it nowadays. But based on the results it's believed that the entire population of cheetahs underwent at least one, if not several bottlenecks, where the population was depleted down to very few individuals from which all current cheetahs descended. As a result, they have almost no genetic diversity, which is critical to facing environmental changes." I finally rolled a chair over to where she was sitting at the hood plating cells. "Oddly though, the species continues, so they are a really fascinating, naturally occurring population to study."

"Now we're learning about the use of microsatellites and DNA analysis, but you didn't have those techniques back then, right? I'd love to hear how you think those studies compare to those done now."

Megan looked up at her with pleading eyes. I know she was trying to rescue her from the emerging lecture.

"Well, there have been so many advances since my day. When I was doing my graduate work –"

"Back when the dinosaurs roamed the Earth," Jamie stomped his feet.

"And DNA was just a figment of Crick's imagination," Megan added.

"And Darwin was still throwing up on the Beagle," Jamie said, being Jamie.

I waited until they were finished.

"As I was saying before those who depend on me for their employment so rudely interrupted, there are thirty-seven species in Family Felidae. Lots of work preceded mine, so I was simply applying the most modern laboratory tools to confirm what most folks using morphology had already determined from fossils and by comparing the structural variation between species."

"Modern at the time," Jamie pointed out.

"Don't you have some sequences to compare?" I shooed him away.

"But morphology can be deceiving," Haley observed.

"Correct, morphology can be deceiving. Just look at the skull of a Yorkie compared to a bulldog and you would be hard pressed to say they were the same species."

"But you don't see that in domestic cats. They're pretty much all the same."

"True. There's not a lot of mystery within the domestic cat when it comes to grouping them as one species, and within the Felidae there are some pretty obvious groupings, like the big cats—

lions, tigers, leopards, jaguars—all of them group well together on one evolutionary branch based on morphology and confirmed by genetics. But there are a lot of smaller wild cats like those making up the domestic cat lineage—European wildcat, African wildcat, jungle cat, sand cat—that don't easily separate out from other small cats like the Pallas' cat, fishing cat, and flat-headed cat that branch off from the domestic cat lineage."

"I don't think I've heard of most of those."

"Neither had I when I started. I used the 'ancient' technique of protein electrophoresis to see if I could resolve some of the ambiguities," I gave Jamie a 'don't you dare' glare.

"Did you?" Haley asked.

"Sort of." I shrugged. "It solidified the close relationship between the cheetah and puma, which though they occur continents apart today, show similarities based on fossils found in North America. There has been a lot of work since mine that has added to the consensus evolutionary tree of the Felidae. Truthfully, I haven't kept track of all of it," I confessed. "I found it interesting to watch it come together and it was cool to confirm their relationships based on a control. We used the hyena as the outgroup since it's a species that is equally distant to all of the cats."

"So the hyena in the cat family?"

"No, it is actually in its own family, but closer to the cats than the dog family. So it should and did show up with equal genetic difference to all the cats."

"Cool."

"There are a bunch of other cool things used to figure out cat evolution." I continued since she was still eager, or at least appeared to be. "Cats group similarly with respect to purring versus roaring. The prevailing theory is that this is due to the ossification of the hyoid bone. Smaller cats have a more rigid hyoid bone better supporting the tongue and larynx, allowing them to purr, and this change occurred in a common ancestor. The smaller cats also group based on endogenous retroviruses."

"Retrovirus, isn't that what AIDS is? "

"Yes, and herpes, and chicken pox. Retroviruses are viruses that insert into the host's DNA to make more copies of themselves. The retro part refers to the fact that they are RNA-based, not DNA, and they bring their own set of tools, like their own enzymes, to make the cell's processes work to assemble a complete virus."

"So the same retroviruses are found in all members of the domestic cat lineage?"

"Correct, but the operative word is *endogenous.* AIDS and herpes are EXogenous retroviruses, meaning they originate outside the host, and are essentially a parasite on that host. An ENdogenous virus is one that has been incorporated into the host's DNA so long ago that it no longer functions, and has become an inert—most of the time—part of the host's genome."

Jamie and Megan jointly rolled their eyes. They had suffered through this story many times before.

"Some species within the Felidae have a set of similar viral sequences that appear in their genome. These sequences are likely from an ancient retrovirus that became non-functional by losing part of its sequence, but remain forever embedded in the cat's DNA. It occurred millions of years ago as the lineage evolved, so all the modern cat species branching from that common ancestor have the same sequences."

"Wow, that's unique, isn't it?"

"Sort of. The two that occur in the Felidae are only seen in those species within the domestic cat branch, but as far as endogenous ancient viruses go, we see the same thing in primates, as well as in many other mammals. Since they were pretty well described before, they weren't important in my work. But endogenous viruses are often used in tissue culture labs to stimulate cells to grow."

"I thought you said they're no longer functional."

"In general they are, but some of them have the ability to stimulate cell growth. You know how the cells you are growing start to die off after several passages, or generations?"

"Yes! That's so frustrating!"

"Well some endogenous retroviruses, when added to the media used to feed cells growing in culture, somehow immortalize the cells, and keep them growing generation after generation."

"That's lit!"

"Uh, okay." I was clearly behind on my lingo. "But like I said, I didn't study them. For my work, mitochondrial DNA was the key to figuring out how all the cats were related."

"And that's DNA that is separate from the DNA in the nucleus."

"Correct. I love how what I only learned in graduate school has become common knowledge for undergraduates or even in high school."

"Exactly! We keep trying to tell you how much harder it is for us these days since we have so much more to learn!" Megan play-acted exhaustion.

"Ignore them. Mitochondrial DNA—or mtDNA—is small and simple. In most mammals it has only thirty-seven genes, and is relatively well conserved within a species but at the same time is variable enough to show differences between species. Similar to how endogenous viral sequences may have become part of another species' genome, the theory on mitochondria and why they have their own DNA is that they were once a separate organism, probably a bacterium, that formed a mutually beneficial relationship inside another cell."

Jamie stuck his head in. "It's a very romantic story."

I felt my lecture ending. "Over time, they simply became a single entity. The bacteria became the mitochondria, which produce all the energy for the cell to use, and still retains its own DNA. The host cell contributes the building blocks—glucose and amino acids to keep it functioning."

"So why is it so well conserved within a species?"

"For one thing there is no recombination. The genome is inherited wholly intact, and as the genes are few and specific, they can't handle a lot of mutation. The combination of these two features means that any genetic change is very telling." Gasping for my last breath I continued, "Also, with rare exceptions, it's maternally inherited and this straight line of inheritance makes it a great tool to track the evolutionary history of populations."

"How does that happen?" she asked. "I mean, the maternal inheritance?"

"Well, mitochondria exist in most cells, including the egg and the sperm, and there are usually many copies per cell. However, in the sperm, they are all in the tail so they can produce the energy the sperm need to swim. But since the tail falls off at fertilization and only the head enters the egg, none of the paternal mtDNA is transferred."

Jamie closed the lecture. "What a poignant ending for all that hard work."

"We can continue this later," I assured Haley.

Megan loudly whispered behind my back, "Trust me, you haven't heard the last of this."

I smiled. My indoctrination had been successful, despite the heckling.

Epidemiology is the search for the source of a disease. The science of epidemiology combines slick, TV-worthy forensic medicine with the intricate, less glamorous field of statistics. Data are collected, maps are overlaid, patterns emerge, connections are made. But it's the statistically significant correlations that hold the key. The Centers for Disease Control and Prevention—CDC—in Atlanta, Georgia, is the US'—and possibly the world's—premier hub for epidemiologists. These scientists have played major roles in piecing together the spread of AIDS from patient zero in the 1980s, tracing the trail of anthrax attacks in the early 2000s, and isolating the sources during threats of human epidemics like SARS and Ebola.

But finding the source differs greatly from finding the cause. Finding the cause is often a progression of fits and starts, following up on hopeful leads, revisiting dead ends, and gut feelings about that oddity that you observed last week that makes you rethink your whole approach. Clinical symptoms can distract from the process, as an organism's defense system may overreact and mask the initial or underlying response that is the important clue.

The interplay of epidemiology and identifying a disease's cause is important, since knowing the routes and rates of transmission can help zero in on the causative agent. But it can still take years to pinpoint the actual cause and even longer to find a prevention or cure. Symptoms of HIV infection were known as far back as 1920. It is believed to have been picked up by humans who ate chimpanzees; the discovery that it was transmitted by bodily fluids supported the theory that it was caused by a virus. Still, it took nearly ten years after it emerged in the US before the actual virus was identified, and decades later we still wait and hope for a vaccine and cure.

Any scientific discovery is the result of many contributors, Nobel Prize work included, building upon an accumulation of data until the scientifically significant *aha* moment. It takes a village—a scientific village. The scientific publication announcing the discovery of the gene for cystic fibrosis, the most common human genetic disease—listed twenty-three authors.

THE DEAD OF WINTER

ANIA LAY on her back, legs spider-like in all directions, spotlighted by the sun radiating through the window, twitching, sound asleep, as I downed my first dose of caffeine. Ancestral genes retained in her species granted her the ability to fall asleep anywhere, anytime, secure in the comfort that she sat at the top of the food chain.

She woke and rose unhurriedly. Like pastry dough gently pulled between two hands, a stretch glided from the tips of her front paws up her neck through her arching back, and flowing through her extended back legs. She stepped out and shook from nose to tail; invigorated by slumber, she locked eyes with me, her tail wiggled, and her face brightened.

Being alone with a dog was like being alone and still feeling loved. That feeling you got when someone you love wrapped their arms around you on a cool, sunny Saturday when you had nothing to do and could simply exhale the world away. She came to me, put her head on my lap, and turned slightly to rub the sleep away. I rubbed her neck and her muzzle, and she kissed my face. "Guess I should get moving, huh?" I asked. For a moment she too seemed to want to take in the feeling, but then she shook it off and beckoned me to the day with a toss of her head. I unfolded myself from the warmth of my cushy robe, stood and stretched as she has taught me to do, and bent down opening my arms to welcome her in our morning embrace.

It was the calm before the storm. Ania, Sofie, and I were all up, finishing the packing, getting the car loaded. They remained hopeful that they would be joining our trip to the Eastern Shore. Forgetting to fully close the front door was all the invitation they needed, and out they bolted to claim their spot among the pillows and blankets and duffle bags in the back of the car, like ET in the closet of toys. They wouldn't care that they wouldn't be allowed to run the beaches in the National Seashore on the Virginia side of Assateague – they wanted only to go with us. There would be lots of stops along the way to frolic on remote stretches as we traveled through the American Indian-named towns that dot the coast. I left them with the car door open, for they would not be moved, and headed in to grab more towels for the stinky, happy wet dogs in our future. The rolling thunder that was my family tumbled down the hall, and we engaged in a flurry of activity before setting off on our journey.

The week moved slowly as we biked the park and rural roads, and took long walks on the beach. The water too cold to swim, still enticed us until our feet turned red and we retreated with the sun. We woke to rain on Thanksgiving, providing an excuse to snuggle in and watch the parade, and catch the dog show that follows, a tradition of ours since before the girls.

Like most dog shows, the event spans five days, with the first days resulting in selection of breed champions and reserves. The

Thanksgiving Day televised show covered the next round—selection of a champion from the breed champions that make up each group—and culminated in the final selection of Best in Show from the seven group winners.

Commentators chattered nervously, albeit briefly, about concerns of CRFS, but concentrated on their script about each breed and vignettes about individual dogs.

"Looks like next up we have a mop on the table," the color commentator chortled.

"Not so! Originally from Hungary; 'compact, vigorous and alert, the Puli is a tough-as-nails herding dog, able to perform its duties across any terrain. The Puli coat is wavy or curly and naturally clumps together into wooly cords, which protects them from harsh weather. Coat colors include black, gray and white. Today's breed champion is a white male, Puli #57, Carpathian Mystic Mountain, but he goes by the name of Bear, and is from Michigan's Upper Peninsula. His owner says that when he's not out on the show circuit, his favorite pastime is herding his small flock of sheep. In the winter she often finds him spread-eagle in the snow making dog snow angels. It must be a challenge to keep his cords clean and dry!"

"I wonder which ones have more hair—the Pulis or the sheep!" Diana exclaimed.

We enjoyed Thanksgiving at Bill's Steak and Seafood, a homey local restaurant that promised turkey and all the fixings just like mom's, a promise well delivered.

All was quiet on the CRFS front until the radio shattered the calm on the way home. Tuned to NPR, an investigative story provided interviews of owners who lost dogs to CRFS. "We were so excited. Josephine had placed best of opposite in her breed, the best she's done at a national show. She was so proud as she pranced around the ring, now she's clinging to life with"—sobs "whatever this is." She was gone by nightfall. Jojo, a Maltese from the toy group, was the first report of what would be thirty-two others from the show; all within the toy, hound, and herding groups. Then the floor fell out of the dog show theory, as reports from shelters, vets, boarding kennels, and countless owners peppered the East Coast epidemiological map. No population was unaffected, and CRFS proved to be an equal opportunity killer, as it took down purebreds and mutts alike. Losses were now in the thousands.

Returning to our daily lives, we tried to focus on the home front. Tess's science fair, and the following weekend production of the girls' school play. But it was hard to ignore that December brought a chill with news of 146 more CRFS-related deaths.

As I walked into the lab, Jamie looked up, surprised, "Hey, did you see your friend Dr. Franklin has left Regnum?'

"Yeah, I saw the announcement in *Science*'s News section." Subject closed.

I had found that curious. Just a little over one month after the big grant competition and potentially a big new research field for Regnum, Neil stepped down as CSO. I wanted to pick up the phone and ask why; was it connected to what happened with Kendal and me? But I couldn't do it. Besides, his career would not have been influenced by one single incident, and he would have immediately pointed out that I was narcissistic thinking it had anything to do with me. If I had wanted to contact him, to start to rebuild our friendship, I would have to wait until the dust settled around him. Did he know it was my technician who spilled the beans to Kendal? Why didn't he call me as a friend to tell me he was changing jobs? I had to admit that my over exaggerated grudge was a likely the reason.

"So what are you all working on today? Were you able to

analyze that sequence from the new batch of Addison's dogs?"

"Yes," Megan pointed to her computer screen. "I was able to assemble the second region we talked about."

"And I have a preliminary analysis on the other segment from last week," Jamie added. "There seems to be variation in the 5' region. But it looks to be similar to the one we saw back in October."

"Another dead end?" I asked.

"I hope not, but we should know in a day or two," Jamie looked confident.

"When are you guys taking off?"

"I'm out of here Thursday morning. I'll help Haley put all the cell lines to bed so nothing turns to mush over the winter break," Jamie gave me a confident look.

"I'm not leaving until Friday," Megan added, "so I can shut down everything else. I'll shut down the water baths and clean them out. We don't have any cells growing, but I'll leave the incubator on. What about the sequencer?"

"Leave that on too. Even if no one is going to use it over the holidays, I don't want to chance messing up the flow of reagents since it's so temperamental."

"I've named her Gladys," Jamie remarked.

"One that got away?" I shouldn't have really asked.

"One that I should have run away from, much quicker than I did," surprisingly revealing a wisp of his private life.

I turned to Megan. "I'll probably still be in over the weekend and a few days a week, so don't worry about getting everything; I can double check when I'm here."

"You're not doing lab work, are you?" Megan asked with worry in her voice, while Jamie looked panicked. Obviously I would never live down my reputation as being all thumbs last time I attempted to join in on the fun in the lab. In my defense, the new automated sequencer was complex, with instructions written in a font size only twenty-year olds can see. They were at an obvious advantage.

"No, don't worry. I wouldn't dare without your supervision. I want to do some extracurricular research on CRFS to see if I might find another way to study it." Their relief was palpable.

"You're not looking to continue with the same approach, are you? Which, by the way, there doesn't seem to be any news on any progress in that area," Jamie pointed out.

"I doubt she wants to follow Dr. Kovach's progress very closely, Jamie."

"Actually, I've been watching, but I've seen nothing. I'm beginning to wonder if it was such a good idea anyway, though truthfully, it might be too soon to expect results."

"Really? Then what are you thinking we could do instead?" Megan asked.

"I don't know. I'm as stumped as the rest of the dog world, but I thought if I came in a few times over the holidays and combed through published articles, news stories, available data and records, anything that I can get my hands on, maybe something will stick out. At this point it's anybody's guess. Maybe since I'm not doing any research in this area I might have a clear head and be open to subtleties that someone immersed in it might miss."

"Would you like some help?" the twins echoed. They really were a solid pair.

"No, not yet. You guys enjoy your break. If I see anything, believe me you will be hit with it the moment you return!"

"I'll be checking my email over the break. I'm happy to come back early if you need me."

"Me too," Megan joined in.

The week closed with no results of interest in our research. Disappointing, but we still had a number of other potential markers to explore starting in January. Exams ended. Like ants exiting a rain-flooded hill, students retreated in all directions, heading home for the holidays. Gray and cold, the deserted campus took on a creepy post-plague movie set look. Brief glimpses of human forms scurrying between parking lots. A car darting faster than normal down the campus main drag, no longer impeded by the bravado of student pedestrians who believed they were invincible. The shortened day pulled away the muted light, leaving a campus cross-hatched by footpaths illuminated by street lights. I closed down my office and the lab, knowing that within a few days I would be back, and hoping to be inspired by the silence and solitude.

Stories I'd read online came to life in my thoughts as I drove home.

A rural vet traveled on Route 13 to 113, down the Delmarva, tending to livestock and pets. The wind blew cold off the Chesapeake Bay, but watermen still headed out for speckled trout and sea bass. A few, on the edge of insanity or maybe brilliance, dove for oysters, hand plucking the thirty-bushel limit with more precision and less potential damage to the fragile beds than the traditional claw method. The vet stopped at the Phillips farm, a small farm handed down through generations, producing melons and a variety of vegetables, the mainstay of the lower peninsula. Two ponies trotted alongside his car, separated from the road by a rundown three-board fence. Adopted in Chincoteague, they had swum in from Assateague Island in the annual pony swim that keeps the island population of wild ponies below carrying capacity, and raises money for the fire department. There were goats, a herd of twenty-two that started from two that Mrs. Phillips got to attempt to make local goat cheese, and which since spent their days frolicking and procreating to feed the growing pet pygmy goat industry. The barn was quiet, warmed and perfumed by composting manure. A tabby greeted him, weaving between his feet; though she was supposed to be a mouser, she preferred her meals supplemented by her mistress Phillips. She walked the beams of her territory inside the barn office and stalls, while other cats more feral, kept the hay barn and tack room free of rodents. Finishing his rounds, the vet returned to the farmer's kitchen to remind her to check two of the pregnant goats, and to not overfeed the ponies or they could founder even with the green grass dying. "Where's Easton?" he asked.

"He passed a few weeks ago, just after you was here last time. Just curled up in the barn office to die," Mrs. Phillips said tearfully. "Found him barely breathing. Blood coming out his nose. Didn't even know I was there. No time to call you, Doc. Mr. Phillips put him out of his misery with one clean shot. I haven't stopped blubbering since."

Easton had been a five-year-old golden retriever with a strong body and heart, her companion from sunup until they retired each night to their respective beds. The vet had described this and several other visits along his route to the online reporter. Nothing out of the ordinary, few of his patients needed more than a vaccination or cleaning and suturing of a wound. But four dogs had died, though he only witnessed one as he took his last breaths; he and Winston's owners stood helpless in goodbye. Their isolation made it impossible to collect useful samples to confirm CRFS as the culprit. But Doc Meyer was convinced.

Then there was the team at the NC State veterinary school who released observations from their research, ahead of any peer-reviewed publication, in the hope that others might be able to quickly confirm and use their results. They had been seeing what they believed were cases of CRFS, and had found an increase in a protein in the blood of some of the victims, but not all. They didn't know if the protein was a cause or an effect. They didn't even know for sure if it was related, as it was not present in all of the victims.

But it did not appear in the unaffected control population. The protein was small, and very unstable, so it could be lost during processing and preserving of some of the samples.

The Wayne County animal shelter in North Carolina was state-of-the-art, with indoor/outdoor dog runs and heated floors, quarantine rooms with separate ventilation systems, adoption testing play rooms and open spaces, and stainless-steel cages that could be easily disinfected. It took in almost any kind of domestic animal including dogs, cats, ferrets, bunnies, hamsters, guinea pigs, birds, goats, potbellied pigs, and horses. The shelter had a co-op of farms that picked up weekly and housed farm animals for holding or long-term sanctuary. But as of December fifteenth, the shelter closed down its dog adoption service, having lost 60% of the dogs in their care to CRFS during the first two weeks of December. At the first hint of the disease, affected dogs were put into the quarantine room or euthanized, but the staff modified their approach within a few days, and pulled all the healthy dogs out of the shelter to private residences willing to take them. All of those survived; none of the ones left behind did.

Then there was the story about the puppies, six of them. I pictured them emerging one by one, limp at first until life was awakened by the experienced licking of their mother. Splattered brown, white, and black, they were a mix of breeds unknown, but they were the lucky ones, as their mother was taken in by Mutt Haven Rescue, which specialized in plucking pregnant bitches from certain euthanasia at shelters across four states. Though dedicated to saving dogs, shelters simply do not have the resources to care for mothers and litters for the six weeks it takes to get them weaned. Eyes still shut, one little guy with black ears and a white splash across his face followed the scent of milk as he rooted for a teat until he latched on, and curled his tongue around to suck in life. He fell asleep still attached. Like a scene I have watched so many times with puppies I have whelped, I could see him with his eyes sealed shut, stir and rock unsteadily, wandering on shaky legs just far enough to lose direction; he cried out and was nudged back into the fold. In less than two weeks his milky brown eyes would peek through, and his world would expand to the walls of the whelping box. At three weeks he was a sponge for information, gradually noticing his feet, his tail, his littermates. He responded to human sweet talk and stumbled towards a voice with the help of his newly unsealed ears and eyes. At four weeks he was a growling, barking, biting, wrestling, wagging, full-on puppy. He should stay with his mom until ten weeks, when his immune system was fully ready to handle the onslaught of modern vaccine benefits. But resources are limited. Mutt Haven Rescue cycled in and out four to six litters a month, a dedicated few screening adoption applications in search of forever homes for each puppy and the mothers. Every successful match was an affirmation of their mission. Dogs are vaccinated before they leave for parvo and distemper. Other than a few unfortunate ones born sick or dead, few were lost. The head of the organization reported that CRFS did not surface in the foster homes, but moms in the shelters did not fare so well, and most of the shelters had been shut down.

Vet clinics in urban communities, those like Anna's, offered a mixed bag of reports. Either they had cases that came in small groups or they had none at all. But no clinic reported total devastation like the shelters.

The information was overwhelming and astounding. I didn't know where to begin. There were obviously many other people out there doing the same thing as I was, combing through hard data and anecdotal evidence. There were countless spreadsheets already available through the AVMA registry and reputable researchers, and a number of others from sources running the spectrum from ignorant to frightening. The largest factor still feeding the conspiracy theorists was that no cases had been reported outside of the United States. None. Not even any in Canada. Even with the international presence at dog shows, none of the dogs that traveled back to their home countries took the disease with them, and there were no credible suspected cases outside of the U.S.

I found myself reading about the Canine Crusaders and marveled at how they were advancing their created-by-terrorists theory on social media and had even gained a few spots on twenty-four-hour news programs looking for sensational filler pieces. They focused their theory on post-market contamination of commonly used products such as shampoos and flea and tick preventatives. While they had not identified the perpetrators, they believed they were an international group hoping to disrupt the U.S. psyche, and were contaminating different products in waves so as not to be traced. Thus explained the initial cases in dog shows, followed by others. It was almost humorous how when unencumbered by facts, they were able to craft a full account of the situation. But it was also a distraction that was disturbing to the public and thus fomenting panic.

The university's break started just when it was time to judge the high school science fair. Chris and I shared a ride and a jug of coffee on the way to the school. Tess had left earlier with her friend Sarah, a senior with a car, which allowed her to avoid any interaction with us before our public display of helicopter parenting.

The judges did our prep work in the teachers' lounge, talking about how to judge, how to score, but mostly how to encourage and inspire. The chemistry teacher reminded us to be mindful of potential bias when talking to girls versus boys, and to kids that may be a minority in their field of interest. Having only daughters, I was confident that if I was biased, it would be the other way. That was until the teacher highlighted the results of a number of studies —girls are more often simply commended for a good idea, while boys are prompted to give more deeper thought to their conclusions and responses. In group situations, like we would have for team projects, girls are more often interrupted, and boys allowed to talk over them.

Yikes, I thought. While trying to be a role model, did having a Type A mom have the same result as gender bias? Instead of trying to serve as a model, did my assertiveness instead quash their self-expression, imagination, independence, and assertiveness, the qualities that I really want to cultivate? Interestingly, Chris was actually the one who inspired through his way of patiently listening and encouraging extended analysis, in both his daughters and his students. While I was there to judge the science fair, it ended up being a mini self-assessment session, leaving me surprisingly flustered as we entered the cafeteria.

A sea of faces turned, peeking around tri-fold displays and small engineering marvels. Faces eager, pensive, vacant, and indifferent, the phenotype based on a formula of variables that included their interest in science, time-management capabilities, parental involvement, and a myriad of social factors.

But behind outward expressions, these kids were refreshing and taught me so much more than I did them. While on the surface these kids were hyper critical of the smallest infraction to political correctness, their unencumbered brashness translated to a hunger for progressive fields like climate change, genetic engineering, and nanotechnology, and they instinctively pushed the boundaries of scientific exploration. I was quickly humbled and in awe of the young minds, with projects that ran the gamut from evaluating the tensile strength of the coating on butterfly wings exposed to various chemicals and UV light, determining the dilution at which the naturally occurring anti-bacterial factors are no longer effective in honey, and designing a computer program to scan images to identify terrorist websites.

I was assigned the youngest ones, the freshman class. Their nervous energy was washed away by the chance to be the center of attention as they presented their work. In some ways they were more free than the older kids, whose thoughts of college applications brought a seriousness to their projects' success.

The day was long, with closed-door judges' discussions about each project and ranking, culminating in tacking ribbons on the posters of the winners, to be revealed to all at the evening open house when the students returned with their families to walk the room and absorb the results. Chris tried to stop me, but I couldn't help but take a final walk through the Juniors' section to quickly glance at Tess's poster. It was adorned with a bright blue ribbon.

"How do you feel about all of this?" I asked Tess on our way home from the open house.

"Winning? Great! I knew that it was one of the better projects, but it was nice to see that the judges felt that way too."

"So now you go on to Regionals –if you want." I tried to be matter of fact.

"Of course I want to! Why wouldn't I? I'm taking this all the way to state."

"That would be great. I just want you to know that if you don't want to take it further, it's okay."

"Wha..? Now I'm really confused," she looked at Chris and they both looked at me quizzically. "You were the one who got me into this project."

I paused, confused in my own thoughts—trying to back off being a pushy mom while trying to encourage my daughter. "Um, you did an amazing job. It is a great project, and you did some pretty complicated and top-notch work, but …"

"But?! What 'but'?"

"But I—I guess I want to make sure that despite my pushing, you're doing this because you want to."

"A little late for that, Mom, isn't it?" Tess's voice was the definition of incredulous.

"Maybe. I'm just saying that it's your choice to continue."

"Really?!" she blurted, then softened at the look of distress on my face. "Mom, if I didn't like it, or really didn't want to do it, I would have spent my time hanging at Lisa's instead of in Dr. Meredith's lab." She leaned forward as far as her seatbelt would let her. "Honestly, this was really exciting for me. I got to work in a college lab, I was treated as an adult, and this project is really interesting. Kinda surprises me how cool I think fruit flies are now. Did I tell you my friends call me 'fruity' now because I talk about it so much?" She plopped backward. "Mom, it's all good, even if you did initially force me into it." I cringed at the operative word.

"Well, parents are supposed to sometimes force their kids to try something a few times if it might be good for them."

Tess laughed. "A few times? Mom, pleeeease! Getting us to try something a few times is one thing, but when you want us to embrace something, you have a way of infusing endless attempts of force feeding, whether it's science or broccoli." She made validating eye contact with Chris in the rearview mirror. "Your nature walks, and" —she air quoted—"'cooking experiments' were about as subtle as your broccoli and cheese soup, broccoli quiche . . ."

"And let's not forget roasted broccoli in quinoa!" Chris added.

"Okay. I guess I can be a bit overbearing," my look daring them to confirm. "I suppose I should consider establishing a savings account for the therapy you're going to eventually need to talk about your tragic upbringing."

"Nah, I'm good, Mom," she reflected, looking out the window, "if you don't tell anyone—especially Diana—I'm kind of glad you pushed me. I probably wouldn't have had much interest in the science fair, or I'd have done a mediocre project, which would have been worse than not doing a project at all."

"As long as you know that I'll support you no matter what you choose to do."

"I do, but it's good to hear, especially in front of a witness!" She leaned forward and patted her dad's shoulder. "Especially when I tell you I've decided to skip therapy and use the money to buy a car!"

We pulled into the driveway. "Guess it's not a good time to bring up all that gender bias stuff, is it?" Chris chided. I felt him colluding with Tess as I helped gather up the day's detritus inside the car.

"The two of you are impossible."

Tess announced, "I've even thought about expanding it next year, comparing the homeobox promoters with the standard TATA-box ones."

"Well if you get good at promoters, maybe you can help Diana out when she becomes an actress!" Chris scored. We rolled our eyes.

I took a few days off around Christmas, snuggled in with the girls and Chris in front of the fire for an evening, visited family, tried to distract myself with trying new recipes. But too often my thoughts drifted and discussion circled back to questions about the devastation across the dog world. Because I worked on dog genes, I became the de facto expert on the latest CRFS news. "Do you think they'll find a cure soon?", "Who do you think did this?", "Do you think it will hit here?", worried friends asked at parties and encounters at the grocery store. I tried my best to keep a positive spin on what I knew about discoveries in the research community, but those closest to me could tell that I was disappointed not being involved directly. The evening news was rarely without a story on the issue, and the twenty-four-hour "news" shows stoked the fire with a parade of self-declared experts who demonstrated ad nauseam how little they knew. The East Coast seemed to be hit harder, and urban areas more than rural.

Typical of their age, the girls only wanted to spend their break with the few friends who hadn't skipped town for vacation. I tried to generate interest in a few house projects that we had planned to do over break, but they seemed more like work than a creative outlet.

I returned to the lab midmorning two days before New Year's Eve. The only others on the campus seemed to be the campus police and a few graduate students desperate for results so they could graduate in the spring. I erased the remnants of our CRFS circles from the board in the lab, and drew four quadrants.

in trying to overlay the cases, no patterns emerged. Dogs moved in and out of the show circuit, back and forth to dog parks and vet clinics, or never even left their homes. So, location or proximity didn't seem to help to determine how they got the disease. And trends had shifted from the original cases in show dogs, to a concentration of cases happening at shelters.

The dogs at the shelters could either have been continuously exposed, or acutely exposed by a single-entry point, I thought, but which was it? CRFS seemed to come in waves, which implied an exposure to something that was highly virulent, affected all exposed animals, but that had a short infectious period, since there were examples of groups of dogs that came in later to shelters and weren't affected. Shelters were an invaluable study population, since the potential exposure routes and timeline could be well defined, and there were control groups of unaffected dogs.

Exposure was one aspect, but what about transmission? I knew it couldn't have been dog-to-dog. Shelter dogs were of no help because they were all bunched together, but dog show animals who returned home to die would have carried the pathogen back to their kennels and infected more dogs if it was contagious, and there were no reports of this. Unless there was a brief period of time when the agent was infectious that would support some of the observations in shelters. Maybe, I thought, though all the dogs were exposed, the infectious period was so short, some of the exposures fell outside that window. But I was still wrestling with the most important factor: what was it? A virus, a bacterium? It couldn't be a toxin or a poison, based on the lack of evidence of any common food or environmental factor, so it seemed more likely that it was a biologically infectious agent.

The most widely published findings came from the veterinary pharmaceutical companies. Likely prompted by their lawyers, they quickly surveyed data on all affected dogs, analyzing vaccination records to determine whether there were any patterns. Perhaps there was a contaminated lot of rabies vaccine, or a modified live viral vaccine that wasn't so modified after all. But there was nothing. No patterns, no common distribution points, no common potential cause, which was probably a relief to everyone, especially company stock holders, though a positive result could have put a quick end to the devastation.

The evening was graying, the girls were sequestered in their basement territory, Chris sat reading Nature on our overstuffed oversized chair. Needing something warm, I made some generic uncaffeinated tea and silently joined him. I opened my computer and let out my exhaustion with a sigh.

"You have to make a decision," Chris didn't look up. "You've been gone for several months now, and it is starting to wear on everyone, especially you."

"I've been here. I just –"

"Barely."

"But it—"

"It's okay, but you can't keep going like this. The girls need you, I need you, and frankly, you need us. I thought when you didn't get the grant from Regnum, things would settle down, but they haven't. It's not like you're working on two projects now, so what is it?" He put down his journal and turning toward me, put his arm across my shoulders. "I thought with winter break we'd see more of you, but it's the opposite. You're in the lab even more than before."

"I'm trying to use this time to dig through online data, news reports, anything that might shed some light on where CRFS is coming from." Now I couldn't look at him.

"So you're working on two projects, but one you're doing all on your own time."

"Yes, without any funding. That's why I'm doing it over the break since it has to be me working on my own time."

"But it's not just on your time. It's on our time."

I took his hand and leaned into him, and we sat silently dealing with the truth.

Sofie sat staring at me. I knew what she was thinking.

Here, have a ball … um … I don't want you to keep it. I want it to inspire you to get off the chair and come outside with me. Hey! I'm looking at you! Maybe you didn't see it. I'll pick it up and drop it by you again. There. See it now? Do you feel the intensity of my focus on you, the ball, you, the ball. Maybe if I spin around you might look away from that thing you are always petting on your lap. Look at me! You're still tapping on that thing. Here, I'll pick it up, throw my head back, and roll it around my mouth some, loudly, and drop it again. It's gooey now. Maybe you don't realize how important this is. I live in the moment. Right now, there is nothing more important than for you to look at me. See the ball! Engage with me! Feel my cold nose? Maybe if I lift up your hand you will disconnect from the thing…tap, tap, tap. I can stare at you forever, or until something else distracts me. Do you know that I chose you to share this special moment? You! Because you are the most important thing in my life right now. Well, you and the ball. I need you to make the ball come alive, like a rabbit. I will chase it across the yard, over and over. You make it happen. I know that. You're still not looking at me. I know you want to. I see your mouth make that shape. It's like when I wag my tail. You don't have a tail. I'll sit over here. Right in front of you. Now a little further away. So you won't miss me if you lift your eyes eeeever so slightly … You sighed! I heard it! Don't pretend you didn't. I have great hearing, you know. I know what that sigh means. It always comes just before you move that thing off your lap and look at me, your face changes, and you give in! See the ball next to you?

I tried, but it was impossible to resist Sofie's plea. With the slightest shift in my sight line, she bolted into overdrive, legs spinning like a cartoon dog in midair. Finally she gained traction and bounded over the back of the chair to the front door, joined by Ania who knows to take her time as I'm the limiting factor. They could hardly contain themselves. I needed to clear my head anyway. I grabbed my coat and opened the front door and they bolted, then turned and waited. They chased the ball until light faded to dark, and we all collapsed in the living room in exhausted ecstasy, snuggling in for the night. Unfortunately, the events of the days ahead would curtail their ball playing for a few weeks.

As if a down pillow had been torn open and flung into the sky, large fluffy clumps of snowflakes floated gently down, drifting in and out of the soft light on our front porch. The world outside would be blanketed in six inches of snow by the morning, dampening sound and placing the world on hold.

New Year's Eve was nice. Thick steaks, big salad, garlic mashed potatoes, and a chocolate truffle cake made by Tess. The girls invited some of their friends over to celebrate and trash the basement with pillows, blankets, electronic devices, junk food, and endlessly streaming movies and episodes of TV reruns. They stayed awake until the wee hours; we didn't make it to midnight. Chris and I reconnected watching Dr. Zhivago, cuddling quietly in our bed with Ania and Sofie filling in the contours of empty spaces around our legs.

Faint traces of cinnamon, nutmeg, and clove wafted down the hall. Bacon soon joined the mix, drawing me out of bed to find Chris in the kitchen making breakfast offering spiced cider, hot chocolate, eggs, pancakes, and grits. Another hour would pass before there were any signs of life from the basement, but I came to life, slowly recharging from a solid night of sleep. The girls and their friends eventually tumbled up the stairs and Chris served as short-order cook, taking on the role full-on, complete with the apron that read "For this I spent four years in college" with his editing of the four to read 10. He successfully embarrassed his daughters with renditions of *That's Amore*, but secretly they loved having the cool, fun dad.

The day passed uneventfully with bowls of black-eyed pea soup, the transition from afternoon to evening unnoticed, and rolling into another deep and restful dream.

January 2nd, embarking on a new year, I woke rested. It was nice to have a break, though the rest of the non-school world was heading back to work. But the calm was slowly drawn away by chatter from the girls about rides to friends, dominion over clothing items, and sisterly conflict.

And the chatter on the news from every direction. The New Year's Day dog show had been cautiously well-attended, though some of the best dogs were missing. The top Irish wolfhound, who was favored to win this year, was pulled by her owner, a veterinarian, when a number of his clients developed CRFS. He didn't want to risk the population of show dogs by potentially exposing them to something he may have encountered in his clinic. He also didn't want to expose his bitch to anything at the show.

There was a brief story in the science section of New York Times, a summary really, about the progress being made by the various pharmaceutical companies' research on CRFS, Regnum included. While Kendal's name was not mentioned, the company she worked for, Xlar, was noted as having made progress at identifying a number of breed-specific SNPs that could be used to identify susceptible populations. I found that odd, as there had not been any reports of breeds with significantly more cases than any others, except when several that attended the same dog show came down with CRFS. But that would more likely be due to similar exposure at the show, as dogs of the same breed were housed in close proximity.

An endless parade of animal rights activists, anti-vaxxers, and self-proclaimed infectious disease conspiracy theorists like the Canine Crusaders crept into the airwaves heightening the panic like others had with Ebola. More reasonable reporting focused on the potential negative impact of CRFS on the economy.

Sofie on one side, Ania on the other, I sat eyes closed, trying to organize my thoughts. Little squares moved up or down and sideways as I tried to create a picture. Data, stories, patterns shuffled in my head as if on a little plastic game that came over on a big ship from China. As the day shifted to evening, Chris relieved me of having to tell him that I needed to go to the lab the next day.

Displacing Ania, who simply moved to the comfort of the

loveseat, Chris placed his arm across my lap. "You should go in tomorrow, spend a few hours, get your thoughts organized. Why don't you plan to do that every day the rest of the week, for a few hours, so you can feel like you have a plan, both in the lab and here."

"Thanks." I leaned into him. "Have I told you lately that you are an amazing person?"

"No. But you're welcome. I'm not saying that I want you to disappear into the night and never surface until the CRFS mystery is solved, but I know you can't ignore it. I'm also concerned that once your lab crew is back you're going to spread yourself thin again."

"Especially if I don't pay attention to eating right." My joke fell flat.

He pulled away just far enough to look me in the eyes. "I'm concerned about your well-being." He acknowledged the inevitable in a pause. "Maybe if you spend a few hours a day in the lab next week you might be more organized when they come back and then maybe, you could pace yourself better when you decide you have to be involved in CRFS."

"Okay. I'll try to go in by ten, home by two." He gave me a half-hearted hug, knowing that my decision to be involved was made months ago.

I headed to the kitchen and spent the next hour lost in the simple pleasure of preparing a meal, finding comfort in the scent of curry and garlic. My canine audience sat anxiously watching behind the invisible line over which they may not cross, one of the rare bits of training that actually stuck. We gathered for an early family dinner at the dining room table, the dogs catching a quick nap since the girls, no longer toddlers, rarely dropped any food worth scavenging. I was reminded of how the girls filled a room with life as they regaled us with stories on the latest movie, music, and teenage gossip. Their chatter was like a smile in the room.

The sound of the house phone, rarely heard, startled us. I would have ignored it except for the faint buzz I heard from my cell phone a minute later. Someone was trying hard to reach me. I excused myself from the table. "Sorry." Chris gave me a wistful look as our family time was over.

"That was Anna," I brushed through heading to the closet to get my coat. "She's been trying to reach me on my cell. She wants me to come by now. She says that she has something she urgently needs to show me."

"She couldn't tell you on the phone," Chris stated more than asked.

"Something is going on. She sounded … distressed, not herself. She said I have to see for myself." I hurriedly shoved on my boots, hat, and gloves, and braced myself for the cold.

"Sounds odd. Need me to do anything?" Chris offered.

I stopped and came back to the table, moving in close to him as he stood. "Just take care of the girls, don't know how long I'll be there. Sorry again about leaving our dinner." I rounded the table, giving each girl a quick hug, not lingering enough to let them pull me back into their lives.

"Mom, you'll let us know if her patients are okay?" Tess asked. "We'll do the dishes."

"I will, my love. Thanks. Sorry to run off."

Chris reached out to offer an embrace but I didn't want it, didn't want contact. I wanted to remain unemotional, disconnected, rote.

"You need this." He pulled me toward him.

I melted into his arms, let him envelop me. My lungs felt like they were burdened by an August day in Virginia, like I was inhaling water. I opened my eyes, inhaled deeply and pulled away. "Thanks."

"My pleasure." He smiled. "But – Is there anything I can do to help you stop taking on the weight of the world, including Anna's world?"

"No. I appreciate the sentiment. I have this ominous feeling that this is going to be heavier than anything I'm carrying right now."

Diana jumped in and threw her arms around me. "Go save the dogs, Mama," she whispered. I kissed her head—which I suddenly noticed was almost at the same level as mine.

Rushing to the car, numbed by the cold and the mechanics of opening the door, I settled into the driver's seat, pushed the button to start the silent engine, shifted into reverse and locked eyes with myself in the rearview mirror. I paused for a moment to take in the confusion on my face. Anna's voice had an ominous tenor to it, a finality. "I need you to come here. I need to show you what I have." She was never one to be overdramatic or emotional. But she also didn't say whether it had to do with Addison's or with CRFS. Whatever it was, she obviously knew it was significant to our work. I backed the car out, confident that Anna would point us in the right direction.

There were no cars in the parking lot—strange, as she said she would be open again right after New Year's Day for people to pick up their boarded pets, and she typically stayed open until seven to cater to her working clients. The doors were locked and the lights were off in the waiting room. As I took out my cell phone to call her, I saw the sign: Due to a rising concern for our dog patients' health, we are temporarily closed for regular appointments. For emergencies, please call the following number. Anna locked eyes with me through the glass door; her keys jangled as she tried to find the keyhole. She let me in and hurriedly locked the door behind me.

"Hey, come on back." She moved stealthily, as if we might be seen, as if a secret might be discovered. "I don't want anyone to see that I'm here."

"That bad?"

"Yes, everyone thinks their dog has CRFS, everyone needs me to calm them down. People are panicking and I've run out of comforting words, and frankly, out of patience."

"I see you've run out of heat too. Why is it so cold in here?"

"I'll show you." I hustled to keep up with her as she switched on lights in front of us and off behind us.

We walked through the hall between the four exam rooms, each equipped with a steel exam table at bar height, and decorated with cheerful colors and abstract pictures of bright yellow cats with pointy ears and blue dogs with thick red collars.

Through the double doors, we entered a narrow chart room, running perpendicular to the hall. Computers and microscopes filled the counters, glass-doored cabinets packed with gauze and gloves and other disposables above on one side, and a bank of light boxes for viewing radiographs on the opposite side. Computer screens that would normally reveal images of chunks of tennis balls lodged in a small intestine or a fractured pelvis from a hit-by-car case were dimmed, keeping their latest diagnosis to themselves. The refrigerator whirred. It was oddly quiet in the clinic. Usually there was a dog or two barking, but all I heard was the machine hum.

I followed her through the second set of double swinging doors into the main exam room—the room they take your pet to when the vet says, "we'll just take him back there for a minute," and when he returns, your pet is beyond grateful to see you and be freed from that scary world.

It's the largest room in the clinic, surrounded by cabinets, full of more gloves, needles, boxes, catheters, thermometers, and with countertops covered in various equipment. A row of exam tables, stainless steel, sparkling clean, run down either side, ten in all. Down the center, a wide aisle, wide enough to push a rolling exam table through on the way to the surgery or x-ray rooms or to the glassed-in recovery room in the back where they keep watch on surgery patients as the technicians and vets hurry throughout the day.

I knew this room, I'd been in the back numerous times. But it was darker than usual. The windows, placed high up to keep prying eyes from distracting the animals, offered only diffused street light through closed blinds. There was an odd smell. Not the medicinal smell of scented antiseptic, but a stale smell, acrid, distasteful. Anna flipped on the light. The two rows of exam tables, all the counters that frame the room, and an extra row of mobile exam tables down the center, were all full. Covered with dead dogs.

A tan and white Jack Russell Terrier, a black lab, a mutt with a speckled face, several golden retrievers, a little brown chihuahua, two poodles, one white mini, and a black standard with unbrushed curls, like my Ania. All victims of CRFS, no longer just stories I read about in the news.

Silence, dead silence. I looked at Anna. Her hand was still on the switch as if prepared to turn the lights off if I couldn't handle the scene. But it was too late. I had seen and will never get that picture out of my mind. She walked over and put her arm across my shoulder. I stepped away to the center of the room, turning slowly to imagine their lives—a child's best friend, a family watch dog, a hunting partner, an elder's companion. My heart ached for them all, owners and dogs.

How many were there? Why were they all here? I knew that when animals died at the clinic, the bodies were placed in cold storage until they were picked up either by the company that provided cremation services, or the one that disposed of the remains. Those services usually came every two or three days. I was confused and maybe a bit angry that Anna hadn't warned me.

"Why are they here?" I asked. "Why aren't they in the cold room?" My eyes darted around the room, not daring to focus again on any one of them, or her.

"There's no more room," her face was expressionless.

"Oh my God. When are they picking up?"

"Not for another day. With the holiday and this happening in a number of clinics, they are so overwhelmed, they can't keep up. I have 139 dogs, close to 30% of my practice, and it's climbing. I have to just hold on to them until they can be picked up, but I can't practice medicine with them here. I've given all of my staff a few days off, my receptionist is coming in to help field phone calls, but I will only take emergencies right now, which when it's a dog, usually just adds one more to the room."

"I'm so sorry, Anna. You must be—" I turned to face her. She had been talking matter-of-factly, staring across the room. She couldn't have warned me; she herself was in shock. We locked eyes and she dissolved.

I enveloped her in my arms. "Oh Claire, I don't know what I'm going to do! I can barely keep it together. Everyone is looking to me for answers, everyone is coming to me to save their dog, and when they die I have to stand calm, sympathetic, unemotional, walk them to the door after they agonize through their goodbyes, and then I carry their baby, their security, their family member back to this! I don't know how much more I can take." She was sobbing and shaking. I was the stoic one for once, trying to keep it contained while I processed the horror in the room. The nightmare of her practice.

We fell silent. I let her sob but only briefly. I knew her and her way of dealing with emotion was to let it take control for only a few minutes, then grab hold of it roughly, shake it violently and toss it aside.

"Goddamn it, this should not be happening. There has to be an explanation. We, you, I, have to do something. I want to show you something." She spun around and stormed through the side doors that led to the lab. I paused to switch off the light. Equipment for analyzing blood and urine sat silent. The shelves were filled with manuals and protocols, post-it notes were stuck on the cabinet doors, reminding staff about chemical orders and problem workarounds, like make sure to hold down the top of the centrifuge when you lock it. Glassed-in cold boxes and incubators held steady their temperature-sensitive contents. At the far end, the walk-in cold room's stainless-steel door failed to lock in the sadness.

"Obviously, I have a ton of blood samples for you." She opened the freezer next to the cold room to reveal neatly arrayed racks of tubes, color-coded and individually labeled with the victim's name, breed, and number. "I've assigned each patient a number, and I've been cataloging as much information as I can on each of them."

"You've done a lot of work."

"One of my technicians has. I don't have much other work for her right now, but she is a whiz on the computer, so I asked her to pull all their records, and start populating spreadsheets with some of the clinical data starting with when they got the disease, and how long it took them to succumb." She paused. "And I noticed at least one interesting trend."

"Really? With just that preliminary information?"

"Yes, but don't get too excited. I haven't a clue what it means, but maybe it will give you some new directions to explore."

She shut the freezer and moved to a computer, shaking the mouse and bringing it to life. With her face illuminated, Anna looked tired, puffy-eyed, drained.

"Stop looking at me," she hissed.

"I just –"

"Stop it. The best thing is for us to help solve this thing. So here's what I have." A chart appeared. "This is a bar graph of the 139 dogs that have died, plus another thirteen that are suspect, but they came in early on and I don't have as detailed notes."

"I trust your instincts."

"Data, not instincts, my dear."

"Oh, aren't we Miss Scientific Integrity?" Sparring, our emotions dropped away, refocusing our thoughts, and our clinical personas emerged.

"The progression of symptoms is similar for all of them. They stop eating, they become depressed, they fade away."

"Like Addison's."

"Yes, but this time instead of Addison's being the great pretender that presents as some other disease, it is CRFS that mimics Addison's."

"You think it's related?" The pounding of my heart grew stronger.

"Not at all, but since it presents in a similar fashion, I'm starting to think that it affects the adrenals in a similar way."

"Why wouldn't you just know?"

"The dogs are too sick to run an ACTH, and every organ becomes affected very quickly. They die so quickly it's hard to tell what is cause and what is symptom. But there does seem to be an interesting correlation in the progression of the disease that is different in Addison's dogs that get it."

"Addison's die quicker?" I asked, proud of my deductive capabilities.

"No—slower," She revealed, curiously. "I think that the adrenals are the first organ targeted. Think about it. We supplement Addison's dogs with corticoids because they have non-functional adrenals."

“Yeah.”

“So, if a disease starts by first destroying the adrenals, the Addison’s dogs would show no signs since they are supplemented. But, the other normal dogs would start spiraling downward in an Addison’s-like crisis, making them more vulnerable and killing them quicker.” Clicking on another spreadsheet, she brought up bar graphs compiled on all the dogs, labeled intake and TOD—time of death.

“Wow. You don’t even need to tell me which are Addison’s and which are normal.”

“It’s stunning, right? It’s three to five days before they die rather than twenty-four to seventy-two hours. I don’t have anything else though. Cindy is putting all of their data – vaccination records, owners’ demographics, surgeries, other animals owned – into an Access database so we can search and compare every which way.”

“Any thoughts on why now? Why is your private practice being hit with so many?”

“I was wondering the same thing,” she spun her stool to face me. ”And why it happened over the holiday. I can’t seem to find anything that correlates. Some were boarded while their owners were away, but most weren’t.”

“Maybe all the owners are feeding them contaminated turkey,” I half joked.

“I thought of that too.”

“Really?”

“Well, not exactly that, but I did glance at the information on what owners had been feeding them.”

“And?”

“Nothing that I can see correlates.”

“Seen any signs of this being contagious?”

Another mouse click and another chart appeared. “No. I haven’t seen owners who lost one dog come back in with another a few days later. Except one breeder that had two die after a local show, but none of hers that stayed home became sick. In fact, now that you mention it, I should run the data to confirm that there is no pattern with those that have multiple dogs just to confirm my observation."

We both stood and stared at the screen. I bundled my coat tighter around me, feeling the cold from all sides. "You should head home," her voice was quiet. "I will pack all the samples and drop them off at your lab whenever you are ready for them. I'm emailing you the spreadsheets now." She pushed send, and closed down all the files.

"One more thing." She looked me dead in the face. "I've sent duplicate samples off to CDC according to the AVMA protocol."

"Good. So I don't have to split up the samples." Her expressionless face said there was something else. "But you haven't sent them your data on observations about the Addison's dogs, have you?"

"No. And I haven't sent them the pre-CRFS samples I've maintained for these dogs. I'm giving you sixty days after your students return."

"I don't—"

"Sixty days. If I send them my thoughts now, they'll swoop in with a pile of researchers, maybe even press, and we'll be out of this. I've thought a lot about this. It's really not a lot of time if you think about what has to be done. And I don't think they'll be able to move as quickly as you nor will they have the insight or instinct, frankly. If you don't find anything earth-shattering in those few weeks, you'll still have a pile of data to hand over to them that will help narrow the search."

"You're putting a lot of faith in me. I'm not sure I agree."

"My samples, my rules, my responsibility. You accept?"

I nodded, just barely.

She closed down the computer and turned off the lights as we headed to the door. I stood in the shadows. "Why did you need me to come here? Why didn't you just tell me on the phone or ask me to meet you at my lab? You could have brought the samples there."

She pondered the question, slowly shaking her head. "I don't know really. It was a gut feeling. Maybe I needed to share this with a friend so we would be starting from the same level of desperation?"

"You, desperate?" I couldn't let her falter now. "I'm going to assume that you needed me, your collaborator, to grasp the magnitude of the situation."

She smiled weakly at me and stroked my arm, her fingers lighting on my hand momentarily, as she closed her eyes, probably, I thought, to make it all go away.

"Hey," I tried to pull her from the bad dream. "What are you going to do this evening? You can't stay here—it's too distressing."

"And creepy," she tried to joke.

"Come on, grab your coat. Let's go get a drink."

Her taillights faded and disappeared. We'd only had one drink, but the steering wheel had gone cold. I turned the car on but didn't want to move. As the seats were heating up, my breath made foggy patterns on the windows and I watched a few people scuttle across the street through the clouds. I pulled one glove off and pushed the center button; my phone glowed as it came to life. I had no choice but to swallow my pride and make the call.

He answered the phone on the second ring.

"Hi," was all I could offer.

"I thought you were still angry with me, haven't heard from you for over a month," Neil stated flatly.

"I am."

"Didn't get a Christmas card."

"No one did."

"Okay. What's up?"

"I need your help. I'm not sure what's going on, but Anna has a bunch of dead dogs and she's made a curious observation in Addison's dogs that have CRFS."

"Are the two related?" he asked, pushing aside the silence of the last few months.

"We don't know. Don't think so, but the Addison's dogs could be key to figuring out the progression, and maybe even the trigger of the disease."

"Why?"

"Because they actually survive CRFS longer since they receive adrenal hormones. It has to be related to the hypothalamic–pituitary–adrenal system. Would it be possible to talk to your friends at Regnum about their interest in supporting this?"

"You don't want to talk to them. They've invested too much on the other ideas. They are not going to entertain a whole new theory."

"It's not a theory, it's a fact. We have proof." Was he doubting me?

"Okay, slow down. Tell me what you have."

"Anna's had more than 139 dogs she thinks died of CRFS, including some that had Addison's. She's been sending CRFS samples to the CDC bank, which then go to big pharma—who, by the way, are hampering the effort to solve this by paying vets to provide samples exclusively to them. She's not taking their offer, though. Just another seedy reality of the race for a cure."

"Stick to the facts."

I rolled my eyes, willing him to see over the phone. "That is a fact. But luckily, some long-term relationships still count for something, and Anna also keeps samples for me."

"Relevant facts, please."

"The symptoms of CRFS are similar to Addison's—lethargy, loss of appetite, quick death. It seems to attack the adrenals, much like Addison's. All the CRFS dogs eventually die from the effects of adrenal failure. But—even though Addison's dogs are also dying of CRFS, they die slower, taking three to five days instead of the one to three. Anna thinks this is because they are receiving supplements to replace the adrenal hormones. Non-Addison's dogs quickly go into an Addison's-like crash and die before anyone can even have a chance to treat the symptoms from adrenal failure to total organ failure. On the other hand, with the Addison's dogs that get CRFS, she is able to see a much clearer and slower progression as it slowly affects the other organs. She is able to see the progression of the disease because they are the only ones that are only mildly sick during the first phase."

"All of them? That's pretty significant."

"I know. She is even keeping the Addison's dogs alive a bit longer because she can catch it in the early stage and increase their adrenal supplements, though there is still 100% mortality."

"So has her insight into the progression given her any leads on the cause?" he said with excitement rising in his voice.

"Not yet. There are so many things to look at, but she's been storing samples on all of the dogs since they were first diagnosed with Addison's, and each time they came in for a checkup. So she has pre-and post-CRFS samples for all of her Addison's dogs that have died of CRFS. I'm going spend the next week before break is over organizing my thoughts and planning our research forward. Maybe then we could talk about the next steps."

"Can you define 'we'?"

"Anna. My lab staff. Me . . . You."

"And my role as part of 'we' is?"

"I don't have any money for this. I can dip into my Addison's grant to look into this a little because there is this anomaly in the Addison's dogs, but I can't ethically spend much more without knowing that it will be paid back. I can't take it any further without dedicated funding. That's why I'm calling you. That's why I need to talk to Regnum."

There was a long pause on the phone. Uncomfortably long during which my mind ran through every possible excuse he was going to give.

"Claire, you can't go to them. You can't trust them."

"Coming from you, isn't that a bit ironic?"

"Stop it. Let me make some calls and get back to you. I will get you the money, just not from them. You can trust me," his terse response put me in my place.

I could picture his stoic face at the Regnum ceremony, and let my exasperation show. "I'm sorry, I don't know what I was thinking. I can't go down this road with you again."

"You called me, remember? You were thinking that we might still have something to salvage. Look, I have enough investors who are willing to take a chance on any recommendation I give them. I can make some calls, and pull together a proposal in a matter of days to secure some venture capital."

"And you'll take your cut if it ends up profitable, right?"

"Have your lawyer draw it up however you want to define my role, or exclude me all together. You might want to consider that sometimes your stubbornness prevents you from seeing that you might not know the whole story."

I accepted that I was being a bit of a jerk. "I really don't care about profit. You're free to make a living. I just want to figure this thing out."

"But not be rich and famous?"

"Not funny. Becoming famous for being the one that figured it out wouldn't be so bad, since it would mean that they stop dying, and more money would flow into Addison's research."

"You can trust me, Claire. I won't let you down."

"Except once," instantly regretting that I couldn't stop myself.

The house was quiet except for the muffled pitter-patter of Sofie's feet as she danced around me. Ania stood in the hallway, sleepy-eyed, her tail slowly waving a tired welcome. "I'll be there in a minute," I told her. She acknowledged and turned and headed down the hall. Sofie trotted alongside me to the kitchen to help me get a glass of water.

I prefer to have overlapping dogs—to feel the ebb and flow of untrained enthusiasm mixed with obedience that serves a mutual purpose.

There is freshness in the over-exuberance, generic puppy response. In puppy feet that know no boundaries, and the bright-eyed eager way the young look for meaning in words, facial expressions, and voice inflection. They remind us to find joy in the simple and the silly. A young dog brings hope.

But there is comfort in the maturity of an old dog whose ways we know; we are adapted to fit together. There is a merging of our spirits as she reads me, and I her. There is a silent exchange between the two of us as we move through our days. An old dog gives me indescribable peace.

One does not replace the other—the old for the young—as people who get a puppy soon after losing their old friend often realize. It takes time to build a life together, to reach a stasis.

It is like that with people too, I reminded myself on the dark drive home. Relationships built over years offered comfort in familiarity and granted concessions without asking. I needed to remember to not bite when a growl will do.

BACK TO BORNEO

I DON'T dwell on their last moments. I try only to remember them vibrant, loving, and healthy. I have let go of many; ones that lived long lives, then one day stopped eating and told me it was time and then helped me walk through the process of acceptance as I helped them leave this world. Others, the young ones, laid a heavy stone on my chest as I struggle, still, to process their leaving. We named one Butterfly. She was just two days old when her lungs filled with fluid and she grew weak. There was no final decision, it was just as it needed to be, but painfully unfair. I have let go of many, but have never forgotten one.

I couldn't get the vision at Anna's clinic out of my head, I couldn't sleep. Dogs, the love of someone's life, so many dogs, so many broken hearts. I didn't even know what day of the week it was. I just knew I couldn't watch without doing something. It was one week before the students returned, leaving little time to get everything set up. I would have to ask them to dive into analyzing Anna's samples right away, ignoring their own research, though that would be unfair to ask of them. They needed to concentrate on their work so they could graduate sometime in the near future, maybe even on time. But I knew that neither Jamie or Megan would put their work before this. Was I being a responsible adviser even asking them?

I headed to the lab before anyone woke up. I left a note saying I would only be in the lab for a few hours. I just needed to get Anna's spreadsheets organized, as well as my thoughts. There was so much to do. I had to set up the lab like a factory for processing the samples. I had to assign duties and everything had to be well-coordinated to ensure that samples were processed quickly, and kept at the right temperature throughout so nothing would degrade.

I needed someone to research any new information on other diseases that started by killing off the adrenal glands, though I pretty much knew them by heart. Someone had to separate the samples allocating portions for protein and DNA extraction. Then someone had to start running the screening for each. What was I thinking? I needed help. I had to pull in some of the other labs in our department. Dr. Martenson's lab down the hall was the only one equipped for toxicology. At least we already had data on all of the animals, with complete blood chemistry profiles, so we knew how their bodies were functioning, or rather were failing to function. We could ignore things like urea, nitrogen, and creatinine levels; we only needed to look for things that were novel and fell outside of known physiological responses.

Over the next week I was in the lab, every day, all day, by myself. Okay, I lied to Chris, or made false promises at least. The day after seeing Anna and the dead dogs, I got home around dinnertime, but I did stop by to pick up something so we could at least have a family dinner. I had called Chris earlier in the day to tell him what happened. As I described in detail the dogs laying still in Anna's clinic, a flood of tears poured out of me. I couldn't exactly read his silence on the phone, but I chose to believe it was because he grasped the magnitude of the situation and was processing through to accepting that our agreement to limit my hours was off.

"Do you understand why I have to be here?"

"Yes," of course he did. "Doesn't mean I have to like it. "He paused like he does so often, to turn his words around. "I'm so sorry. I know that must have been awful."

"Thank you. I'm sorry too that it's going to pull me away for a while. I'll make sure to not work over the weekend so we can spend time together with the girls."

"At least call them. Let them know you're there if they need you. I don't want them to feel like you're sequestered with no contact with the outside world."

"Maybe you could bring them by?" I suggested.

"They would rather stick forks in their eyes than have to pretend any interest in our lab work. You know that," he countered.

"You're right, at least your lab has cool vats of little fishes."

"Yes, way cooler than water baths and incubators. Good luck," he said. "I'll miss you."

"I love you," I said as he hung up.

"I found you some money," Neil stated.

"Do I want to know from whom and what it is going to cost me?"

"Well, I have two contributors. Basically, what I propose is that we set you up as an equal investment partner, contributing your research in-kind. I'll be contributing most of the funding."

"You?" My emotions were mixed.

"Yes. I have money from my settlement with Regnum that I've been looking to invest. I can't think of a better cause."

"Guess you really do love those dogs of yours, don't you?"

"Yes, and you. The other investor is Johnathan Oros."

"The guy who was the CSO at Regnum before you?" I asked, a bit surprised.

"Yeah, he's a friend now. He started his own company and we talk often about the plusses and minuses of owning your own business. His company, though small, has a few grants to work on two orphan diseases. You know, those that very few people have and only the federal government will invest in. They pay enough to keep the lights on. But he also is an FDA contract lab and is set up to test and produce vaccines during national emergencies. If your findings pan out, he thinks he can get FDA to give him approvals quickly to move through the phases of any clinical trials that need to be done on a vaccine or treatment, so you can get it out to the public quickly. He is willing to provide some of his own investment money and set you up as part owner in his company so you'll share in anything that comes of this."

"Wow, that's a sweet deal . . . um, but . . ."

"You don't need to justify taking a share. It's okay to make money. I learned that long ago. You academics can pretend that the two are not heavily intertwined until a great discovery slips through your hands and someone else makes money on it. Then you want to cry foul."

"I was just going to say thanks."

"That will do. But it will cost you one more thing."

"My heart and soul?" I asked.

"Close.; Our friendship. I want that back, and in better condition than it was when you gave it up."

"I gave it up?" I asked incredulously, but caught myself. "Can I give it to you in installments? I don't know if I can afford the whole thing right away."

"All or nothing. That's the deal," his offer final.

"I—"

"I'm serious. I know you are still angry—some of it may be

justified because I didn't warn you, but the rest is not. But if we're going to do this together you need to drop the anger that perfuses every conversation. You women can hold a grudge awfully long."

"And you men can stir up the deepest of emotions with your silence."

"I miss you too. Love you, all that crap. Now let's get busy. I'm having my lawyer pull together a legal agreement for us in the next day or two, and in the meantime I'll be working with my finance guy to set up a funding stream. Don't know if we need to set up a foundation or what, but let me worry about that." He paused. "Claire, friend to friend, how sure of this are you?"

"Now you're asking?" I laughed. "As sure as we can be that we are on to something significant, whether we can find it with our small team or whether we will need a lot more help remains to be seen."

"My money's on you," he assured me. "Make sure your staff have non-disclosures."

"Already thought of that. When they come back from vacation Anna and I plan to meet with them and have them all sign a non-disclosure agreement." I smiled to myself. "See I can think like a business woman even if I am just a researcher."

"Never doubted that. I'll try to involve you as little as needed in the paperwork process so you can concentrate on the work, but you will have to meet with Jim at least once to finalize the agreement. Can you get away for an afternoon to go to Philly to meet him in the next few days?"

"Sure, just say when."

The Acela express train up the East Coast forces you to think. It can be crowded or you can luck out and get an empty row, but it is quiet and rhythmic, and a respite from the outside world. After reading the newspaper and catching up on emails, motivation ebbs, scenery floats past, the mind wanders, and things that matter surface for clarity. Why anyone would hopscotch up the East Coast in a plane baffles me. How much further is Canada? I contemplated the possibility of riding off to a new country, a new life, devoid of dead dogs and needed work to rekindle my marriage.

As sure as I was that I married for life, I was also sure that there were risks to that life being a happy one. It would have been easy to push my marriage off a cliff. Not by a freight train barreling into it and splintering the foundation, but by slow, quiet, collective deterioration as the mechanics of the day replace meaningful interaction. By taking advantage, failing to appreciate, carelessly tossing around harsh words. Big events happen in all marriages that temporarily distract—children enter, illnesses invade, careers demand, children leave. But you have to keep clearing a path around those big rocks to keep the flow. I could see it, I knew it, but I couldn't seem to focus on the anything but the mounding debris. We had moved so far away from the rhythm of the sailboat that brought us together many years ago.

Sipadan island lies 35km off the northeast coast of Borneo. Tourists traveled there back then by a converted fishing boat, whose engine roared and billowed diesel exhaust for three hours solid.

The water changed from light to dark deep blue as we left the continental shelf of the Semporna archipelago for the depth of the Celebes Sea. I watched this breathtaking transition while facing the water, lying on the deck, retching my guts out as the boat cavorted over wave after wave, joyously laughing at me as it played with what was left of the contents of my stomach. I couldn't imagine life continuing. I wanted nothing more than for the boat to heel just enough for me to slide into the water, sending me into the cool depths and Davy Jones' arms. But it was not to be. The boat crew would not have it, bad for business, and they sustained my life by bringing me small cups of foul-tasting water and saying "drink, drink" in thickly accented English. And I did. All the while knowing that in about a day, I might pay dearly for allowing a new mixture of foreign microbes to explore my digestive system. Though I threw most of it up. The blue below beckoned.

We arrived to an overly cheery bunch of Malaysian greeters, their smiling voices announcing "Welcome to Sipadan" as they scraped me off the boat deck and laid me on the dock alongside several others who barely survived our adventure. A bowl of plain white rice appeared in front of me—"eat, eat"—and I did, and within minutes I was sitting up, able to focus, and taking in the smiling hopeful faces of my hosts. This was obviously a common ritual.

Sipadan straddles Malaysian and Indonesian territorial waters, and at the time there was a dispute over who owned it. The Malaysians had been the first to overtly claim it, establishing a diving operation and tourist attraction there, and eventually they were awarded ownership by an international court in 2002. There was only one permanent resident on the island, an old turtle egg hunter who was allowed to continue to collect and sell turtle eggs by permission and limitations of the government, leaving the remaining hatchlings to emerge from the sand as little pancakes with finned feet struggling back to the sea in the hope of continuing the species.

The island is only thirty acres in size, with a small tropical forest packed into the center that was ringed by bleached white sand sprinkled with perfectly intact shells. From almost the water's edge, a coral reef thickened as the water gradually deepened, and then the reef abruptly dropped off a cliff into a two-thousand-foot abyss. It was a diver's paradise. Pristine soft corals waved their long fingers and fanned the marine inhabitants with the gentle sway of the currents. Like Haight-Ashbury in the 1960s, the reef was a psychedelic collage of apple-green scales, purple velvet-tipped fins, and giant eyes outlined in Day-Glo orange. Color combinations my mother told me didn't go well together were boldly displayed by curious fish. Feather duster worms retracted their long lashes in the blink of an eye. And the turtles, big smiling turtles, came from below, rose out of the water with dreamy eyes, and submerged to fade into the deep blue distance. There were no words to adequately describe this place.

I was there for five days. I had heard about it from some Australians who passed through the wildlife sanctuary where I was collecting skin samples from the wild cats of Borneo—the clouded leopard, flat-headed cat, marbled cat, leopard cat, and the rarer bay cat. My lab director and the Malaysian wildlife department worked out an agreement; we would do the genetic analysis if they would provide the samples. I had waited to do field work almost my entire graduate career, and had already used samples from zoos. Of course they could send the samples, but allowing me, a graduate student, to travel to the jungles and work side by side with the researches in Borneo was part of the deal—even if it was just a glimpse at their world. When I overheard the Aussies talking about the majesty of Sipadan, I drove my hosts crazy until they connected me to Borneo Divers so I could spend my precious days off there.

Chris was one of the smiling faces on the dock. Those no longer dying from the journey joined the unaffected in the dining hut, and I, being the last, asked him if there was anywhere that I could go to die.

"I suggest that you choose another activity here. You don't really want to spend a lot of money to get here just to become fish bait."

"No, guess not. I suppose you're here as part of the welcoming committee to tell me my options."

"Yes and no. I'm not officially part of the operation, but I help out the best I can." He extended a tan arm, covered in hair bleached by the sun and sprinkled in sea salt. A margarita came to mind. I was feeling better. He helped me up and we walked to the dining hut. As I sat down to introduce myself to a few of the other visitors, he disappeared into the palm trees.

The dining hut was right out of an Annette Funicello beach party movie, with a single large open room framed by bamboo and palm fronds, but unlike a Hollywood set, it was built to withstand heavy tropical winds. Two rows of long tables up front offered prime ocean views for our dining pleasure. A long bar lined one side wall, the other side wall was open, and a buffet table in the back offered a Malaysian feast. A door on the back wall led to the kitchen where steam billowed from pots kept ready. We were to make ourselves at home, writing down anything we drank from the bar in the little book; they would tally on the morning of our departure. There were four kitchen staff who sat patiently all day to fix us whatever we wanted. Eggs collected from the chickens roaming the grounds, scrambled, over easy, soft boiled. Mangosteen. Coconut. Durian. Jackfruit. Papaya. Rambutan. Starfruit. Soups for lunch, noodles, and rice, always rice. Each night a buffet dinner was prepared; staff standing behind boiling heating trays were eager to serve fresh fish caught each day.

Sign up for a fishing trip, learn to dive, or venture out on my own. Two dive masters and an island manager ran the place and were there for anything we needed.

Only thirty people total were allowed on the island at a time, which meant that there was room for only twenty guests. Workers could radio the mainland, and there was a speedboat that brought supplies in twice weekly and was available to shuttle a weary guest back in little over an hour. The diesel stinkpot that brought us here and would take us back came once a week.

I could walk around the island in twenty minutes, keeping watch in the evenings for a swath of disturbed sand, signs that a female turtle came ashore to nest. Step carefully to avoid pancakes making their way to the sea. At night with flashlights in hand, researchers rotating from the university on the mainland led small groups to witness a female turtle, exhausted from digging, drop seventy or eighty eggs into her open nest. She ignored us in this, her sanctuary.

And there was entertainment. Several evenings a week the staff shared their culture with local songs and dance. Guests were invited to share their own talents and willingly participated once enough alcohol was consumed.

My room consisted of a grass A-frame hut with a double bed, a little table, a stand for my duffle bag, and a lamp. The door was covered in opaque linen, and woven palm fronds could be pulled closed for privacy. I slept ten feet from the sea. A Biblical paradise. I needed nothing more.

Chris spent his afternoons under sail shuttling guests to the outer edges of the thickest part of the reef on the other side of the island, docking as the colors of the setting sun blended with Australian wine and local cheeses. On my second morning he sat alone in the dining hut, coffee cup in hand, writing in a notebook. I didn't want to disturb him so I filled my cup, picked up a banana and sat on a bench on the outer edge of the hut. My back to the table and him, I faced the water and massaged the sand with my toes.

"It's always interesting to try to guess what someone is like based on that first encounter on the dock. I figured you for the more friendly type."

I was surprised and admittedly intrigued by his directness. Not turning around, I said, "You would be right, but I'm also the type to respect people's privacy so I was giving you some space."

"Ah, you don't have to do that here. I get all the privacy I need."

I found that odd as he must spend so many hours entertaining island guests on his boat. Wasn't privacy a daily nutrient for solo sailors? I turned to look at him and felt my heart rate increase. "May I join you then?" I asked.

He closed his notebook and stood up. "I'll join you." He had on bathing trunks and a tee-shirt from Borneo Divers. He straddled the bench facing me, tempting my personal space and me. His directness boarded on being forward, but I kind of liked it. He extended his hand. "Chris. We were never formally introduced."

"Hi, Chris, I'm Claire."

"Yes, I know, from Virginia." He smirked as color rose on my face. "I review the guest list before folks get here so I have an idea what I'm facing."

"We're that bad are we?" I asked.

"Rarely. But it helps to know if there are families or couples or singles traveling alone."

Ah. Now I understood. He gets to know the guests so he can figure out ways to connect with them and thus increase his tips.

"I want to try to avoid saying something stupid." He adopted a character expression. "So, would you and your daughter like to take a sail around the island?" he turned to the imaginary people sitting across from us. "Oh, this isn't my daughter sir, this is my wife! That kind of stuff." He turned back and fixed his stare, challenging me to react.

I blushed again at my misjudgment of his motives. My heart rate quickened. He was younger than I realized, closer to my age, and with a rugged attractiveness softened by sky blue eyes. His thick, wavy brown hair had a personality of its own. I felt like a school girl who bumped into the most popular guy in the class and dropped her books. A common reaction which I was sure he had experienced.

"Are you interested in a sail?"

"No, I'm not interested in anything—that didn't sound right—I'm most interested in doing nothing, for once."

"Busy life?"

"I'm finishing my degree so I'm in the last leg of a data-collecting marathon."

"A sailing trip might help." He swept his arm across our view to his boat quietly swaying and speaking to us in its rigging-clanking language.

"Despite making my way here to paradise, I live the life of a poor grad student."

"Ah, the operative word being poor," his face spoke genuine kindness. "I don't have any bookings this afternoon, so it's at my invitation. No charge."

I stared blankly at him. He was not easy to read, though his smile was light, his manner affable, and he seemed genuine in his offer.

"It's free," he emphasized.

"Won't your employers be unhappy?" I looked over to the office hut.

"Oh, them?" He tossed his head over his shoulder. "They're not my employers actually. I sailed over here one day and we reached an agreement that I could stay in exchange for helping with the guests. They get a cut of each cruise, I get fed, the guests don't go bonkers."

"Here? Go bonkers with what?"

"Boredom. You'd be surprised. Folks think it is paradise until about the third or fourth day when they have seen their thousandth parrot fish, finished War and Peace, and completed their shell collection. Unless they have learned to relax, which few people do, they are looking for something to do. And they start dri- . . ."

"Driving you and other staff crazy," I guessed.

"Yup."

We set sail around two. It was quiet, and gentle, and exquisite. So was he. He moved from line to line like a brachiating gibbon. He was easygoing and accepted me as crew after I neatly coiled the line when we shoved off. He exuded the confidence required of a captain, but seemed to lack any sense of ego or need to be in control. Our bare feet scrambled on the deck as we changed tack; we made a great team.

We talked about the places we'd been, current world news, and the island. He knew a lot about the local ecology, ocean science, science in general. We steered away from talk of personal lives, and jockeyed around weighty issues until we determined that our politics leaned the same way, as did our ideologies. I felt we had a synergy.

We stretched out on the bow enjoying some of the fruit he had gathered from the dining hall for our foray. We were a relaxed fit and I felt emboldened.

"So, I imagine that you lead the perfect life. No one stays for long, you provide the perfect image of the solitary man in need of comfort, and have your pick of the young women." It seemed a natural and inevitable question for me to pose.

"Imagine all you want, but I can tell you that is far from the truth."

"Which part?" I asked.

"All of it. I am not the lonely man who travels the seas looking for a place or woman or life that will save me from myself. Most days I meet some nice people, nice families, and learn something new from them. Most nights I read a book on my deck, maybe share a drink with someone new, and go to sleep alone."

"Most nights?" I couldn't help myself.

"Why does that seem to be the most intriguing part of my story? Interested?"

"Um, no, sorry, I guess I just . . ."

"It's the image again. It's not me though. And besides, I don't think my hosts would find it acceptable, but rather distasteful, if I made sailing trysts one of their special offerings."

I must have looked disappointed.

"Everyone always wants to believe what fulfills their fantasies, not mine. Not that I don't get approached more often than I would like, but it is a bit predictable and not really appealing." He was not boastful, just factual.

We sat in silence for a while. A comfortable silence, made uncomfortable only by my realization that I was completely content.

"So what's the rest of your story Chris? You're American by your accent, and you're obviously well educated. Is it self-taught or did you do time in an academic institution?"

"Both I suppose, but I'm actually currently committed to an institution. I'm on sabbatical for a year."

"Oh. So you . . ."

"So I am not what you imagined, again. Sorry, I'm not a societal dropout. I'm simply a college professor who always dreamed of spending his life sailing but was not committed enough to give up the life of luxury that a high-paying professorship supports." I laughed at his sarcasm. "I finally got on a tenure track, and decided I could risk being away."

"So what is your field of expertise? Let me guess, aerospace engineering."

"Marine biology, thus the diving, the fish knowledge. Made this place an easy fit."

We talked of careers. He was only five years older, but was ahead of me since I had worked for a few years before going to graduate school and he had flown through his dissertation. His current research was on the Chesapeake Bay, mine in cat genetics. I told him of the postdocs I was applying for. He avoided acknowledging any of them as his. Both East Coasters, both scientists, there were no limits to our discovery of topics of interests we shared. He had flown to Australia, chartered a boat, made it as far as Borneo and Sipadan and had one month to go before he had to head back to the States and his parallel life. We talked deep about perspectives on life, opinions on science and politics, but left the personal details of our lives a mystery.

We swam, we snorkeled, and dived. He was a master diver, I a novice. My eyes widened and I gave a bubbly thumbs up to surface as we paddled out over the reef's edge. "What's wrong?" he asked.

"My brain is saying cliff!"

"You won't fall," was all he said as he took my hand. We dropped slowly along the wall for thirty-two feet, just enough for my ears to pop and for all color fade to blue, but also enough so we could peer into one of the caves that burrowed beneath the island. The sun was setting when we surfaced; he scrambled up the ladder and pulled me from the water. The physical contact felt natural and right.

We sailed back around the island, joining the other guests for dinner and entertainment. Traditional rebana ubi, or hand drums, hypnotized with rhythmic beats. Dancers grabbed a partner for the joget and native voices sang the traditional Ulek Mayang, telling the story of the Bomoh (shaman) who tries to undo a spell placed on a fisherman by a sea princess in love with him. She calls for her sisters to help her, until the high princess tells them all—Enough! Those from the sea return to the sea, those from the land return to the land.

Stomp by stomp the bamboo poles dared our feet to keep up. Eyes closed, I drifted side to side, transported to an island in the

Pacific a million miles from reality. Chris sat on a stool towards the back of the bar watching me, laughing as I whirled with one of the Malay women, and spun off balance. He caught me with his smile.

As the party disintegrated into guest karaoke, he slid in next to me at the table, chatted with the other guests, and leaned in whispering, "Care to join my private party on the boat in fifteen minutes?" Not looking at him, I nodded yes.

I stopped by my hut first to change out of shorts into a long dress that flowed as the evening wind began to pick up. From a distance, I could see light and movement on the boat. I arrived to find two other couples and another woman; the not so private party already in progress. He smiled as he took my hand to help me aboard and announce my arrival. It was a delightful night, really, despite my initial disappointment in our different interpretation of the word *private*. He had chosen like-minded people from Australia and Canada, and a woman from Argentina. Conversation flowed with the tide, we told stories and laughed at our differences despite our similarities. The couples retired sooner, Gabrielle gracefully conceded shortly thereafter. I was to learn later that she had invited herself.

As she receded into the darkness, he extended his hand, inviting me to join him on the long transom bench. I stretched my legs alongside him, and leaned back as he enveloped me in his arms. We lay like this for an eternity: talking, and listening, and being one.

The morning was overcast and cooler. I woke slowly, registering sound first, then light, then my surroundings. Chris was down below. Like a groundhog, he popped his head up when he heard me move, then disappeared again. He emerged with two cups of coffee, mine cream no sugar.

I took a sip. "How did you know?" I asked.

"I'm a quick study. I was watching closely yesterday morning."

"Ah. Sorry I fell asleep on you, literally."

"My pleasure." He sat down and looked out over the ocean. "Every morning that I have been here I try to let this setting take hold in my mind. It's a world away, isn't it?"

"It is." I relaxed in the moment until I realized the sun had risen to full-on morning. "What time is it?"

"Unfortunately, time for me to start getting ready. I have a sail scheduled this morning and probably another at noon." He must have registered my faint pout. "Would you like to spend the evening together? I should be back around six."

"Sure, I'd love that!" showing more enthusiasm than intended.

He grinned and leaned in, kissing me gently but only briefly. I gathered my arms around his neck and pulled him to me. He joined me in the transom and we enjoyed each other for a few minutes before he pulled away and mumbled, "It's going to be a long day,"

Chris found me around noon reading on the steps of my hut. "Hey, my noon cancelled."

"They found a more exciting option?"

"No, the wife is already fearful of the water and is too worried about the storms. Want to head out for a sail?"

"And the storms?"

"Sounds like there will just be some small squalls early this evening, clearing up overnight, then the fun stuff will move in tomorrow afternoon."

"Oh great, so I will be heading back in that." And for an instant we acknowledged what little time we had left.

I tossed my dress below, ready on deck in a bathing suit that left little to the imagination. We set sail to explore the other side of the island, though just out of sight of the resort. He scuttled across the deck and squatted beside me. "Want to fly?" the playful boy asked with a shit-eating grin.

"You're the captain!" I replied, scrambling to my feet.

"Let's trim her up then!"

And I obeyed his every command. The wind blew steadily and Sipadan diminished to a spot on the horizon. We raced the flying fish that skittered across the water's surface, and danced between crest and swell. We were alone on a canvas of blue.

Toward late afternoon, a gray wall began to form in the distance, so we came around and headed in. Chris reefed the main and hove-to, suspending us on the sea. He unfolded onto the deck in the joy of exhaustion. I laid my head on his chest and we relaxed in our brief interlude, as we watched Sipadan slowly return to us. The sea was eerily calm before the storm as we skated on glass to the edge of the reef and tied off on the far side of the island at one of the permanent moorings. Orange and yellow from the setting sun converged with a light rain and we stood on deck and watched the show as it washed over us. Only a green flash would make the scene more perfect.

Drenched in the rain and the moment, we stood on the bow and Chris turned me around to face him. The back of his hand stroked down my face to my back, and he kissed me, at first tentative, then with intent. My bathing suit top fell away as his other hand trailed down over my breast and grazed the fabric between my legs. My arms went around his neck, his tongue caressed deeper, and he drew my hips firmly against his. He was strong and hard, and I was dripping wet.

He disengaged, taking my hand and guiding me onto the deck; standing over me he removed his shorts, then my bottoms, and I anticipated the weight of his body on mine. Slowly, savoring every detail, we explored each other with our mouths, our tongues, our hands, our skin. His fingers slowly traced circles along edges and in folds, he glided into me and I arched my back at the moment of climax engulfing him in waves of my own. He raised his face to look at me, casting a net of blue entangling my every sense. His breathing quickened, and he closed his eyes, burrowing his face against my neck as he pulsed and released.

We spent the hours laying in each other's arms, moving about the boat, and making love over and over. I in my early thirties, he in his mid-, we were both experienced and appreciative. Several more curtains of rain washed over us and we went below, exploring each other in the berth. Late in the evening, the sky cleared and a billion stars speckled the night's sky. The three-quarter moon reflected a path home on the water. We returned to the resort dock, tied up, and retreated below, exhausted in each other's arms. The boat's tiny fan blew whispers across our entangled bodies.

The pinging of the rigging and scent of coffee woke me. Two cups sat by the pot, but Chris was not there. I called out his name as I slipped on my dress, and peered out through the forward hatch. No Chris. But the speedboat was there with supplies. The sounds of breakfast, dishes rattling, voices chattering, and the smell of morning cooking awakened me fully. He probably had to go check on his schedule, I thought, so I filled my cup and waited in the cockpit, curled around the warmth of my cup. Schools of swirling jack fish and barracuda tickled the surface of the water, turtles poked their heads out to welcome the morning, and the sun rose lazily.

After a half hour I decided to join the others for breakfast, maybe go pack, so Chris and I could spend the remainder of the day together. I was scheduled to leave around four o'clock.

"Oh, Miss Claire!" one of our hosts exclaimed. "Good you are here! We unfortunately have to alter our departure plans for this afternoon. There is a fairly big storm coming, and we need to get back to the mainland before noon. We will take the speedboat. I hope this won't inconvenience you."

"What? Um, no, sure, a storm, I understand." But I didn't.

"Good, good. If it is not too much trouble, we would like to have your luggage ready at your hut by 9:30, so we could shove off around 10."

"Oh! What time is it now?"

"Eight o'clock, plenty of time. Again, so sorry for any inconvenience."

Two more hours? That's all I had left and I had no idea where Chris was. I grabbed some fruit and a glass of juice. Other guests beckoned me to join them, and I stood and chatted for an obligatory amount of time.

"I must be off though, as I guess we are leaving early so I need to pack. Anyone else leaving today?"

Only two others, the rest were staying in paradise a few more days. "We're looking forward to experiencing the storm!" one of them announced.

I practically ran to my hut and packed my things, then realized that my bathing suit, sandals, and underwear were still on the boat. I sat down to take in what was happening. I was heading home and he was staying. The intensity of my feelings for him was something I'd never felt before. But the awkwardness of a morning after a one-night stand slowly crushed any hope. A one-night stand. Was that really what it was? It seemed ridiculous to leave him my number. I didn't even know at what school he taught. It felt too much like contriving a future to ask for details, though he did talk about his work on the Chesapeake, so that narrowed it to just a few places. I told myself I should simply be thankful for a magical evening, and leave it at that. I sat down. Slowed down. Slowed my breathing and closed my eyes for a few minutes as I tried to smile at what was now becoming a lovely memory.

I bolted up. Twenty minutes. I would take twenty minutes to walk the island one last time, plenty of time for Chris to settle his schedule, and for me to settle down. Plenty of time left for us to say . . . whatever it was we were going to say. I shoved everything into my bag and dropped it outside my hut, and headed out down the beach away from the hub of Sipadan activity. The island was like a merry-go-round, the seascape revolving with each footprint I left in the sand. As the distant muted shape of Borneo's mountains faded behind me, an outcrop of tropical trees bowed in the wind, beckoning me to a bleached shore that raced to mingle with the vibrant reef which morphed into a cobalt ocean that danced with a gray sky. On the far side of the island, nothing but water and sky. I stood still and let the wind dance around me, communing with the Celebes Sea.

With acceptance, I came around the final curve, and the end of my journey came in view. The dining room, the huts lined up along the beach, mine at the far end, just out of view, and the dock, already a few suitcases waiting. Chris' boat was gone. I started to run only to realize how stupid I looked when I caught sight of one of the resort workers.

"Good morning Miss Claire! Did you sleep well?!"

I blurted a response and scurried past.

I sat in the dining hut with the others scheduled to leave, they lamenting leaving our fantasy world, I silent and agonizing over leaving what was very real. The crew loaded the speedboat and came to get us, lowering each of us down into the cramped boat that sat too close to the water. Our luggage was piled at the stern and we were seated at the bow. I noticed a plastic bag with my bathing suit and sandals tied to my suitcase, but all I could do was watch it flail in the wind as we bounced across the rough seas.

Our hosts politely transferred our bags to be loaded below on our bus, leaving me tortured for another half hour as we rode back to their mainland office. Finally, my possessions in my care, I stood to the side of the group and tore open the bag in search of something more, a note maybe. But nothing. I walked out into the downpour to catch a taxi, incredulous with myself that I didn't leave a note either.

Google was an infant back then, so finding Chris took more work than a few key strokes. Knowing that he would not be back in the U.S. for another month, I tried to put it out of my mind, but I soon found myself requesting a MEDLINE search of his publications from the university librarian. His most recent, and rather impressive, article led straight to his academic affiliation. As the fall semester began, one long distance phone call and I was connected to his department, and was given his schedule from a student overly happy to have a part-time job where she knew the pattern of every professor's day.

On a Friday in October, I drove mindlessly for two hours and made my way up the formidable staircase leading to the marine science building. I collected myself inside the main entrance and time stood still. Everything around me continued to move, people walked by, the door ker-chunked open, bam closed, voices but no words. My life was either about to be uplifted or I was to be horribly embarrassed.

I peeked around the doorway watching him walk back and forth lecturing to his class; mesmerized that it was the same man who had held me in his arms a world away three months ago. He looked out of place in street clothes in a classroom. Then I realized that I filled the frame of the doorway. I wasn't discreetly peering in to see when he was going to finish up, I was centered in a frame of view like a stripper dancing in the cage above the crowd. Look at me, look at me! And the entire class was. Following their eyes, he went silent and his expression changed from distraction to recognition. A slight smile rose on his face and he turned back to his students. I dove out of view, mortified.

"So we've got only five minutes left. Let's stop here. Remember to turn in your lab notes and proposals on Monday, and don't forget the exam next Friday. Study session Wednesday at seven."

Notebooks snapped shut, papers shuffled, and students started pouring through the door. I heard a sugary-sweet voice say "Um, Professor Thompson? What if we can't make Wednesday's session?"

"Then I guess you'll have to prepare the old-fashioned way —study."

"But, I have another . . ."

"Study." He sounded exasperated. "And if you have specific questions you can leave me a note or call my office. If you still don't understand something, you can make an appointment."

"Can I just make an appointment now?"

"Do you know what questions you have?"

"Um, no."

"Then you don't know if you need an appointment." I could see other students' eyes rolling as they pressed out the door. I couldn't tell if they looked disgusted at her or him. He was ruggedly attractive, and I'm sure that there were rumors, but I wondered if he cared enough to try to make an effort to set the record straight. That didn't seem like him—but what did I really know about him? She humphed past me.

The room was suddenly silent.

"You still there?" His voice loud enough to carry into the hall.

"Yes," I responded, stuck to the wall.

"Good, I was thinking that I have finally reached my breaking point and become delusional."

"Maybe it's time for a sabbatical," I braced myself and I poked my head around the doorway.

"I tried that," he said as he moved toward me.

"Oh? Was it helpful?"

"In some ways, but I had my heart broken."

I started to ask by how many women, but the look on his face was sincere. We were now face to face, inches away. "Hi, Chris."

"Hi, Claire." And he opened his arms and I stepped towards him, embracing as water merges with the sand. Eyes closed, our syncopated hearts felt like that moment when you awake from an afternoon nap. Momentarily blissful, I tried to stave off the heady prospect of having to become fully awake. I held tight for one more moment of contentment before facing the truth. He tightened his arms around me.

Still enveloped in each other's arms, we separated, just a kiss away. And then the moment was gone. Who pulled away first?

"Wow, this is quite a surprise," his look was unreadable.

"Oh dear God! I didn't mean to interrupt your class. I was just looking in to see if I could tell when it would be over and I sort of got carried away watching you."

"It was rather amusing. But a welcome distraction. As well as a surprising one."

"You said that. I'm sorry, was this a bad idea?"

He let go, turned and picked up his things off the lectern, walked back toward the door, and looking deep in thought, turned off the lights. I followed him into the hall. He turned and stopped and faced me dead on. He looked too serious. "I'm not sure. It depends on why you're here." He held my gaze only for a moment, and we turned and walked side by side down the main hall, past other lecture rooms, and turned towards the labs, silently. "I need to lock up my office and lab. Can you hang on a minute?"

I silently shook my head yes, but all I wanted was to catch the next speedboat to another world.

His lab was impressive. State of the art equipment, well organized, and lots of bubbling tanks and glowing lights. "Want the quick tour?" He had perked up.

"Absolutely!"

"So our main research agendas right now are invasive species and oyster decline. Major issues in the Chesapeake."

"I know, I read some of your papers."

He gave his stalker a curious look. "So we have three main tanks to house each of the three stages of oyster growth. We're working to move these back out to reseed some of the old oyster beds. We also started to look at the zebra mussel, a fairly recent invasive species from the Caspian Sea. We're also participants in Mussel Watch, which is a nationwide annual collection of bivalves to track changes in response to on environmental stressors. As they are the filters of our waterways, their stories are pretty telling."

"How many graduate students do you have?"

"Enough. Five right now, but one who might be finding a new career."

"Science or personal issues?"

"A little of both. Every time he seems to make some progress in his research project it seems the next crisis du jour hits—the girlfriend, the roommate. It almost feels like he knows he won't make it to the end so he's subconsciously self-destructing."

"Have you talked to him about it?" I asked.

"I'm exhausted. Frankly, my sabbatical left me with a newfound intolerance for first-world problems."

"Really?"

"Yeah, surprised me too. Hopefully it's a phase, but I find I have little patience for people who have a great life and seem to mess it up. My student is smart and personable. If you want to change your life, change it. If you want to screw it up, don't involve me." He shook his head as if to shake off his hard edge. He seemed different. He moved in close and ran the back of his hand down my arm, lighting his fingers on mine and gently entwining my hand. "You free for dinner?"

I had made the right decision to come.

We headed out of town to avoid dining under the watchful eye of any of his students. His car was impressive. A twenty-year-old mustard yellow Volvo that said, while I like good cars, I'm not going to spend a lot of money on one.

"Why didn't you leave a note?" he finally asked as we sat at an outside table enjoying the last of the season's warm days.

"Because I thought I was going to see you again. I just left for a few minutes to see if I could find you in the dining hut and they told me that we had to leave earlier. So I went to pack. When I came out your boat was gone." Turning the question on him, I asked, "Why didn't you leave a note in my bag of things?"

"Same reason, I thought I was going to see you again. I left just to find out if they needed me that morning, and when I came back you had left the boat. I waited since I thought you would come back for your things, but before I knew it, the woman who cancelled the day before asked if I could take them for a quick sail. There was no time to look for you."

"So she lost her fear of water and storms?"

"More like she had a big fight with her husband. Before I knew it they were on board and I was scrambling to pick up your clothes strewn about my boat." He grinned. "And off we went. I didn't know you were leaving earlier than originally planned. I thought I would see you around noon, so I just gave the bag, discreetly, to one of the workers so you could pack it."

"Discretely?" I smirked. "It was tied to my bag the whole ride back, waving in the breeze for the world to see."

"Ha! The Sipadan team were a pretty fun bunch. Very quiet and respectful, but with a sleepy, sneaky sense of humor. They were famous for pulling pranks on each other and me once they felt comfortable."

"I should confess that I actually went for a last walk around the island to clear my head, and I was startled to see your boat gone when I came around the last bend. " I felt the shock all over again. "Everything happened so fast and before I knew it, Sipadan was fading in the distance." He reached for my hand and I met his touch. "As we skittered over the ocean—in a very scary speedboat I might add—it occurred to me that there were two coffee cups waiting when I woke up, but . . ."

"You wondered if just leaving it as a memory was best," he completed my sentence.

"Yes." I smiled at our renewed synergy. "I wasn't sure this was the right thing, contacting you."

"I'm glad you're here—and I'll confess that I have your phone number, address, the whole—"

"You do? How?"

"Your registration with the resort." I must have looked mortified. "And it took some sleuthing to get it without the company finding out." His tone changed to wistful. "But I had to concentrate on my remaining days on the island and the two-week solo sail ahead to return the boat. Once home the semester started, and I accepted that this is my real life. I convinced myself that you would have left a note, sent a message back through Borneo Divers, or done something if you wanted to see me again."

"Or show up at your classroom months later?"

He took both my hands and captured me once again with his eyes, "I hadn't considered that. But it works."

We dated for three years, at first long distance as I finished the final semester of my Ph.D. I moved closer when I landed a postdoc at a nearby university, and then moved in. We married and I landed a tenure track position. All the while, Chris remained at his college, and we split the difference in commuting time by finding a home off one of the creeks that feed the Chesapeake watershed. We have been blessed with children, dogs, and successful careers. I loved him from the moment he smiled at me on the dock. I love him still. But the seasons change, some things die away, others bloom again, invaders alter the landscape and make survival challenging, yet new growth emerges. As the train rocked and the urban landscape rolled by, I committed to clearing the debris.

In 2000, members of an armed Filipino Islamic separatist group arrived on Sipadan Island, taking twenty-one of the twenty-three vacationers and hosts hostage. They were transported to Jolo Island where they were held with several other hostages taken from other archipelago islands over subsequent months. They were eventually rescued and released through a series of negotiations, ransoms, and military actions. While still a popular site for day trips and diving, Sipadan is no longer a place one can stay. Eden cannot last forever.

A COLD DAY IN HELL

I HAD everything ready. All the background research done, a schedule, assignments, and documents for signatures. Assembly line organized, the students returned and Anna delivered the samples in person. Behind closed doors we told the story and I asked everyone for their commitment and silence. Joining us were Drs. Martenson and Pierce who would run the toxicology and endocrinology assays. Participation was unanimous.

We explored the ethics of sharing only those samples from the CRFS dogs. Everyone had an opinion. While Jamie didn't think there was any use in sending non-CRFS samples to CDC, even if they were from dogs that eventually got CRFS, Anna felt that there was value in looking at these in the context of looking for differences in the same dogs pre- and post-infection. It was critical that we eventually share these samples. Martenson and Pierce saw legitimacy in her argument, but pointed out that since the CDC was not collecting these from other vets, there wasn't an established pool of like samples and ours would not make up a statistically valid population in the context of the thousands of other samples in their bank. Megan and I both felt that we should submit the samples eventually, but Anna's team—our team—should at least get first crack at them since she made the initial observation. We came to a consensus that we would conduct our research and if we didn't find anything in our initial analysis, we would contact the CDC and see if they were interested in taking these samples. Anna would at least make a note in the files of submitted samples from Addison's dogs with CRFS that they seemed to die more slowly than dogs that didn't have Addison's.

We were not alone in this. If we found something we would follow it closely, but we had to let others contribute their expertise. The thought that Regnum and thus Kendal would likely gain access to our work made me sick to my stomach, but I had to just deal with, or better, just ignore it. Even if we were inclined to keep the samples initially to ourselves, considering the endless possibilities and seeing the vision of all those dead dogs, there is no way we could expect to do this on our own. We needed to do the initial work and prepare for scientific collaboration beyond our team.

Messenger RNA (mRNA) extraction had to be done first since it is very unstable. When a gene is activated, short pieces of mRNA are created from the gene's template, which is then read by the ribosomes to make proteins. Changes in the amount of mRNA for a particular gene suggests that the organism has a reason to make more or less of that specific protein.

Proteins were next. They are fragile and degrade quickly if samples are not kept cold. There's always a fear that an elusive protein wasn't found not because it wasn't there, but because the sample had degraded. Again, changes in levels or structure of a protein can point to how the dogs' bodies are reacting to CRFS. Evidence of a foreign protein could point to the agent of CRFS itself.

Lastly, DNA. It is made up of a complex of molecules involving some of the strongest bonds in chemistry, and it's sturdy as hell. Its covalent bonds are simple but strong, and the scaffold made by the double-stranded helical structure further physically protects the bonds, making it difficult to break them. By contrast, single-stranded mRNA leaves bonds exposed; thus they are oxidized easily and the strand degrades quickly. DNA is so stable that it has been pulled from such paleontological finds as bone marrow of 38,000-year-old saber-toothed cats permeated with tar from the La Brea tar pits of California, a femur and teeth of a 430,000-year-old pre-human found in Spain, and bones of a 700,000-year-old horse from the Canadian permafrost.

Extracted DNA can be kept indefinitely. It can be frozen, dried, stored in alcohol, or left in a vial on a benchtop. Just don't heat it above 94C or the complementary strands that make up DNA will break apart. Capitalizing on this feature, a controlled denaturing of DNA is the initial step in one of the most commonly performed DNA analyses, the polymerase chain reaction (PCR). In this procedure, DNA is heated until the two strands fall apart; the tube containing the denatured DNA also contains the building blocks for more DNA along with other required enzymes and primers. As the temperature is subsequently lowered, new strands are assembled off the template of the original single strands of DNA, making a second copy. Successive cycles of this result in hundreds of thousands of copies of the targeted piece of DNA.

It took the best of two weeks to set up protocols, process all the samples, and begin the analysis phase. With mRNA, proteins, and DNA in hand, we set out to see if we could detect any differences between normal dogs with and without CRFS, and Addison's dogs with and without CRFS.

We spent the next four weeks in a factory-like process to conduct every possible type of laboratory procedure on the samples, and meticulous data entry and analysis of every correlation we could think of. Everyone was working full-time on their part of the assembly line, to the detriment of their own research. The regimented process was punctuated by thrilling moments when there seemed to be an intriguing result, followed by a reality check when it proved to not be statistically valid.

Throughout February came a blizzard of dogs lost to CRFS. While the outbreak was still largely isolated to the East Coast, no population of dogs was left unaffected. Purebreds and mutts, pampered city dogs and working dogs in rural communities all fell victim with scattered losses that still seemed to show no pattern. There were mass losses at shelters, many of which temporarily stopped taking in dogs. Curiously, dog rescue centers were still largely untouched, even as they took in those dogs that would have gone to the shelters.

Two weeks before spring break and still nothing significant. The sun had set, closing another work week, but no one bothered to turn on the lights. Thinking that I might go home early for once and catch the girls before they engaged in their weekend plans, I headed out through the lab to find Megan and Jamie, huddled in the luminosity of computers and equipment monitors, hovering over output from the DNA sequencer. The energy was palpable.

I crept up behind them. "What are you two conspiring over?" I whispered. Megan yelped. "Whoa, I was only kidding. You find something?"

"Maybe." Jamie motioned me over with a rapidly waving hand. He looked strangely serious, even for him.

Megan looked up, as excited as Sofie finding a mole hole. "If it is what we think, then we have something very interesting."

I wedged in between them. The three of us focused on the computer screen covered with rows and rows of thin lines making hundreds of little colored peaks, each indicating which nucleotide base was at what position in the sequence. Running underneath each row was the resulting sequence of A's, T's, C's, and G's. On a separate monitor were statistics of the peaks telling us the concentration of the nucleotide at each position. Jamie searched the screen for the pattern of interest, and pointed out the peaks and corresponding statistics on the intensity. "See? Right here."

"Whoa, sorry guys, my eyes are too old for this," I walked to the wall and flipped on the lights.

Blinking fast to adjust to the light he focused back to the sequences he had highlighted. "We've been looking at a particular mRNA that appears to increase in amount in all the dogs with CRFS. See here how the intensity indicates a large number of copies?" I'd hardly taken it in when he switched the sheet for another screen with rows and rows of the same sequence.

"See here, the first few rows? These are the normal dogs that don't have Addison's. We've matched these to the next few samples which are the same dogs after they got CRFS.

Then below these are the Addison's dogs, again the first few samples before they got CRFS, the next are the same dogs after getting CRFS.

"We of course also have control dogs that are healthy and did not get CRFS. And see? Every dog has this same short sequence." He pointed to rows and rows of the same series of letters, and grinned broadly.

I was not yet in on the secret. "So, every dog has this sequence. Then I would say that it's just a dog sequence, but I'm sure you're setting me up." He shifted to his sneaky boyish, wait-for-it look.

"Oh!" It hit me. "You said you see an increase in the number of copies of the sequence in the dogs with CRFS."

"Correct, they all have the sequence, but when we look at the intensity statistics, there's an increase in the amount in the CRFS dogs, though the increase is very slight. Megan has the quantitative data." He beamed at his teammate. "Show her."

She rapidly swapped out his spreadsheets for hers, trading lines of letters for numbers representing the concentrations of mRNA sequence. "See here? These are the matched sets of healthy dogs to those with CRFS. Both the normal and one's with Addison's show an increase in the mRNA level when they have CRFS."

"Hold on. You said you have matched sets for normal dogs. The same normal dog pre- and post CRFS infection?"

"Uh-huh." Megan smiled.

"I thought all we got from normal dogs were samples after they got the disease. How did you get matched sets for these dogs?"

"Anna gave them to us. She's been collecting blood from any patient that came in, with the owner's permission of course, telling them that she wants it just in case, and that it may help find the cause. She said no one had refused. So even though we don't have matching sets for every normal dog that died of CRFS, she has a fairly decent number of samples. See these, here? There are eighteen samples from normal dogs that eventually got CRFS."

Anna was amazing. She'd thought of everything. I plopped down on the stool, shaking my head as I slowly processed the implications of the data. "Do you know what the sequence codes for?"

"Not yet. Jamie started picking this up yesterday and we've spent the day repeating the analysis, running every sample through a second time to be sure." Megan clicked to a spreadsheet of the samples.

"We'll have to run comparisons through the NIH NCBI databases tonight and tomorrow, but we have a theory. Want to venture a guess?" Jamie teased. They looked like two little kids who put the frog in the teacher's desk.

"Is the amount of mRNA the same in dogs that you say are healthy, or without CRFS, regardless of whether they're normal or have Addison's?"

"Yes!" Megan pounced. Obviously she and Jamie thought they

had the answer. I thought I did too, but it was worth carefully considering each detail to make sure every angle was covered.

"Okay, since Anna says the dogs are first affected by adrenal failure, her theory is that CRFS messes up something in the overall hypothalamic–pituitary–adrenal system—the HPA."

"Correct," Megan said.

"And, since the Addison's dogs don't have functioning adrenal glands, they get medication to replace the adrenal hormones. So even if CRFS were to directly affect the adrenals, Addison's dogs would probably be protected."

"Correct." Jamie nodded rapidly.

I continued, "But since you did see a difference in Addison's dogs that get CRFS, and since they obviously do get it, CRFS can't be directly acting on the adrenal glands, but probably somewhere else in the HPA other than the adrenals.

"That's what we're thinking," Megan agreed. "But there is definitely a difference between how normal and Addison's dogs respond."

"How so?"

"Well, see the numbers here? Even though both types of sick dogs show an increase in gene expression, the dogs with Addison's show a slightly lower level."

"So you also validated Anna's clinical observations with mRNA evidence." The slow trickle of thought started churning into whitewater. "This should be relatively easy to identify. Why didn't you start running it through NCBI's database when you first suspected something!?"

"Because we wanted to be sure!" Megan letting me know they were sticking to protocol.

"We've been checking and rechecking all day to make sure that we have all the samples correctly categorized, and all the sequences match, and that all the levels of mRNA are confirmed, since the difference is very small," Jamie added. "We were actually holding off on searching the databases to see what it was, sort of as a reward to ourselves once we had it all confirmed. We were just about to come tell—"

"You didn't have to, I could feel something was up from across the room!"

We looked at one another in stunned silence, the excitement hovering between elation and realization of the implications of their finding. We could have a major clue to the process, or even be close to finding the cause. Each step from here would have to be carefully calculated so we didn't waste a lot of time chasing phantom links.

NO WHINING ON THE YACHT

TRUMPING STORIES of war and falling economies, when a well-to-do American systematically killed Cecil the Lion for the sole purpose of having a wall trophy, the clamoring for the offender's head was deafening. For a brief time, Cecil's story drowned out those of starvation in Ethiopia and the Central African Republic, and mass migration of refugees from the Sudan, even though all of these stories originated from the same continent half a world away. To be honest, those who questioned our collective sympathetic priorities did have a point. Those of us who love our dogs and toss out phrases like "they are my family," "they are like my children" speak from the privilege of first-world problems and the luxury of isolation from the impact of world events that don't directly touch our lives, unless we choose to post a related picture on Facebook to show how in touch we are.

It is estimated that 40% of American households own a collective seventy-five million dogs, spending money on everything from the purchase of their pet, to food, vet care, toys, accessories, and services like boarding and grooming. Americans spend over $60 billion a year on our pets—more than the gross domestic product of most countries in the world. Our pets have become more than companions; they have become a reflection of our capitalist indulgences, proudly signifying that their owners have achieved the American dream. Simple food and shelter have been replaced with multi-level cat apartments, doggy daycare, and an assortment of outfits and costumes to celebrate every conceivable occasion.

When a dog is dying you will know it is time when it stops eating. But often we extend their lives with veterinary interventions that may call into question who the care really benefits. We love our dogs, but sometimes love is blind.

The slowly creeping downstream economic impact of CRFS first and most significantly hit the dog show world, with groomers and handlers and breed clubs practically shut down and out of work. Then business dropped precipitously for national pet store chains, as the fear of contaminated products from overseas grew, while cottage industries surfaced, including many who locally produced raw dog food. All of this happened without the slightest link to the cause.

While it was clear that CRFS was a problem of an economically advanced nation, the economic impact was felt worldwide, as American owners hunkered down and stopped buying everything from collars from China, and toys from India. But though sympathies abounded for those who mourned the loss of their pets, they did not extend to those who were affected downstream, and whose lives depended on a meager percentage of industry revenues.

At least at first. There was a slow-growing social media movement afoot to highlight the absurdities of our obsession with our pets, juxtapositioning images of owners agonizing over their dying pets with those of mothers agonizing over their starving children. The movement's position, in some ways valid, was that there should be no whining on the yacht.

Another text, my fourth of the day. *Can you pick Tess up after rehearsal?*

Of course.

I could feel the irritated force of Chris' typing. It had been more than two months and his patience was wearing thin, especially since until now we hadn't made any breakthroughs. But he did not know yet about the hope.

I'm sorry, again. We're on to something that is looking pretty interesting and I can't just walk out in the middle our discussion, so I don't know what time I will be home.

My phone sounded *Moondance*, Chris' ringtone.

"Hi, I'm sorry," I wanted absolution. "I just can't stop. I completely forgot she had rehearsal. Can you get her?"

"It's okay," his voice emotionless. "She told me this morning and we worked it out." There was a numbness to his voice.

"She did? But I told her that I would take care of it."

"Well apparently she is learning not to depend on you either." I deserved that, but it still pissed me off.

"That's not fair. It's a critical time."

"It's always a critical time for you."

His point was not lost on me. Each step, each node of progress, whether forward or backward, was critical. No matter how small. So it *was* always a critical time, to me at least.

"I know I keep saying that, I just—Anna's samples are showing something really interesting and we need to determine what to do next, quickly. We're just about out of time."

"What are you seeing?"

"I'll tell you later when I know something more definitive."

"Sorry, I forgot. I'm just the chauffeur." I knew that he wanted to add "and the cook and the maid."

"Don't be that way. I just don't know what we have yet."

"But you have something. You could simply share that with me, remind me that I play a role in your life. Say something of interest —after all I have nothing better to do while I wait for rehearsal to be over since I cancelled my cigar night with the boys."

His timing was masterful, his aim precise, the guilt was surgically extracted. Dead silence.

"I'm sorry."

"You've said that." He wasn't going to bail me out.

"What can I do?"

"A little conversation. Less texting like I'm your servant. Make an attempt to connect."

"You're right. I just—"

"Fewer excuses."

We both felt the buzzing of my phone's timer. Megan's final run repeating the quantitation of those with different treatments for Addison's should be ready. The discussion was over.

As he always does, Chris let me off the hook. "Can you plan to hang around a little in the morning so we can spend some time together?"

"Yes, I will. That would be nice." For a split second I could feel the much-needed shift it would give us.

"And bring your work. I'd like to hear about it. I don't know if you remember, but I'm a scientist too—I have an interest and might even be able to help."

"I remember. And I remember that I love you."

"That would be good too."

The loud snort woke me. Unfortunately, it was my own. It was a terrible consequence of getting older.

Chris was in the kitchen—no sign of the girls. The clock

showed an hour that I rarely saw in my kitchen on a Tuesday. Eight o'clock.

"Wow, did I sleep!"

"Oh, you were sleeping? I thought you were buzz-sawing down a forest, or maybe herding warthogs."

I ignored his attempt at humor. "Why did you let me sleep so late?"

He shrugged. I supposed it was a rhetorical question.

"Breakfast will be ready in a minute, coffee is out in the sun room. I put the heater on to warm it up a bit."

I started towards the sliding doors, then changed course for a much-needed connection. I wrapped my arms around him, turning my head slightly so I could feel my whole body connecting with his back and syncing with him.

"I'm sorry," I offered.

"Thank you," he accepted.

The sunroom was our escape from the world. From on top of a hill, the view rolled down to a patch of woods on one side, and a pasture with our barn on the other. The bare trees and blanket of fresh snow presented a landscape in grayscale, that equalized my emotions. Here you breathed deeper and your heart rate slowed.

We talked of the girls. Diana apparently had a new crush but he was being held captive by a girl that he didn't even like but he felt guilty about dumping, and Tess needed new character shoes, black ones.

"You know what those are?" he asked.

"Yes, dance shoes with heels. I can take her this weekend, and the neighbors are having another one of their wine tasting parties Saturday. We should go but we need to promise to keep an eye on each other so we don't consume so much. Every time we go, I end up with a wine headache the next day."

"Then drink water." He made it sound so simple.

"I do, but somehow I keep finding my wine glass filled by someone again so I just keep drinking."

"You don't have to."

"But their wine is always so good, and really expensive. It's a good thing we walk home."

"So do the girls have their full rehearsal schedule yet?"

"Yes, I put it on the calendar."

And on and on . . . the tiny fibers that made up our joint life got stitched back together to patch the holes.

"So, tell me, what have you been up to lately in the lab?" Chris asked, smirking as he knew I'd been waiting for him to bring up my work.

"Oh nothing, you?" I'd play for a while.

"Same old. Any big scientific breakthroughs?"

"Don't know yet, but something came up yesterday that looks interesting."

"What does?" His game face slipped and he was no longer playing. "I know you don't think I can help, but at least humor me. Or do you not want me involved, except as your partner in life."

"It's not that."

"Then what is it?" he asked, with some frustration showing.

"I don't know. Maybe it's the sharing thing altogether."

"With me?"

"With anyone. After what happened with Kendal and Kate, I don't want to let anyone know what's going on until I am certain."

"Except Neil. Wait, Kate?"

"Oh geez, I forgot to tell you that she is the one who told Kendal about our proposal. It was an accident, but I got a new lab tech because of it."

"You fired her? When did this happen?"

"No, she quit. Didn't even give me a chance to talk her out of it. It was months ago."

"That's a shame, I liked her . . . Months ago?" He looked at me and it registered with both of us how this one fact illustrated how the gulf between us had widened over the past few months.

"I liked her too," I felt genuine regret. "Sorry I didn't tell you."

We sat in silence for a bit. Finally he leaned forward, putting his folded hands on the table, preparing to fully engage. "Let's just talk about here and now," he started.

"If I stop to think about it, it would be nice to be able to talk to someone about it," admitting it to myself as much as to him. "I really have no one except my lab team and Anna. I could really use some other scientific exchange. I just have to make that leap of faith."

"I think you made that leap when you married me," I could feel him shifting. "Look, do you want to be famous?"

"What? No, that's not why I'm doing this."

"Really?" He was setting me up for some point he wanted to make. Fine. He deserved the chance to walk me though my thoughts.

"I'm doing this because I want to find out what's killing these dogs and I want to stop it from happening to others."

"That's great, that's noble—and selfish."

"I know where you're going with this."

"You do? Then tell me, Einstein, how are you going to come up with the theory of relativity all by yourself? Which by the way, he did not do by himself, you know. Michelson, Lorentz, Planck and a bunch of others—But I digress. Why are you chasing down every possible path before bouncing your ideas off others in the field?"

"You're right. I can't do this by myself. I shouldn't do it by myself. I just struggle with how to share the science without losing the edge that will get us some more funding. We're burning through Neil's money pretty fast."

"Do what you love, the money will follow, as Lee Iacocca was known to say."

"Wow, you are Mr. Wikipedia today. I don't think he was talking about grant money."

"That's Dr. Wikipedia."

"Ah, you point that out for a reason. The reason being that you do have some standing in a discussion about the merits of scientific exchange."

"I do believe you are on to something!" He'd become that smug kid who answered all the questions, waving his hand to be called on. I bet his teachers had either loved him or hated him.

"You promise you won't steal my idea and compete for funding?"

He went silent and serious. I was struck by how, no matter how long you have been with someone, there were still triggers that drew emotions when you least expected. "Why so serious?"

He looked over at Ania and Sophie sleeping, curled up on their big chairs, having exhausted themselves with their morning routine of ball chasing and biscuit eating while I slept. "I love those dogs you know," with slight surprise in his voice. "They are a constant smile in this house. I can't imagine if they get this disease and we lose either of them. I want to help find a cure too. I could care less about any credit or funding."

I wanted to say I was sorry, but that was all used up. Instead, I acknowledged the obvious by reaching for my computer bag that I brought home the previous night that was somehow miraculously sitting on the table this morning. He was a master of the set-up.

I explained that we had analyzed all the samples of blood that Anna gave us, looking for differences in mRNA, DNA, and proteins in the blood of CRFS and unaffected dogs, the same as the rest of the research community, but there were no obviously noticeable differences between a group of dogs that were affected and different group that were not.

Chris reminded me that it wasn't a waste of time: negative results were critical at this juncture to understand what was not happening. Still, it was the positive result that gave rise to a surge of adrenaline and created an atmosphere of excitement in the lab and propelled us forward.

I turned on my computer, "but wait." I opened the file of the sequences Jamie showed me the previous evening and slid my computer in front of him. "We are in a unique position because we can compare samples from the same dog before and after it got CRFS. Anna has been collecting samples from all her Addison's dogs. In many cases she has samples that cover their lifespan, including after they got CRFS."

"And you can see a difference before and after they got it?"

"Yes, a slight increase in a mRNA, but so slight that it would have just been assumed to be an anomaly within the standard variation for any two populations of dogs. Except that our populations are pre- and post-disease samples from the same dogs. Also, we see this difference in 100% of same-dog comparisons. Not one that doesn't show it."

"Geez. That's striking." He stood and tilted the screen upwards, studying the string of letters, then looked at me. "Okay, but what does this have to do with Addison's?"

"Actually nothing. We think. We just happened to have not only matched sets of samples from normal dogs, but also matched sets from dogs with Addison's.

"Wait, why did Anna have samples from normal dogs taken before they got CRFS?"

"Well Amazing Anna had the forethought to ask her clients to let her take wellness blood samples early on in this epidemic, so she also had samples from eighteen normal, non-Addison's dogs, pre-

and post-CRFS infection. They have the same type of increase, only ever so slightly lower than the increase we saw with the Addison's dogs."

"So just to cover all angles, why hasn't anyone else seen this?"

"Three reasons. Like I said, the increases we see are so slight that other researchers might not have considered it significant. All those samples sent to CDC would have been from hundreds of different vets, and would likely have inherent variation in processing—like how quickly samples were preserved, and whether there was any degradation, which would obviously cause a change in the amount of mRNA remaining in the sample."

"And the second reason?"

"Our matched sets with pre-disease samples from the same dogs. I doubt anyone has those, so again, they wouldn't notice the minor change in mRNA concentration as important."

"And third?"

"Addison's dogs. They confirm that CRFS is acting on the HPA system."

Chris' mouth dropped open ever so slightly, and he sat back down, still staring at the screen. Sometimes it was painful to listen to the silence of his thinking. I was the type to think somewhat out loud, so people often knew my thoughts in real time. Someone might not be able to follow my circuitous logic, but they would have a sense of how many different directions my thoughts were going. But Chris? For all I know he could have been thinking of when he could reschedule his cigar night. Finally he furrowed his brow and unveiled his thoughts.

"So, you found a transcript of a gene that exists in all dogs, with and without Addison's. You also know that the number of copies of this transcript is elevated in dogs with CRFS, more so in dogs with Addison's."

"Exactly. The really interesting part is the clinical observation that goes along with this."

"There's more?" he asked.

"Yes, do you remember me telling you that Anna noticed that the dogs with Addison's actually succumbed to CRFS slower than the dogs without?"

"You mean faster."

"No. *Slower.* Which would indicate that they can stave off the disease a bit longer."

He registered the fact. "Slower. So they are somewhat protected. What, because of their medication?"

"Yup. The Addison's dogs are somewhat protected by their daily treatment. So as the normal dogs are starting to succumb to CRFS and their whole HPA system starts to fail, the Addison's dogs are able to still respond to the stress of CRFS and produce more copies of the mRNA transcript."

He finally looked away from his study of the sequences and looked me dead on. "What does the sequence look like? Does it match to any known sequence within the HPA?"

"We don't know. That's what I was doing when you called last night. Helping set up the comparison to all the sequences in Genbank."

He hesitated and then relented. "Well played, my love." An acknowledgment that I might have been justified in staying late. "But you could have just made that today's work." He must have registered the disappointment in my face. "Maybe not."

"Yes we could have, but I wanted the results early this morning—Shit! What time is it?!"

Standing in the shower, scarcely taking the time to rinse the soap out of my hair, he had me trapped. The glass door slid open, and he stepped in.

"If I say I don't have time, will it ruin the morning?" I asked.

"No. Actually that's not why I'm here. I just want to remind you I'm here. That I want to help, that I can help." He reached up and redirected the water from my face.

"I know. Thank you. I'll keep that in mind." He looked at me with that yeah, right look. "Okay, I will—if you remind me." He reached for the shampoo.

Damn. He really was there to shower.

Just as I decided to take my time and get ready at a normal pace, my phone rang.

"That was Jamie. He's identified the sequence. I told him not to say anything till I got there." My heart was pounding. Chris gave a hopeful smile. I tilted my head and smiled back, "Want to come with me?" I asked. He closed his computer and beat me to the door.

We arrived at the lab to find Jamie kicked back in his chair, feet propped on a pulled-out bench drawer, chatting—no, laughing—with Megan.

"My, you two look positively radiant!" I moved aside as Chris worked his way past me to shake Jamie and Megan's hands. They were without gloves in computer analysis mode.

Chris came to my side and put his arm around me.

Jamie was now failing at looking casual.

"Okay," I thought about playing with him but couldn't, "spill it. What did you find?"

"We're on the right track." His expression became serious. "Like you thought, it's a gene for a protein that is a critical part of the HPA."

"You're sure?" I wasn't asking for my sake, but for his. He would have to defend the findings soon.

"I can solidly prove it to you. In 100% of the samples. Care to guess which gene?"

I had been thinking all night, but there were more than a dozen possibilities. "I think we don't have time for me to guess. If this is it, we're going to need every moment we have to chase this puppy."

Jamie looked at Megan and nodded for her to do the honors. "There's an increase in the glucocorticoid receptor transcript."

"Really? The GR? That's the most ubiquitous component of the HPA. It's present all over the body! It's what stands ready to activate and shuttle stress response hormones wherever they are needed. Fuck with that gene and—"

"You're fucked," Chris concluded. Jamie and Megan grinned.

"Whoa," was all I could come up with. Jamie and Megan obviously had processed the observation and had moved from shock to planning our next move.

Chris was right, mess with GR and you are done for. We knew that this normal gene was in overdrive as a result of CRFS, and we knew this caused a deadly cascade of responses resulting in 100% mortality.

We called Anna. When I told her what Jamie found, I felt the weight of the next round of decisions. Did we let the rest of the scientific community know, or did we keep it to ourselves, for just a little longer? Would that be selfish or unethical? Anna made the executive decision to give us a few more weeks, defined more by our need to work through a few more steps of discovery rather than by an arbitrary, self-imposed deadline. I wasn't as confident as she was in our chances of making any great strides in the next few weeks—it had taken us three months to find the GR anomaly, and knowing the effect was far different from discovering the cause. But we were collaborators and she was the most confident in her position, so I wasn't about to argue with her. In truth I wanted to press on, wanted us to be "the ones," but the cost in dog lives as the days ticked by was daunting. We owed it to the dogs to chase this hard and fast.

But we owe them so much more.

We owe dogs a lifetime of care. Our domestication of their species comes with that promise.

We owe them food since we have bred out much of their hunting instinct, at least in most breeds, leaving them with no real knowledge of hunting and killing for survival. We selected out the extraordinary teeth and jaws of the wolf that allow them to shatter bones and shear through meat. While Ania and Sofie are relentless hunters of moles, and frogs, and baby birds, they are only in it for fun. And for praise; they demand praise when they present their quarry. Feral dogs rarely are found running through the woods looking for bunnies and small game, but instead they wander the cities and urban environments scrounging for scraps out of human refuse.

We owe dogs shelter, and a clean, safe space for them to nest, though it doesn't have to be on the bed that mine are convinced they are entitled to. It is estimated that dogs spend twelve to fourteen hours a day—half their lives—sleeping, up to a tenth of it in a deep, REM sleep. On a good day, when food is plentiful, wolves will sleep for a third of the day, but rarely do they sleep deeply. To survive, dogs need a place to call home where they can snuggle in. Our domestication has ingrained in them the need to be close to us to feel at home, regardless of whether we actually care for them. Abandoned dogs don't typically dig dens for themselves, but instead they eke out an existence under human discards.

We owe dogs a bath. While there is nothing happier than a muddy dog, we have created coats that are like Velcro for dirt and burrs, and we have essentially erased grooming behavior critical to keep them sufficiently coiffed; though curiously it is retained in cats. Wild canids—wolves, foxes, maned wolves, dingoes—all thirty-four species, may be found with tiny flora and fauna making a home imbedded in the animal's fur, but for the most part canids keep themselves clean and beautifully groomed. They depend on growing and shedding undercoats, to keep them warm and cool, and even to communicate, raising their hackles to show aggression. Dogs wouldn't be caught dead, or rather would be dead, without a well-cared-for coat. Mine don't know the art of grooming other than the slicker brush that strokes them to sleep in front of the TV. Rarely do they wash the day from even their paws. I think the flavor of dirt is distasteful to them.

We owe dogs veterinary medicine. We owe them vaccinations against disease, treatments for parasites, and a mess of other preventatives, therapies, and cures. After all, we traded their genetic diversity for short-muzzled, wrinkly-faced curly-tailed pugs, lean-legged greyhounds, and wrinkled shar-peis. We have bred into them expressed traits—phenotypes—that make us happy, and we have bred out of them unknown genes that could have been advantageous when facing emerging diseases. As they are our closest buddies, it makes sense that we have created in them a situation no different from what we have created in our own species. The paradox of the benefits of modern medicine, veterinary medicine included, is survival of the not-so-fittest. Take hemophilia for example; modern medicine facilitates the survival of individuals with this disease, and thus the retention of these deleterious genes in the species. Through selective breeding to create the domestic dog, much like with ourselves, we eliminated the naturally-occurring species.

Make no mistake, there is still a lot of genetic diversity in the domestic dog. A study that compared thirty breeds living the comfy life, dogs from African shelters that had been freely outbreeding for generations, and other members of the Canidae (wolves, jackals, and coyotes) found a remarkable amount of genetic diversity, or heterozygosity, particularly for large gene complexes that code for body size and shape and for hair and pigmentation traits. The effect of domestication and artificial selection on the dog is a dominance of a few genes with a large effect. In another study of genetic diseases in 114,000 domestic dogs, surprisingly only three breeds—the bull terrier, miniature bull terrier, and boxer—were found to have a low heterozygosity.

Yes, we have narrowed the gene pool in the population, and clearly some breeds suffer because of it, routinely requiring interventions like C-sections or operations to correct eye and nasal issues, all due to the look we have created. A recent study looking at dogs' medical records indicated that for the majority of diseases, there was no significant difference between purebred and mixed breed in the prevalence of disease. The few diseases that did show a difference were found more often in purebreds. These could and should be removed from the breeding population.

So, we also owe dogs ethical breeding. We owe them genetic testing of potential parents to avoid passing on genes for diseases like degenerative myelopathy, progressive retinal atrophy, and von Willebrand's disease. We owe them evaluation of the structure of their hips to avoid perpetuating crippling hip dysplasia, and we owe them decisions on what animals to breed based on hard science.

The concept of "outbreeding" the domestic dog to improve the gene pool is not scientifically supported, and in fact it can cause additional complications. One can easily imagine that crossing a Chihuahua and Great Dane would more than likely create a combination of body structures that would be debilitating for the offspring. While it is not as obvious, there can be similar problems when crossing poodles and Labrador retrievers or Australian shepherds, which are all built very differently both physically—for example, in the placement of the legs and carriage of the chest—and behaviorally, with distinct differences in their retrieving and herding instincts. These differences may be subtle, but the resulting offspring can be unbalanced in their structure and their behavior. The road we have journeyed with dogs is well traveled. We owe them our careful consideration of what we allow to pass on to future generations of puppies and companions.

Sometimes I do feel sorry for my dogs as they spend their days curled in slumber with nothing to do but wait for me to play with them, feed them, connect with them. But they sleep contentedly, which is a valuable gift.

"It's really quite elegant."

"Elegant?" Jamie scoffed from the other side of the bench. His black-and-white view of science leaves no room for modifiers like elegant, intriguing, or fascinating—though I have heard him mumble an occasional "Cool."

Ignoring him, I turned back to Haley and the white board. Having worked for these few weeks in an Addison's research lab she has absorbed some understanding of the disease progression and mechanisms of the adrenal system, but inserting the effect of CRFS introduced a whole new layer of complexity. "Yes, finely balanced and simple or elegant."

"Geez I can't keep any of this straight," Haley scribbled frantically.

"Let me draw it out for you. There are three areas in the body that are involved: The hypothalamus region in the brain, pituitary gland at the base of the brain, and adrenal glands on the kidneys. These three talk to each other through chemical and electronic pathways." I did my best to sketch them on the board.

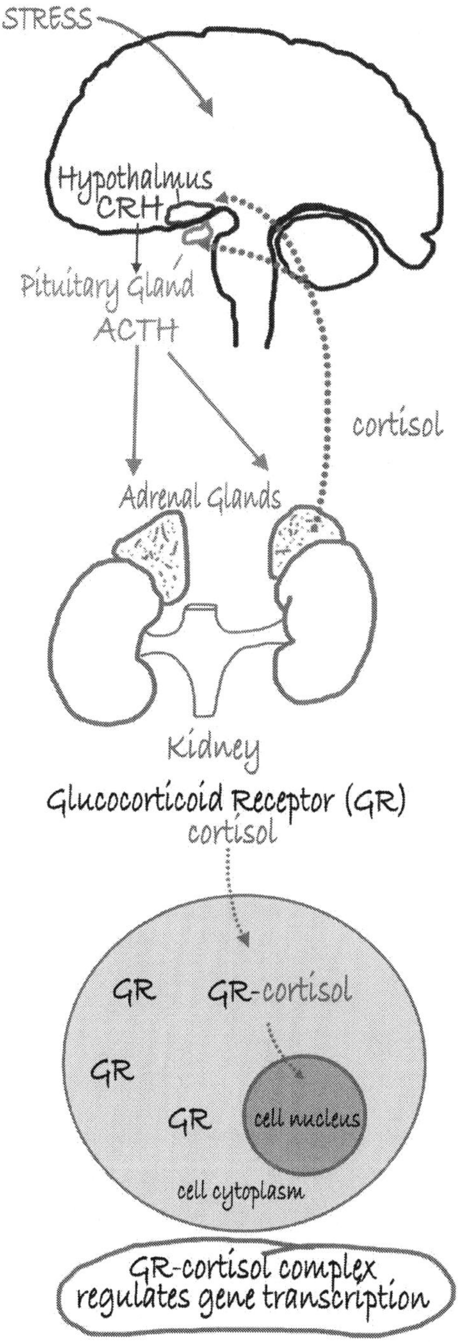
STRESS
Hypothalmus
CRH
Pituitary Gland
ACTH
cortisol
Adrenal Glands
Kidney
Glucocorticoid Receptor (GR)
cortisol
GR
GR-cortisol
GR
GR
cell nucleus
cell cytoplasm
GR-cortisol complex
regulates gene transcription

"When an animal gets stressed—and stress can come in a lot of forms like immediate fear or excitement, or slow-rising anxiety—"

"Like a semester-long paper," an obvious assignment of Haley's.

"Or a charging pack of Chihuahuas," Jamie teased.

I ignored them and continued, "Stress triggers the hypothalamus to release the chemical CRH or corticotropin-releasing hormone." I drew a red stress arrow and a blue CRH flow arrow. "CRH then triggers the pituitary to release ACTH or adrenocorticotropic hormone."

"I'll never remember these names."

"You will eventually. For now, concentrate on the organs and acronyms." I drew arrows to the adrenal glands on top of the kidneys. "Finally, ACTH triggers the adrenals to release cortisol."

"And cortisol is the Chicken Little of the stress response, running all over the place and causing everyone to get excited," Jamie flailed his hands in the air.

Megan joined him, throwing her hands in the air and swaying round and round for a moment, then dropped her arms to her lap, "That is, as long as there is enough glucocorticoid receptor or GR to go around." I wrote that one on the board.

Jamie took the ball and continued. "Yeah, cortisol is carried by the blood all over the body but it can't do anything at the cellular level until it binds to GR inside the cell. Once the two bind together they enter the nucleus and trigger the stress response activity." He hiked an imaginary ball to me.

"Yup," catching the ball, "Once in the nucleus it triggers gene transcription, resulting in lots of stress reacting proteins."

"That's neat." Haley was clearly amused by them.

"Yes, very neat," I smiled. "About the cortisol, but also how you two can still get excited about explaining the process." The co-conspirators, proud of their performance, returned to their work, allowing me to continue my lecture to my audience of one. "Actually, there are all kinds of other chemicals and pathways that are triggered, like adrenaline, but cortisol starts the biggest cascade of responses."

"Got it." Haley studied the board locking it all in.

"So, what do you think happens when the stress goes away? Do you think the body still needs to keep the system turned up to full speed, sending cortisol all over the place, keeping the heart racing, keeping the muscles contracted and ready for flight?"

"No. So I guess somehow the system knows when it's produced enough cortisol?"

"Bingo. Cortisol's binding to GR also serves as a built-in feedback mechanism to help the system return to normal. As we said, cortisol goes all over the body connecting with GR in each cell and activating stress responses. But when all the GR is bound up and can't take on any more cortisol, the cortisol levels start to increase in the blood. The hypothalamus is sensitive to this, and shuts down the release of CRH and the whole cascade of responses stops."

"That makes sense."

"Exactly. There is only a set amount of GR in a cell, and once it gets bound by cortisol, no additional cortisol gets in."

"So no more GR, cortisol builds up, and feedback to the hypothalamus turns off the system," Haley said.

"Correct. This is an oversimplification because, like I said, there are a bunch of other reactions going on. But this is the biggest part of the delicate balancing act."

"It's all so elegant," Jamie holding a beaker like a tea cup, his pinky extended.

"And you all are thinking that somehow CRFS has an impact on the GR gene, causing it to what? Become turned on, making more GR and messing up the feedback loop?" Haley asked.

"Yes!" I responded, pleased that she'd worked it out. "Each cell makes and has ready a set amount of GR, and when it binds to cortisol, it's unavailable to pick up more, setting a maximum limit of cortisol-activated activity. You don't see an increase in GR production as a response to stress, as it is part of the regulation of the response. But in dogs with CRFS, something is telling the cells to produce more GR, and with more available, it keeps activating cortisol all over the body, and the whole system goes out of whack. Tissues and organs are thrown into overdrive and quickly start to fail."

"Okay, I think I get it. Too much GR means the cortisol keeps getting removed from the blood and the system doesn't sense cortisol is at maximum acceptable levels and should shut down."

"Correct. So, in the normal dogs that get CRFS the adrenals start to fall apart from the constant surge of ACTH and over-activity to produce more cortisol, then the rest of the cells in the various organs start to fail."

"And the Addison's dogs?"

"There aren't functioning adrenal glands to receive the ACTH and produce cortisol. Instead, there is a constant level of cortisol-like steroids that are part of the medications they receive, that keeps them at a steady state of low-level response."

"Doesn't the constant level of cortisol hurt them?"

"No. It is a very low level compared to actual stress levels, but without the adrenals they are not able to respond well to stress. That's why we call them soft dogs, because they fold into themselves in stressful situations. They are unable to take it."

"Poor things," Haley's face saddened.

"Not completely. It makes them really cuddly companions, and with medication and proper care, they can thrive. But with respect to CRFS, since there is nothing to keep producing cortisol, extra GR in the system doesn't do anything initially."

"So what happens eventually?"

"Well, eventually the extra GR takes up all the cortisol that is there from the medication and with nothing left, they fall into a typical Addison's crash."

"But why do Addison's dogs with CRFS have a higher increase in the GR gene? You said that, right?" asked Haley.

"I'm thinking that since they are slower to respond to CRFS—that their system simply has a little more time to overproduce GR before they collapse."

I turned to Megan and Jamie. "That reminds me you guys, we need to ask Anna if she's seen any difference in the rate of disease progression between the Addison's dogs that receive monthly hormone/daily prednisone injections versus those who are treated with that uber-expensive daily fludrocortisone acetate oral treatment. Does she even have any of those?" Jamie and Megan looked at each other then looked at me. "I take it I don't have to ask her. You guys already know the answer."

"Yes! I mean, no, you don't need to ask. We already have that information on the samples!" Megan rapidly leafed through papers scanning for the correct data. "We saw two different levels of increased mRNA but thought maybe it was a time of day thing since the whole HPA system works on a circadian rhythm." She opened the binders and pulled out a page, smacked it on the lab bench, and motioned me over. "Here they are! See? These eight dog samples show a slightly higher level than the other forty-three. And I can easily cross check them back to the prescription data that we have for all of the Addison's dogs!"

"I'm betting the data will match perfectly to disease progression, with the ones that get daily treatment holding steady longer than the ones that get a monthly injection," I had no doubt. "This won't tell us anything new but will at least confirm again of our theory on the mechanism of how CRFS attacks the body."

"And will add credibility for a really cool paper?"

Our heads all snapped in Jamie's direction.

I smiled. "It's okay, you can think like that, but only after your comment about how it moves us one step closer to saving a lot of dogs."

"Of course, I meant that! It was implied since I'm such a dog lover."

We all groaned and settled in to our own thoughts on the work ahead.

Sure enough, dogs getting daily meds were less affected initially and had the highest levels of GR, which made sense since those receiving monthly meds could be anywhere in the cycle: having just received their dose or being close to needing it. Still despite all our efforts, despite knowing what the symptoms were at the biochemical and molecular level, we still couldn't figure out the cause. The levels of GR were increasing, causing the body to quickly shut down as the feedback mechanisms that regulate the system faltered. But what was causing the increase?

We knew we were looking for something that was kicking the GR gene into high gear. The next step was to look at the DNA sequence that codes for the mRNA to see if anything was wrong with it. We pulled out the corresponding DNA fragment, including pieces on either side of the gene to determine whether something was wrong with the promoter—the tiny sequence prior to the gene that regulates production—or the stop codon that indicates the end of the gene.

By the day before the university's spring break, we still had nothing.

OUT OF THE MOUTHS OF BABES

I AM a dog person. Of course, that's what my dogs would claim too. And though they are happy to believe this since they are treated like members of the family, I am not one of those people who says that my dogs are my children. Not because I have children, but because I think we do animals a disservice when we anthropomorphize them too much instead of appreciating their uniqueness as totally different species. We marvel at discoveries of how whales communicate through song or how other primates use tools. Yet right under our own roof, we are granted insight into the innermost secrets of the dog and its instincts—and we too often feel compelled to see them in the context of our species. We want to tuck them in the same pocket of our heart where we place kids, when dogs belong in their own space. While I often fail, I try to keep them separate. In some odd way it helps me to accept when they die that their place is different and their time with us was always destined to be shorter. I love my children and I love my dogs, but differently. And that is what makes dogs all the more special.

Diana's cough was persistent. Annoyingly persistent. I had to check myself. My personal stresses were overriding the empathy I was supposed to feel as her mother. Sometimes I'm just not that good of a person. My daughter had a cold—worse than that: a sore throat and a fever that challenged me to time perfectly the alternating doses of ibuprofen and acetaminophen, lest her temperature skyrocket towards 103 and we have to bring in a different kind of doctor. Having already coaxed her to school for the first two days of her illness (knowingly exposing her classmates for my own selfish reasons), I realized I should assume the role of full-time mother, so I nestled her in a stack of pillows and blankets in the living room where she could drift in and out of sleep and SpongeBob's pineapple world under the sea. The day also brought over-salted chicken noodle soup and warm milk with honey and butter, in the tradition of generations of my maternal ancestors.

Lucky for Diana, this was not her spring break. Unfortunately for me, it was mine at the university.

Ania, sensing the need for her nursing abilities and finally seeing an opening, she stepped up to take her place at Diana's feet.

"No, Ania, you go sleep over there on the floor," Diana shoved her feet to block the open space.

"What's up, you don't want her next to you?" I asked. "She probably senses you're out of sorts and wants to help."

"I know. I want to cuddle with her too, but I don't want her to get my cold."

"Dogs don't get human colds," I motioned to Diana to scrunch up, and patted the couch to invite Ania to the claim her spot.

"Why?"—she must have sensed the inevitable science lecture coming—"The short version please. I'm sick. Remember?"

"Well, the Reader's Digest version is that different species are susceptible to different viruses. Since different cell types of different species each have different receptors—those little proteins on the surface—viruses can only connect to and invade those cells that have receptors that fit, so they're species-specific."

"Oh yeah, I remember you told me before that fish can't get rabies, but all mammals can."

"Yup."

"Even dolphins? Dolphins are mammals, right?"

"Yup and yup."

"But if I'm a mammal and I have this cold virus, why don't other mammals like a dog get it?"

"Good question. Some viruses are just more specific. Some of it has to do with how quickly the virus or the host, or both, evolve. Some viruses evolve alongside, or rather inside of their host species, without doing a lot of harm so they essentially co-evolve." Diana picked up the remote and the channels started to change. "Other viruses rapidly evolve, like the influenza virus or the rhinovirus or coronavirus that causes colds, and their host species, us, don't ever get a chance to co-evolve an immunity. Add in modern medicine, which changes the way we adapt and all application of standard evolutionary theory goes out the—"

"Mom." She silenced me, feigning imminent death. I picked up her dirty dishes, leaned over to press my cheek against hers to feel her temperature, and stood up, blocking her view of the screen.

"Bottom line is it is not cool to kill off your host, so sooner or later you should establish a more symbiotic relationship with them if you are an infecting agent and you want to survive.

"Viruses don't have brains, Mom. And mine might explode if you try to put any more into it today and that would be really gross."

"Oh my poor dear, I wouldn't want you to spew your brain all over the place and make the rest of us sick! Let me just add that there is a lot of DNA in a species that actually came from viruses that originally inserted themselves into the genome to use the host to create more copies, but over time mutated to the point of being inactive and incorporated into—"

"Mom? You done?"

"Finished. I'm not a cake. Remember?" Diana buried her face in her pillows, imitating a seizure. I left the room content in having scored a few educational points. I peeked back in, just to make sure she was faking. I'm actually not that bad a mom. She was back in her cartoon world and I felt a sudden sense of urgency to get back to mine and let myself get pulled back into my laptop.

Ania was curled up against her feet, keeping close, standing by, solidifying her pack.

They have trendy clothes, use phrases and words that are foreign to me, and are experts in navigating the latest social media app within moments of release. I sometimes look at my daughters and wonder, "How did we end up here?" With both Chris and me being environmentalists, I had visions of Birkenstock-wearing, tree-hugging clones of us that would eagerly await the weekend we were going to go help plant sea grass that we grew at home as part of the Chesapeake Bay Foundation's restoration effort. And we did that, though they were barely old enough to remember now. We had a dead animal collection, starting with the sun-dried Pipistrelle bat—one of the smallest, cutest of bats—we found stuck on our window screen. Our collection grew as we found a snake skin (though technically not a dead animal), exoskeletons of a horseshoe crab and some seventeen-year cicadas, and countless beetles and other cool critters. The girls were licked in the face by dogs and consumed dirt along the way: things we firmly believed were necessary to build a child's immune system and character.

We are fortunate to both have good jobs; we're not wealthy, but solidly middle class. Though sometimes, I know that all our efforts to provide my daughters a comfortable life have also done them a disservice. Their busy lives revolve around their needs, and their volunteerism meets their schools service hour requirements, though falls short of instilling in them social responsibility. We imprinted in them the importance of family, loyalty, tolerance, and conservation. We tried but failed to teach them to turn the lights off when they left a room.

Surrounded by dogs from the moment they were born, Tess and Diana developed respect and love of animals and compassion for fellow humans. Those were non-negotiable. They are happy, kind, funny, and self-centered. But our ability to influence them slowly slips away as they navigate their way through public school, peer pressure, pop culture, and a world of outside influences. I had no idea at the time that those first five years would be so critical in establishing a foundation of morals, beliefs, and communication. I see glimpses of our influence in their evolving opinions, but I have had to accept the disintegration of my vision of how my children would be, just as I accepted the disintegration into dust of our dead animal collection by the tiny live organisms feeding on it. I watch, react, support, hold my tongue, and recalibrate when I can. My daughters have a totally different vantage point, giving them a perspective unlike mine. I hold on tight as their personalities develop, jagged edges worn down as the waves of life wash over them, and wait for beautiful smooth beach glass to emerge.

Diana was asleep, Tess was prepping for the regional science fair in two weeks, and I was sitting in the dark staring at my computer.

Chris, on the other side of the room in the big chair, was staring at our dim reflection in the sunroom glass doors. He looked tired and disengaged, or rather, distracted. In a rare exchange of our roles of late, he came home after dark, and we ate dinner in relative silence, except for my cute story about Diana and the science lecture. As a stay-at-home mom today, I had called to check on the progress of Jamie's analysis of the GR sequences to see if there were any anomalies, but nothing had revealed itself. It was frustrating, as it looked like we had uncovered CRFS' mode of action, but not the cause. Maybe it could at least lead to a treatment, if not a cure. But that would mean involving other scientists. Which would be okay.

Chris didn't seem to have the energy to register the small events of the day. It registered with me that this was how I acted lately, and how he must have felt my absence.

Without turning to look at me, he asked, "How far upstream of the GR gene have you sequenced?"

"What?" I shook my head to register his words. "Um, I'm not sure, but I would guess slightly before the promoter region all the way through and slightly past the stop codon to confirm that we definitely had a full gene sequence."

"Can you find out? And if you don't have another two to three thousand bases past the promoter and stop, can you ask them to get it?" His movements were measured, his speech deliberate; he was containing something huge.

I picked up my laptop and moved closer to him. "Okay, I'll send them an email now so they can get started first thing in the morning." I tilted my head: concerned or confused or both. "Want to give me a hint what's going on in that powerful brain of yours?"

He moved to the edge of his chair, and faced me, his expression one of a mad scientist plotting a maniacal plan. "Diana may not be that far off in her confusion about cross-species infection." He raised one eyebrow.

"So you were listening to my story."

"Every word, and more." He stood up, towering over me. "I might be way off base, but if Megan and Jamie get more of the sequence, can they send it to me right away so I can explore my idea?"

"Sure, Sherlock. You going to clue me in?"

"Can I keep it a surprise for another twelve hours? I don't want to get overly excited, or get you overly excited on something that might be a dead end."

"Too late. And it's not like we haven't had a pile of dead ends. But, beware, if I ask them to do this, they'll also be analyzing the data as it comes off the sequencer. You'll have competition from those two and they'll be at an obvious advantage having the data in hand before you.

"Bring it on."

I stood and wrapped my arms around him, holding him tight, hearing his heart pound. I pulled away just far enough to look him in the eyes. "Kind of fun working together again, isn't it?"

"Yeah," and he pulled me back in.

I waited until almost midnight to email Jamie and Megan because I knew they would have likely left the lab. If I sent it before they left, regardless of how late, they would have spent the entire night working on my request. I wanted them well rested.

Megan started processing samples before she took off her coat, but it still took us the entire day to process enough samples to feel confident that we sequenced the whole GR gene and controlling ends. Jamie, meanwhile, alternated between attempting to do some benchwork and sitting at his computer bouncing his knee like one of those balls on a string on a paddle. By four o'clock, he was finally uploading the sequence data to the National Center for Biotechnology Information database to compare against the dog genome sequence, and sending a copy to Chris. The race was on.

Diana was much better, and Chris stayed home. I had gone to

the lab to offer help, but there really wasn't anything I could do. I busied myself with updating our rapidly diminishing budget, and searching for any news on CRFS research discoveries. Google returned pages of reports on more dog deaths—in the thousands—and the impact on dog parks and pet stores, and the rise of fears that there was a new virus created by China, socialists, ISIS, or some other group that supposedly wanted to destroy our world. I headed home early to see what was happening on the receiving end of Jamie's data.

When I walked into the house, I was greeted by a subdued poodle party, a common variant on their greeting when the garbage has been their entertainment, or when something else is amiss in the house. The place was dark except for Chris' computer in the sunroom, and the lights at the end of the hall in Diana and Tess's rooms. I headed down the hall.

"You feeling better, babe?" I asked Diana.

"Yeah, much. Dad made us pizza and has been pacing the sunroom. Now both of my parents have abandoned me." She put the back of her hand to her brow and collapsed on her pillows, ever the actress.

"You're fed, warm, and now apparently healthy enough to go back to school tomorrow. What more could you want?" I sat down on the end of the bed. "How'd your day go?"

"Okay. Wish I could stay home one more day though." She fake coughed.

"Sorry, you have stuff to do before your spring break. Where's your sister? Her light is on, but she's not in her room."

"Out, I guess. She has a life." I gave her back one of her oh, pleeeease looks. "I think she went across the street to work on her project with Lisa, or something like that."

"Okay. You need anything?"

"No. Glad you're home though Mom. Oh, maybe some ice cream?"

"You got it." I headed to the kitchen, turning off the light in Tess's room.

The first poodle my mother bred was Abby. Unlike me, Abby was a good mom, the best of moms we ever had. When her first puppy was born, it took twenty seconds for her instincts to kick in, cleaning and nursing it with such care, even while simultaneously delivering another. She mothered her puppies longer than other moms, tolerating their needle-like teeth and sharpening claws, wincing as they fought to suck out one more snack. She played with her puppies with such joy, high-stepping and gently springing aside to avoid hurting them. She taught them boundaries with a soft mouth on their muzzle or a quick sharp growl. I learned from her how to paint the blank canvas of a puppy. While some bitches will rebuff and even kill the puppies of another, she embraced her ancestral role as the matriarch and treated pups from my other females as a loving aunt should. Most telling was her desire to provide for them even as her artificial environment gave her few opportunities. I had a display full of my Steiff stuffed animals just within her reach, and each day she gently put her feet on the shelf to capture her quarry, carrying them one by one to create a stack of fresh kills outside the puppies' pen. Abby was the best of moms.

At least I delivered the ice cream.

Chris paced, phone to his ear. He put the phone on speaker and sat down, mouse clicking back and forth. Then he was back on his phone. I watched him for a few moments until he saw me and motioned me in. The dogs cautiously trotted behind me.

"It's awfully dark in here. Can I turn on a light?"

"Oh, yeah, sure. Jamie's on the phone. Say hi." He put the phone back on speaker and put it on his computer, and stood.

"Hi Jamie," I moved in facing Chris, the computer-phone combination on the table between us. They went eerily silent. "What's up, guys?" The dogs set up a perimeter of curled up warmth.

Jamie was hesitant "Claire, Chris and I—I'm sorry. Chris, do you want to tell her?"

"No, you go ahead, Jamie. This is your discovery. I'm only here to troubleshoot and help validate."

"Jamie?" I half-pleaded.

"It's unequivocal. Just under 2,500 bases ahead of the regular promoter, there is a second, foreign promoter that we think is turning the GR gene on overdrive."

I sat down, staring at the phone then at Chris as he too sat.

"Did you hear me?" Jamie asked tentatively.

"Yes, yes I did, I'm just not sure what to . . ."

"Say? Do? Think?" Chris asked.

"Pretty much. Jamie, you said unequivocal. Explain."

"It is in every sample that Megan's processed so far—seventeen of the CRFS-infected dogs. It does not occur in any samples from dogs prior to infection. Megan should have the rest of the samples ready by tomorrow evening."

"Okay. You said it was a foreign promoter. How do you know that?"

"Because when we compare it to the entire dog genome sequence it does not match anything. It has to come from the outside."

"And do you have any idea where it came from?"

"Yes," they said in unison.

I retrieved Tess from Lisa's, and she was ecstatic. "Mom, if a promoter has something to do with CRFS, I so want to be involved!"

"Me too!" Diana added. "Dad said I gave him the idea to look outside the dog, whatever that means."

"I'll keep you guys posted." I gave them each a meaningful hug, and cracked a smile at the two of them sitting on Diana's bed. "You two are the best."

"You go Mom, we'll be fine." Diana brightened. "We can call Lisa's mom if we need anything." They looked so mature as they grasped the enormity of my excitement.

I called Anna trying to contain myself. "Anna, we have to meet with you! We've picked up an extra sequence in 100% of the affected individuals we've looked at so far. We need to get together."

"I closed at six. I'll come—"

"We'll come to you. Can we meet you at your clinic? We want to see if there is anything in your records that might be related."

"You have all my data." She pointed out the obvious.

"Maybe," I responded.

Chris and I pulled into her clinic parking lot just as she was unlocking the door. She ushered us in and locked the door behind us. "I'm closing early these days," shaking her head. "With half my practice gone, I've become a cat clinic."

There was no need to comment. She'd just needed to say it. We made our way to the back room. The exam tables were cold and bare. We spread out our findings on one of the bench tops.

"Use one of the tables. They have better lighting and are easier to work around," Anna called out as she detoured into the lab area. Though the room was cleared of dead dogs the image was still vivid. I had to shake it off.

She returned with a laptop and set it on the exam table. "So whatcha got?"

"Well, Megan extracted pieces of DNA sequence that were longer on both ends than the original sequence we looked at, and Jamie then ran what looks to be an extra promoter on the GR gene through GenBank to see if he could match it to any known gene sequence. Chris has been working with him to validate his analysis."

"Quite a team you've got," she congratulated me. Turning to Chris, she asked, "And you and Jamie found . . ?"

He dangled his printed stats, "There is an extra promoter but it looks nothing like the typical GR gene promoter. It doesn't even look like a promoter for any gene found in the dog, so it doesn't look to be just a random duplication of another dog gene's promoter."

"I feel a *but* coming on."

"Yes, but a good but."

"Kind of like mine." I smiled at both of them.

Ignoring me, Chris continued, "I found a similar promoter on an unrelated gene."

"You just said it didn't look like any other promoter in the dog."

"I did, correct. It's not from any species in the dog family." He paused for effect. "The promoter matches the promoter for an endogenous retrovirus in one of the Felidae species."

He looked to me to deliver the final punch line. "The domestic cat lineage."

We watched as Anna's face transformed from curious to knowing—but not surprised, which seemed odd.

"So what we are wondering is—"

"Shh!" She held up one finger to silence me. She opened her laptop, clicked closed spreadsheets, and opened up access to her client records. "I already know where to look. I had ever-so-slightly suspected a connection early on but dismissed it as other things stuck out more," she impatiently banged on keys, "Damn it."

"Suspected what? We didn't even ask a question," she was one step ahead of us.

"There were a handful of cases in which I saw the owner one week when they brought in their cat, and the next week they brought in their dying dog. I remember them because when they brought the dog in I asked about the cat that I had just seen, but none of them reported that the cat was sick."

She had read my mind, "We were going to ask is whether you saw any sick cats in the same households."

"They weren't sick," she repeated abruptly.

"So you thought it was a coincidence that they came in two weeks in a row?"

"No, you know I don't believe in coincidences when it comes to science. I thought there had to be some sort of connection, but my fear was that by them coming here with their cat, they picked up something and took it home to their dog. Damn it, why didn't I pay more attention to this?!" I saw tears welling up in her eyes as she was clicking through patient records. "I was so afraid that our clinic was contaminated and the cat owners were picking something up on their shoes or hands and taking it home to their dogs. I drove my technicians crazy with implementing an overly stringent disinfection regimen."

"Don't kick yourself! You had no way—"

"I should have mentioned it to you guys. Frankly I just put it out of my mind because I started to see other cases of CRFS that didn't seem to have this cat connection."

"How many do you think you have?" I knew she had those data.

"Cases with a cat I saw and then a sick dog? I'm checking."

Out of the corner of my eye I could see Chris' face evolve into a look of almost panic. "Anna, can you pull up one or two? What were the cats brought in for?"

She was laser-focused on her computer. "That's what I'm looking for." She clicked to open up two client records, side by side. She scanned them and sat down, deflated, locking knowing eyes with Chris.

"Someone want to clue me in?" I asked.

Chris lowered his eyes. Anna murmured, barely audibly, "Vaccinations."

"The same vaccination," Chris said as a statement, not a question.

"Yes. FeLV," Anna closed her eyes tight.

I understood then. "And Feline Leukemia Virus vaccination is a mod—"

"A modified live vaccine, containing a modified version of FeLV," Anna opened her eyes to her computer screen, "Which is shed to the cat's environment the first twenty-four hours after vaccination."

We all sat in dead silence, taking in the gravity of the connection. We could not confirm how vaccinating a cat against a virus that was completely unrelated to anything in the dog could lead to CRFS without further tests, but we all knew this was the smoking gun.

Chris and I cuddled for a bit while the girls slept. Ania lay regal and aloof next to me, quietly reminding me with her warmth that it was not my job to convince people of the merits of her breed, it was hers.

She is a standard poodle. An incredible breed loved by those who know it, much maligned and misunderstood by those who can only see a goofy haircut on a pampered white poodle dyed pink, wearing bows in her hair, nails painted, with an owner who insists she demands such attention. "Have you ever actually seen a poodle in that haircut?" I'll ask. "No," the response always is. "I've only seen them on TV, but so-and-so had one when I was growing up that was really nasty."

We poodle people know what you are really thinking.

It is rather goofy, this caricature of the original hunt cut from the time when a dog's hair was kept long on the chest and joints to keep it warm in the water, while the hind legs were shaved to help it move through the water, and two patches were left on the hips to keep the kidneys warm. Poodles were bred to be water retrievers, complete with webbed feet and water repellent hair—not fur. But someone who is curious enough to get close at a dog show will see what really goes into crafting these dogs into regal athletes. In addition to careful breeding, there is an artistry to the grooming and a discipline to training that gets lost in the cartoon. And if you are looking for different type of competition, there are also those who participate in grooming completions where they sculpt poodle coats into colorful scenery or to other animals, tis another interesting side of the poodle world.

I fell in love with the breed by chance, having grown up with a miniature poodle, who was appropriately named for the 1960s Pierre. My college rebellion against everything parental resulted in my owning dogs of two other breeds who shed, smelled odd, and died young of some malady from poor genetics. I loved them each dearly, and anguished over losing them. But by my late twenties I came back home to the poodle, and now I marvel every day at their intelligence and physical ability. They don't drool, they don't smell, and they are kickass smart, making them easily corruptible into spoiled and demanding creatures if they are not trained right. They are fiercely loyal, and uniquely intuitive about their surroundings and human companions.

And they have a great sense of humor. Sofie only needs to find my purse and dig out something to parade around the room to get my attention and make me laugh. Having bred poodles, and watched many reluctant family members and friends become staunch defenders of the breed, I am long past being sensitive to people who don't get them. And I love their curls!

In 1998, the first animal genome was sequenced, that of the nematode worm, which consisted of just under one million bases. Next was the *Drosophila* fruit fly in 2000, with 165 million bases. These early efforts involved a painstaking set of procedures of cloning short pieces of DNA and piecing together the genome from an overlapping puzzle of strands. By the turn of the twenty-first century, a revolution in techniques and laboratory equipment automated the process. It facilitated the sequencing of the human genome in 2003, at over three billion bases, as well as genomes of other species of significance to laboratory research, including the mouse, frog, and dog. While there is controversy over their use, beagles are the most common laboratory dog, with several different lines that have been maintained for decades. Interestingly, the first draft of the dog genome sequence was from a standard poodle named Shadow, because the researcher leading the project wanted to use his own dog. Ultimately, the first complete sequence of a domestic dog, published in 2005, was of a boxer named Tasha. The boxer was chosen because there is very little variation between individuals in the breed, allowing verification of conserved regions of DNA with just a few individuals.

Ania is tenacious and persistent, and committed to going after what she wants. A ball under the couch has no chance of hiding for long. Neither does a lizard scampering across the rocks. A raptor perched on a wire surveying a field has nothing on Ania's vantage point from the sunroom. She bolts out the dog door from her ready state and the poor lizard is obliterated. She is relentless in reminding me that my morning coffee is served with a biscuit for her and that the basement door is to be opened in the afternoon to usher in the afternoon ball chase. She is driven like Anna.

I sat quietly, staring blankly out at the empty campus. Silent, Anna stood at my office door, hugging a small cooler, waiting for me to notice, or maybe simply allowing me a final moment of peace. She looked oddly calm.

"You're early," I hugged her and the box.

"Actually late, months late, but let's get to it."

We went into the lab and unpacked the box on Megan's bench. I grabbed markers and labels while Anna laid out spreadsheets and opened her laptop. Everything was already well organized and there was no need for us to rearrange the samples to set up the study, just to put lab-specific accession numbers on them and get started. Megan and Jamie showed up within the hour, excited at the prospect of making a critical connection. Their goal was to pull the modified viruses from the vaccination vials and sequence them the same way they would any sample. I silently hoped to find a match to the promoter sequence we found in the CRFS study dogs.

A LINE IN THE SAND

FROM LION to lamb, March in Virginia shifts from frost-covered dawns and frigid nights to mornings perfect for standing on the deck enjoying the warmth of the sun awakening the world. Crocuses poke their purple heads through the softening ground, yellow daffodils open their mouths to sing in the lengthening days. A soft green haze overlays the gray trees. As winter unclenches its stubborn hold, spring quietly takes the stage. By the beginning of April, the season is in full bloom. Spring in Virginia is like a muted fall. Instead of deep oranges, reds, and yellows there are the pale pink feather dusters of the mimosa blooms and cherry blossom petals, faint yellow flowers of tulip poplars, purple redbuds, and white crosses of the dogwoods. A full pastel watercolor palette tints the landscape.

The dogs too come alive, relentless in their efforts to capitalize on creatures emerging from their underground world. They stand alert in the middle of the yard, heads cocked, listening for the rumble beneath the grass that only their highly attuned ears can hear. They pounce, dig, stop, listen for a change in direction, and repeat. They excavate the tunnels with precision; the moles have no chance. The yard looks like an ant farm. Orange mud oozes from their muzzles, sticks between their toes, and stuffs up their noses. Reluctantly, they make their way to the tub on the command of "shower"—but I know they are secretly giggling.

The origins of CRFS had lain dormant for six months but once it began to germinate, a cascade of discoveries brought it to full bloom. Neil and I had not spoken in the last few weeks—he wanted to keep in the background—though we did communicate through short texts punctuated with key findings.

I got straight to the point. *Found a sequence definitely related.*

His response was immediate. *And?*

Sequence associated with the HPA.

Are you talking about CRFS or Addison's?

CRFS. The sequence codes for GR.

In the pause I could feel him thinking. *Are you sure?*

Yes. Think we found the smoking gun.

What next?

When can you get here?

It had taken the better part of two weeks to know, definitively, that we had identified the cause. Neil flew in Saturday night in preparation for an all-day, heavy discussion at our house on Sunday. We told the girls what was going on. They were filled with questions, concerns, and to our delight, genuine interest. As they tried to understand the nuances of our explanation, they were guinea pigs for our eventual presentation to the public. Armed with ninth and eleventh grade educations, they understood most of it and helped us to clarify for the lay public, those concepts that as scientists we took for granted. Genomes, DNA, Addison's, retrovirus. We needed a glossary of terms. It would be the same if I were to listen to experts in finance or information technology talk their talk.

We all gathered for cocktails and hors d'oeuvres on the deck consisting of soda water and whatever cheese we had left in the refrigerator. We needed clear minds to work through the night, and worked out our game plan while we waited for dinner to cook. Ania dropped the ball at Neil's feet. He picked it up and balanced it on his knee for a few seconds, then let it roll down his bent leg and bounce off his toe. She darted after it, pounced, and proudly brought it back to him; again, he let it roll down his leg. "Careful, don't get her started unless you're inclined to do that all night," Chris spoke from experience.

"But she's having such a ball," Neil retorted.

"And she looks so fetching doing it, don't you think?" Chris said without a hint of shame.

Dinner was calming and rejuvenating. My favorite friends, Anna and Neil, and my family, the loves of my life. The girls were comfortable at a table of adults, entertaining with their syncopated storytelling, and engaging with their fresh perspectives on everything from politics to science to Hollywood gossip. A momentary shrill from the kitchen followed by "mom I dropped my phone in the pie!", was truncated by Neil's "Oh! Are we having baked apple?"

There was a synergy between Anna and I that added hidden meaning to our interchanges, a momentary catch of the eye or subtle knowing smile. The guys competed mercilessly for the role of pun master.

The girls cleared the table and even did the dishes as the rest of us turned our dining area into a conference room, with stacks of documents and notebooks, and several laptops open and ready for the presentation. Anna, Chris and I planned to walk Neil through all the details of our findings, and tried to anticipate any questions he would have. I knew this was a dress rehearsal as we would be grilled on our data and conclusions many times in the coming weeks. "So you know that Anna had samples from 139 dead dogs," I began.

"But I've put a stop to that," she added.

"And she carefully collected and catalogued all of the data on these animals."

"I always liked you," Neil with grinned with sarcasm, or maybe something else? "What kind of data?"

"Everything," Anna looked him straight on. "All the information leading up to their deaths, blood work, physical profile, vaccinations, treatments, diet. Demographic data like breed, age, information on their owners, other animals in the house."

Turning to me he asked, "Okay, other than that she is stunningly beautiful, how does that make her different from all the other researchers with samples of their own or who received samples from the CDC?"

I looked at her bemused. Neil has never been sexist in the least, and it was an odd time to be flirting. Anna seemed unfazed and answered for me. "You are correct that my good looks separate me from the rest. That and my Addison's samples. My CRFS sample population includes fifty-two dogs that died which also had Addison's. I also had stored samples of their blood pre-CRFS, often from different stages of their life and death. But you already know all this. It's the analyses that are telling."

Anna stood, and like a pizza chef in the window of a restaurant, arranged the ingredients of papers and notebooks on the table creating a centerpiece for her story. We all moved to one side of the table to get a better view. I opened and slid to her the notebook that contained all of her spreadsheets: pages of color-coded highlights, dog-eared and scribbled upon. Anna walked Neil through her original findings, that Addison's dogs lived a bit longer, but eventually succumbed to the disease.

Seeming to hang on her every word, Neil tipped back a bit and looked at me behind her back. "That's when you called me."

I nodded. He leaned back to the table and Anna talked on. She had called colleagues across the country, and she and I had gone over all of the information that I collected over the holidays. There seemed to be little rhyme or reason to the pockets of outbreaks.

I walked Neil through our process of elimination as we worked through all the possible laboratory analyses. There was nothing from the toxicology folks, no elevated proteins in the blood, no unusual DNA sequences. Nothing.

"So from nothing you discovered everything," Neil's rising anticipation was palpable.

"Well, to be fair," Chris added, "it wasn't completely nothing. Claire's team screened hundreds of blood samples for changes in DNA, and finally noticed a slight barely perceptible, but definite difference not in the DNA, but in a short mRNA sequence that came from transcribing a gene needed to make more of the protein GR."

Neil looked at me, "Barely perceptible?" He needed proof.

"Barely," I locked eyes with him. "In fact, it's not a matter of a change in the sequence of the mRNA, but instead, in the number of copies."

"Well, that's only part of the change," Anna inserted.

"Don't spoil my presentation," I brushed her away. "I'm going for a big climax."

"You were taking too long."

"Since when are you the one who is in a hurry? I Usually I have to do the set director's speed it up sign when you're telling—

"You digress," Neil interrupted. He shook his head, dismissing us, and turned to Chris to rescue him. "So Chris, there is a difference in the number of copies. What else?"

"Once we'd noted that the number of copies increased, the question became why. Was it in response to CRFS, or was it linked to the cause of CRFS. So the next thing to look at was the sequence itself."

"And?" Neil asked.

"And, while it is true the actual mRNA sequence is unaltered, there is an extra promoter upstream of the normal promoter."

"An extra promoter. And that caused . . ?"

"That caused the increase in production of GR RNA transcripts."

"And you see this extra promoter only in CRFS animals."

Our three voices answered in unison. "Yup. Yes. Uh-huh"

"Okay folks," Neil was not happy to be on the outside. "Let's hear the punch line because I feel like I have three Cheshire cats hovering over me. What does this extra promoter look like?"

"Ooh, good analogy," I said.

"Yes, purrrrfect," Anna cooed.

Neil looked to Chris for relief from their shared purgatory. "It's a cat virus promoter," Chris the spoiler put an end to our fun.

Neil turned and took a few steps away from us towards the window. When he turned back to face us he looked genuinely shocked. "Are you suggesting that there is a cat virus sequence that has jumped to dogs? Do we have a new parvo on our hands?"

Anna continued. "Yes about the cat sequence, but no on parvo. The extra promoter isn't from a current cat virus like parvo was, but is an ancient one that became part of the cat genome, so it is technically from a cat sequence."

"You've lost me."

I jumped in. "The promoter is from an endogenous retrovirus of the cat. From an ancient virus that long ago got incorporated into the cat's genome and forever sits there quietly—like a Cheshire cat."

Neil wasn't allowing the humor. "What? Wait, if it is endogenous then it's inactive. Like you said, forever sitting quietly. How exactly are you proposing that it got turned on then jumped into the dog? That's a pretty wild assertion."

"I didn't say it did. We only see the promoter part of the sequence, forty-three bases, in front of the GR gene, no other part of the retrovirus," Anna said. "We also believe the endogenous sequence didn't just get messed up in the cat and then suddenly jump to the dog."

"Then how . . ." Shaking his head, Neil walked back to us and plopped into a chair; slowly the rest of us descended into ours.

Anna pulled a blank sheet of paper in front of him and began to illustrate the sequence of events. "Here's what we think happened. A vaccine was created using standard modified live technique." She drew a vaccine vial and an arrow to a cat. "When it was injected into cats it triggered the typical immune response, which includes shedding the modified virus into the environment through urine, feces or saliva, for maybe twenty-four to forty-eight hours, and the dog then picked it up. Since the vaccine is based on a modified cat virus that doesn't normally affect dogs, it should have had no effect on the dog, except to wander around the body looking for trouble.

"But this was not normal."

"Correct. The vaccine was contaminated with an extra promoter, so it found trouble in the dog by dropping off the promoter. As it happens, it did so at a location just upstream from the GR gene." She added a dog to the illustration and a blown-up block with a squiggly double helix and a dot for the GR gene.

"And the dogs are exposed how?"

"They have to be inhaling it through those magnificent noses," I could envision Ania, nose to the ground. "That's the lowest common denominator of all the cases—they are sniffing around recently-vaccinated cats."

"And this modified vaccine with the aberrant promoter has no effect on the cat?"

"Not likely," I said. "Even if the promoter came from an endogenous cat virus, cats have evolved with the sequence so it is likely harmless, but we actually haven't had time to look at that."

Turning back to Anna, Neil asked, "So it's in the dog, then what?" He had been a Chief Scientific Officer at a major vaccine-producing company. He knew these answers, but he also clearly knew that we would need to be able to explain every detail.

"The promoter triggers the overproduction of GR all over the body, which most immediately sets up an imbalance in the stress feedback loop and sends the dogs into an Addison's-like adrenal failure."

Standing again, Neil surveyed Anna's illustration and pointed to her rendition of a dog. "If the production of GR is in overdrive, wouldn't everyone researching this be seeing this same increase in the number of mRNA transcripts, or be suspicious of an increase in the GR protein made from them?"

"Sure," I confirmed.

He eyed me over his shoulder. "So then why hasn't anyone come to the same conclusion as you, which by the way, I still am not quite clear on."

"Because it is a normal gene. Everyone is looking for something abnormal," Anna sat forward, ready for his questions.

"But the number of copies would be abnormal," Neil observed.

"Compared to what?" I asked.

"Compared to what is produced normally," there was frustration rising in his voice.

"Right."

He sat down, "I'm starting to feel like I'm in an Abbott and Costello routine."

"Everyone and their donkey has been comparing the population of affected individuals with the unaffected," I nodded, acknowledging he needed us to be straight-forward. "But remember, the increase is very slight, and changes in the levels would vary naturally from dog to dog as each responds in a different way to stress."

"So unless you are comparing the same dog before and after CRFS, which we don't think anyone is, it wouldn't be significant," Anna added.

He looked over at Anna and grinned, "Which you were able to do because you have pre- and post- samples from all the Addison's dogs who are in your study."

"Exactly."

"That still doesn't explain why no one has at least suspected something from the elevated levels." He was playing devil's advocate now.

Anna added her view from the clinical side. "I suspect that when anyone has seen GR elevated they are thinking that this is just how the dogs were reacting to CRFS as their whole system was going out of whack. No one is thinking this *is* CRFS."

"Okay, so you have a gene being transcribed at higher than normal rates. How did you connect this back to a contaminated vaccine from a cat?"

"It was surprisingly quick," I looked to Chris. "For about a day we thought we hit a brick wall since the gene sequence looked normal. At one point we did start to believe that it was just a symptom, but then Chris had an epiphany, and suggested that we look further upstream and downstream of the GR gene."

Neil turned to Chris, "And that's how you connected the dots to the cat endogenous retrovirus?"

"Actually Diana helped. Out of the mouths of babes came the

discussion of cross species viruses, evolution, and endogenous retroviruses, so we're making the kid a co-author."

"You're talking to your fourteen-year-old about endogenous retroviruses? Geez, you're a fun family." Neil shook his head. "Continue."

"Actually I wasn't thinking it was anything as bizarre as what they found. I was simply thinking maybe there's a yet-to-be-discovered CRFS virus that was influencing transcription of the GR, and that walking up and down the intervening sequences around the GR gene might reveal something."

I continued, "The GR coding sequence has a typical promoter, 300 bases upstream of the gene, but when we sequenced past that there was another promoter with a small sequence that did not match anything in the dog. Chris and Jamie then had a race to find out what it was, and confirmed within hours that it was from one of the cat's endogenous retroviruses."

"That still doesn't explain how it got into a cat vaccine."

"It doesn't. We thought it was from a cat, so we went back to Anna to see if she could scour her records and see if she saw anything going on with cats at the same time. I was hoping that maybe there was something that turned on the endogenous virus in cats, that mildly affected the cat but was deadly to the dog."

"But that was not the case." I could tell that he knew.

"Correct," Anna continued. "When they came to me and told me about the cat sequence, I suspected a vaccine right away because I remembered that several of my cases were very similar. I had a number of clients bring in their dogs dying of CRFS within days of seeing them to vaccinate their cat." Her shoulders dropped. "I'm still kicking myself for not paying more attention to that."

Neil gave her a moment. "I suspect if your records had not been so meticulous you wouldn't have been able to make the connection." There was a gentleness in his voice that I rarely heard. "So the obvious questions are how did you confirm it and how did it get in the vaccine." Neil was no longer asking questions. He was walking down the long road of inevitability.

"Let's start with how it got in the vaccine." Anna gathered herself and flipped some pages in one of her notebooks. "We think we know that."

"Of course." Neil smoothed out Anna's drawing on the table and placed both his hands on it. He looked Anna squarely in the eyes. "You have the entire thing figured out, don't you?"

"It sounds masterful, but it is pretty straightforward with all the pieces in front of us."

"Don't kid yourselves, millions of dollars are being spent on this, and no one even has a clue, much less a solution." He sat down next to her and looked around to each of us.

Waving off his declaration, Anna plodded on. "My guess is that a single run or a few lots of the vaccine were contaminated as it was being produced."

"How? And feel free to detail your lecture for the masses; I think you're going to be giving a lot of them."

Inhaling slowly, absorbing the weight of that reality, Anna continued, "This came from the Feline Leukemia Virus or the FeLV vaccine. The vaccine is produced using a modified live virus. They make the vaccine by inoculating cells growing in culture to produce the modified virus and then extract it from the media solution that the cells are growing in."

"But you think the contaminant is actually a sequence not from FeLV?" Neil asked.

"Uh-huh," Anna answered. We think that the cell culture that was used to produce the modified FeLV virus was contaminated, but we are only guessing at how. They probably didn't use a cat cell culture to produce a cat vaccine, but probably something closely related."

I pulled open a notebook to another set of spreadsheets with numbers and sequences and placed it so both Neil and Anna could see it.

"Contaminated how and with what?" he asked cautiously.

Anna continued. "Well, you know how cells in culture tend to peter out after several generations of replication? They start to accumulate too many mutations and slowly die off?"

"Yes." Of course he did.

"And you know how there is a technique to sort of immortalize these cultures with endogenous retroviruses from other species which somehow keeps them going."

Neil shook his head to the affirmative, "And you think that the cell cultures used to produce the FeLV vaccine became contaminated with a piece of an endogenous retrovirus that was used to immortalize the cell culture."

"Yes. We actually *know* that the contaminated vaccine carries the extra promoter sequence. The same extra promoter that appears in the CRFS GR gene."

Neil stood up and began to pace the living room. He walked across the room and sat down sideways at the piano. Looking down at the keys, he plunked out random notes. We all watched in silence. His expression released and he tilted his head just enough so we could see his face. "I'm taking it that brilliant Anna also keeps vials of all the vaccines she's used in her clinic."

She sat up straight, "One from every lot."

"And you, quote, know that the vaccine has an extra promoter because you have already sequenced said vaccine?"

"Every vial," I confirmed. "Megan is a whiz at the bench and was able to pull the modified FeLV out of each vaccine vial. She found the extra promoter in each one. In a few cases she could confirm from several samples in the same lot."

"Ah, more than one vial." Neil locked eyes with Anna. "Nice job."

"Thank you," she said without pride.

I motioned him over to come see the printouts. He stood but didn't move. "You don't have to look if you don't want to," Neil just looked from me to Anna and said nothing. He looked down. Black and white keys: all pretty clear.

I stood quietly left the room and felt Neil move towards her as if swimming upstream against a storm current. Their voices quiet, Anna walked him through the vaccine data. Chris followed me into the kitchen.

His voice hushed, he asked, "You think he is taking this personally?"

"How could he not. He hasn't asked the question, but he's brilliant and I'm sure he's figured it out."

Returning with a fresh pot of coffee, I put down a trivet, the pot, and a few cups. It was going to be a long night. Chris followed with milk and sugar, and a plate of odd munchies that he pulled from our refrigerator, questionable if edible. Neil stood staring down at Anna's drawing on the table. We sat down across from him, Anna sat next to him, he remained standing. Anna quietly watched him, her face soft, perhaps with relief because the end was in sight. She caught me staring at her and gave a weak smile.

Neil placed both hands on the table and steeled himself for the question, turning his face slightly and locking eyes with Anna. "The name of the pharmaceutical company on the bottle?"

Anna's whole demeanor softened, "Regnum;" she put her hand on his. He looked crestfallen, even though he had to have known it was coming. This happened under his watch, while he was the Chief Scientific Officer at Regnum. Regardless of whether production of the contaminated vaccine continued after he left, he was in charge when it all started. Quality control and quality assurance fell many rungs down the ladder from where he sat, but he was still ultimately responsible for the quality of the science at Regnum. And he was never one to shy away from responsibility.

"So Regnum caused this, and they hold the key for putting an end to this."

"They do," Anna's voice was barely audible.

He looked from Anna, to Chris, to me and registered our collective affirmation.

"God damn it," He said angrily as he pulled his hand away and shut his eyes.

"Yup." I looked down studying the pattern in the hardwood floors.

We continued on for several more hours. Neil wanted to see everything. Raw data. Photographs of gels showing the increased intensity of mRNA sequences, printouts of sequence data, statistics from sequence comparisons in GenBank. He questioned each conclusion, requiring solid linkage to significant data, without excessive extrapolation. He was relentless in his demand for duplicate results and tight controls and steadfast in his goal to ensure there were no holes in the data and that our conclusions were the only possible outcome. It was clear why he was the CSO at Regnum, past tense noted.

"So, now help me to understand the epidemiology of the outbreak. Why did it start with dog shows?" Neil asked.

Anna showed no signs of becoming exhausted by his challenges, in fact she seemed to be baiting him to keep it going. "Well, it makes sense in terms of concentration of newly vaccinated animals. A lot of cat fanciers keep their cats inside so they don't fully vaccinate, but once they want to take them to shows, they are required to vaccinate, so with each show there is a significant concentration of the newly vaccinated."

"How does that relate to dogs that became infected?"

"We looked back at the venues that held dog shows where dogs first came down with CRFS, and most hosted cat shows just prior to the dog shows. In other cases, like where the show was held at 4H centers or county fairs, there are a lot of barn cats, and dog show organizers are very strict about booking only where they guarantee to keep those semi-feral animals vaccinated. There is a lot of concern about rabies and especially parvo as some strains of the virus are believed to have originally come from the cat feline panleukopenia virus. Then there are the shelters. They have a constant stream of cats that are vaccinated upon arrival. A number of shelters have been decimated with cases of CRFS. We haven't really looked into a lot of cases. They are adding up too fast. But where we have looked, over and over we can make a direct link to recently vaccinated cats. The only thing we haven't figured out is why it started mainly on the East Coast with a smattering of incidents across the country."

Chris added, "That's one of the questions for Regnum, but we suspect that it has to do with the timing of them releasing different vaccine lots and where they were distributed. We are thinking that the contaminated lots were first released regionally to vets, but maybe also to some cat breeders on the East Coast."

Anna jumped in. "That makes the most sense. Like with show dogs, the cat breeders tend to do their own vaccinations, ordering them online. The question is whether mail order companies also distributed certain lots to certain areas. That would explain there being fewer cases outside the east."

"For not being epidemiologists, you sure do have a good handle on the spread of the disease," Neil confirmed our assumptions. "It is common practice to distribute lots regionally in case of this exact type of situation." He paused. "It helps to contain any problem that might result in a recall."

"So Neil, how do you think a vaccine lot got contaminated in the first place?" Chris asked. "We're not just looking at a common contaminant like a bacterium that might result from unsanitary conditions. It has to be a flaw in the standard practice."

"I don't know. You were correct when you said that they probably wouldn't have used a cat cell line to grow the vaccine. They would have used rabbit kidney cells. And they wouldn't have used a cat endogenous virus to immortalize the cells. It's not good practice to use materials from a species to produce a vaccine for that species. Keep in mind that Regnum follows strict protocols and has a very intense quality assurance program to verify compliance with its protocols in order to keep FDA approval."

All three of us groaned at his defense of his former employer.

"Look, they are not a bad company."

"They just made some really bad decisions," I crossed my arms.

"And they are going to pay for it," Neil said. "I suspect that if you are right about where it came from, they will pay a lot. I'll have to think about the possibilities, but I wouldn't rule out something intentional."

"You serious?" I sat forward. "Could someone possibly have designed this just for kicks?"

"I'm not ruling anything out. My brain is a bit jumbled, but after some sleep I'll try to walk through each of the steps and think about the possible points of entry. I'll have to think about each of the people that I knew there and whether any of them would have A) been capable and B) been motivated to do this."

"So how do we bring this to Regnum so that they listen and take the right action, namely pull the vaccine right away?" I asked. "I suspect that once they learn about this they will start building some mighty big walls."

"You can be sure of that," Neil acknowledged. "This is going to take some finesse. Who else knows about this? Have you told Johnathan Oros?"

"I think we need to leave him out," I realized we hadn't thought about this. "I know you brought him in at the beginning and he has offered some funding, but as of yet, he hasn't been involved at all, and based on Regnum's vaccine being the cause, his lab won't be needed."

"Your call, I just want to make sure that when the press finds out, that—I just think it is critical that we are all on the same page. Claire, you should be the spokesperson, and everyone should refer all questions to you." He looked at Anna and she nodded yes.

"Actually, I'm going to have to coordinate with the university communications office, and probably the legal office, and—this is going to be way bigger than any of us have really allowed ourselves to think about." I shook my head to shake out the complexities.

Chris shouldered me. "It's going to be huge." He shook me gently. "Neil is right, you have to make sure everyone is of a single mind in how this will be addressed publicly and with Regnum. Everyone has to be committed to one goal."

"Stopping the dog deaths," Anna sat back, finally looking a bit weary.

Neil put his arm around her. "We will. You all have found the culprit, now we need to bring this to an end, quickly."

"And hope that the folks at Regnum are as committed," I pursed my lips at the thought.

We all looked at Neil.

He nodded hopefully. "Ending this is—"

Anna and I alternated. "Simple."

"Stop using the vaccine."

"Millions of dollars, millions of research hours," Chris look disgusted.

"And thousands of dogs," Anna added

"I get it," Neil backed away. "The solution is straightforward, but not really simple. I take it that you all grasp the implications?"

"We grasp the implications for you, yes," Anna said, and Neil shook his head no, not a concern. "And for Regnum. But mostly we grasp the implications if this continues even one more day. I'm concerned that with prolonged exposures that sooner or later some dogs are going to show some immunity, and may become carriers, and we will have a real epidemic on our hands. There are millions of dogs out there."

"We'll give you one week." Chris startled us with his declaration directed at Neil.

"That's not much time to work through the machinery of a multi-billion-dollar company."

"One week. Until next Monday." Chris was adamant. We had discussed this as our likely timeline, but it was obvious from the look on his face that he meant business. Good for him. "They go public in one week regardless of Regnum's actions and they will have to deal with it then. Even one week is going to mean the deaths of hundreds more dogs, and everyone is very uncomfortable with that, but I think we all understand that they will have to have some time to confirm our findings. They won't just take Claire's word for it. But they will have only a short window of time to do the right thing."

Neil leaned back in his chair, stretched his arms up, and folded them behind his neck, tipping his chair back. "Okay, they get one week—what time is it?" He looked at this watch. "Geez, it's one in the morning! I don't know about you kids, but I don't stay up this late any more. Anna, can you—"

"Already have," Anna pulled out a black notebook buried in the stack. This one was different. It had a formal cover on it that simply read Confidential, with the first page in the form of a letter I wrote summarizing our findings. The rest of the two-inch-thick binder held summary sheets of each part of our study—sequences found, variations in mRNA concentration, serial numbers of the lots of vaccine that had tested positive for the promoter.

Neil stood and quickly leafed through the pages with a nod of admiration, and looked to me.

"I'm the only one whose name appears in this document," I was emboldened. "However, if Regnum gets any ideas that they can keep this quiet, I prepared duplicate copies for my Dean and the President of my university which I'll deliver to them next Monday."

Anna walked Neil to his car, with a single notebook in her arms. Neil leaned with his back against the door, as the two of them stood and talked for some time while Chris and I packed the notebooks into two boxes. Anna's drawing remained alone on the table. Chris picked it up and sat down. "If it weren't so heartbreaking, this would be really cool."

"It is. It will be especially interesting to find out how the promoter got into the vaccine." I shook my head. "I never considered it could have been deliberate. By the way, stop saying them, it's we. You are a part of this."

I left him sitting at the table and carried the pot and cups into the kitchen. The simplicity of rinsing the dishes and putting things in the dishwasher gave me a moment of solace. I gathered up the shriveled remains of the munchies and dropped them in their final resting place in the kitchen trash. Everything was put away. I turned off the kitchen light and walked toward the front door.

The light was off in the entry way and I stood and watched Anna and Neil still outside, leaning side by side on the car looking up at the clear night's sky. Their exchanges were few. I tried to imagine the heavy burden we were sending off with Neil to carry, and I couldn't imagine anything that Anna or any of us could offer as comfort.

I looked towards the dining room, Chris looked up from Anna's drawing on the table. He stood and walked toward me, switching off the dining room light on the way. We wrapped up in each other's arms and breathed slow and deep, both knowing that we would need to hold tight to one another, to Anna, to Neil and the rest of our team over the next few weeks. The lights from Neil's rental car pulled away.

Anna silently opened and closed the door and walked past us without a glance. The dogs remained curled up on their beds too invested in sleep to give notice. In the dark she put on her coat, picked up her purse, and joined us in the entryway. She gave Chris an embrace and a kiss on the cheek and turned to me. Her eyes were red and swollen. She must have finally let herself cry with Neil at her side.

"At least I stopped this at my clinic." She had pulled all the contaminated vials from use. "I'm going to call a few others who I can trust to keep this confidential and have them do the same."

"Do you think that's . . ." Her pained expression ended my words.

She put her arms around me and held me tight. The enormity of our discovery and the personal toll of having dealt with the repercussions of CRFS surged in my head and the dam broke open, releasing a flood of tears. "If only we could be this successful with Addison's," she whispered.

"If only." I could barely speak.

She let go, shook it off. "I'll call you in the morning. Love you guys." And she quietly headed out into what remained of the night.

Sniveling as I brushed my teeth, I put on a T-shirt, crawled into bed, and turned off the light, hoping that sleep would take the place of exhaustion, but it was not to be. I resigned myself to my kindle and couch.

The softness of her paws on the hardwood floors ruffle the silence of the night. I know it's her by the distinct sound of her gait, and because for thirteen years, this magnificent creature has been my constant companion, my heart-dog. Ania stops at the end of the hall and lifts her head, scanning the living room for me, then continues her journey. She gently places her front feet on the couch. I lean forward and offer my cheek. She snuffles, content, and climbs up next to me, collecting her legs around her, morphing into a warm, fuzzy ball. But before she tucks in her muzzle like a snow goose in a winter storm, she looks back at me and asks with her big brown eyes "You okay?" I rest my hand on her, absorbing the calm she radiates. She sighs, curls in, and falls sleep.

I exhale and settle into this perfect moment.

I close my eyes. A kaleidoscope of thoughts spin around in my head creating fleeting patterns, but none of them seem the right fit, leaving unanswered questions. Where is CRFS coming from and how can it be stopped?

Dogs are dying. By the thousands. And no one has yet figured out why.

Until now.

SCENT MARKING

IN HAVANA, Cuba, feral dogs roam the streets wearing collars with tags. Every year, the dogs are rounded up, vaccinated, sterilized, and released with shiny new accessories. They walk in and out of stores, scrounge at the edge of restaurants, but mostly congregate in the parks looking fairly well-fed and behaved. Similarly in Asuncion, Paraguay, the more fortunate feral dogs are claimed by shopkeepers and residents on a designated day each year and a sweep is done to clear the city of unclaimed dogs. The lucky ones are vaccinated, sterilized, and released. There's a philosophy that a nation shall be judged by the way it treats its most vulnerable members. While animal shelters are a luxury for many countries, I am humbled by the ways those with limited resources still find ways to live up to the promise owed through domestication, and treat their street dogs with compassion. Wrapped in the generic brownness of their coats and eyes lies the unspoken agreement to always be beside you.

Monday to Tuesday, Days 1 and 2

The lab hours are eerily simple and short. We've shelved all further efforts on CRFS and returned to our regular research, which seems less satisfying than the frenzied pace of the past three months.

I've heard nothing from Neil for close to forty-eight hours. I trust him to move quickly to help end this, but I'm starting to get concerned that we have thrown him to the wolves. I'm sitting at my desk looking over my computer out across the darkened campus. Evasive shadows skulk from path to path and into colorless buildings. March will hold a solid, cold grip on spring until the very last days.

Neil's face lights up my phone screen. The fuzzy picture snapped three years ago, begrudgingly.

"Hi, you okay? I've been a bit worried."

"I've been in meeting after meeting with Regnum."

"I bet they haven't been too happy to see you."

"It's been a bit of a mixed reaction. I started with a phone call to Jon Bosto who took over as CSO. Good guy, great scientist."

"I remember him. We met two years ago when I was out for the vet med conference." A split second of thought on what happened at the meeting this year flashes through my mind. I need to be more forgiving.

"He got it, and had me meet in their Washington office with some of their Board in person, while he and few others video conferenced in. He was ready to pull the lot even without confirmation."

"But they didn't? Are they serious?"

"The Board voted to investigate first."

"Big of them."

"Big *to* them. Huge. They see a big financial loss as a consequence of your findings and they felt they need to be able to claim their own role in investigating. They have their research arm testing all lots for contamination, doing a blind study, so they haven't released the information to their in-house investigators on what lots are suspect."

"Unbiased results are good, but this is going to take time. And it is all unnecessary."

"You understand how monumental this is, correct?"

"Yes, I can picture a room full of dead dogs. Anything else?"

"No."

"They have five days left."

Wednesday, Day 3

Mid-afternoon less than twenty-four hours later, Neil is calling again. John flew in from California last night, and the entire Board has also arrived. "They've confirmed your results. They have stopped production, destroyed most of the lots, and recalled all that have been released for use."

"Did they explain why in the recall?"

"No, they never do unless forced to."

"Perhaps this time it might help stress the urgency. Anna says that it's a pain when a recall comes in as you have to go through all the records, contact all the owners whose animals may have been affected and report all of this when you return the vials. It's a lot of work for vets. In many cases, they are not inclined to do this; they simply just destroy what they have left and move on. She said the pharma companies actually like this as it results in less claims against them. They might not even get the link to CRFS if Regnum doesn't disclose the association, and we will lose important data, and maybe more dogs."

"I'm not in the position to agree or disagree with them or you. Just reporting the facts."

"Wow. Okay. Did they offer you any Kool-Aid while you were there?"

"No . . . It's just . . ." I've never heard him sound tentative.

"What? You're creeping me out!"

"They want to talk to you."

I'm thinking—trying to think—but there are a million possible reactions I could have. "Really, what else?"

"They would like to see your data."

I snort. "They have the summaries, but they are not getting any of my raw data. What else?"

"They . . ." He's hesitating, he's concerned. I know him well.

A light bulb goes off in my head. "They would like to buy my silence."

"They would like to reimburse you for your efforts and provide you compensation for your contribution."

"You have got to be kidding me! This is the message that they asked you to convey?"

"Their exact words." There is a seriousness in his tone that is unnerving.

"And you have no problem bringing me that message."

"I didn't say that. I'm just the middleman."

"Middle? That implies that you are as close to our side as theirs. Does the middleman have an opinion? Off the record?"

"He does. He is advised by his and Regnum's lawyers that he signed a non-disclosure agreement and that this happened on his watch."

My heart is pounding and I feel a surge of fear—no, anger. "Are you fucking kidding me?! Are they threatening you?"

"Do you hear any chuckle in my voice? No, not kidding." His voice is actually trembling.

Quieting my tone, I ask, "Neil, are you scared or are you angry?"

"Both." He hesitates. "They would also like to know who the members of your team are. Who else knows about this?"

"Like hell I will tell them."

"They will find out on their own. It's not hard to figure out."

"Let them. What the hell are you saying?"

"Claire, it's getting pretty weird. I have never experienced anything like this. The consequences to Regnum are huge. This could actually bring a multi-billion-dollar company to its knees just in terms of recalls and lawsuits, never mind how their stock will plummet if the public finds out."

"You mean *when* the public finds out."

"Obviously they are hoping for *if*."

"And they think they can buy my silence?"

"They have pretty deep pockets."

"They have a lot of pockets to fill. Mine, Anna's, Megan's, Jamie's, all the folks down the hall, and you."

"I'm not a factor."

"You're doing this for fun?"

"I'm simply the messenger."

"A messenger maybe. A liar you are not."

"Perhaps we should have lunch. After you meet with them."

"I'm not going to meet with them. They can go fuck themselves if they think I am going to let them go quietly into the night with the secret of the origin of CRFS."

"They won't go quietly, trust me on that."

"Is that a threat?"

"I sense that is not beyond their thinking."

"Oh my God! Do they think that they can keep close to a dozen people quiet with money and threats? Are they going to just pull the lots and not tell anyone about the connection to CRFS? This is the stuff of a bad movie."

"You can't make this stuff up. Perhaps we can sell the rights to this one someday." There is a flatness to his voice.

Ignoring his attempt at easing some of the tension, I say, "Let's just say that in their wildest dreams, we were all interested in a big house on the lake. With a big endowment for our research. What about the public, what about all the people who lost dogs, what about the scientific community that will spend millions more chasing a ghost that no longer exists, money that could go towards other real research needs?"

"What about folks who will never trust a vaccine again, and the unvaccinated dogs that will die? What about putting out of business a company that for the most part, has saved countless dog lives with cutting-edge discoveries?"

"Are those your words or theirs?"

"Mine actually. I just thought of them. Do you like?"

"No I don't. Whose side are you on? Ours or theirs. Pick one."

"You know where my allegiance is, but at this point, I'd rather help in the best way I can, by trying to facilitate an agreement."

"Sorry, I'm not playing. Not if they start the game by writing all the rules in their favor. Besides, there's no agreement to be made. They need to announce the origin of CRFS and their plans for moving forward."

"You should at least know what you are dealing with. You need to meet with them."

"Then I am adding another person to my team."

"I can't join you."

"Not you. A very good lawyer. One that they will be paying for by the time this is all over."

I call Anna to fill her in on my call with Neil. "They are scent-marking," she declares. "They think this is all their territory and they are making sure we know it." She is ready for a fight.

Thursday, Day 4

Spring brings renewal, hope. The morning is only chilly and Chris and I sit wrapped in blankets at the table on the porch warming our hands around our mugs. The morning light is not yet firmly in place; everything is veiled in a yellow hue. We watch the dogs float down the hill half-heartedly giving chase to the deer who spring away, bouncing over the fence as if attached to a bungee cord. Ania and Sofie trot back, content to start their day with a good romp.

I get up, ask if he wants any more coffee. Chris stares at me as if it is a monumental decision. "Are you worried?" I ask.

"No, you got this."

"Then?"

"I'm thinking what a waste. What a ridiculous amount of energy and angst we will expend in the next few days, when we all know how this is going to end. They are going to have to go public to convince the public it is over."

"But it's all about control. He who controls the message wins."

"I suppose. But while we want to control the integrity of science, they want to control their profit margin."

"Yup. That's what we each win if we control the message."

I put on my only suit. That's the good thing about business attire, it forestalls any initial assumptions about who I am based on the way I dress. I am not giving away anything.

We gather our pack, picking Anna up. It's at least a two-hour drive, but in Washington traffic, it could be days. Anna looks radiant, confident. There will not be another CRFS death in her clinic. We talk of everything except the looming conflict.

Our lawyer, Rachelle Swavek, waits for us. She's an old friend of Neil's who was occasionally opposing counsel on cases against Regnum. Big companies are always the target for someone's get-rich-quick scheme, but Neil said she only took valid cases and has an instinct that made Regnum settle them quickly, out of court. Apparently, Neil had called her two days ago and asked her to stand by, and at my mention of a lawyer on our call, he gave me her contact information. I spoke with her only briefly last night but she assured me she knows how to end this quickly.

We are sitting in the coffee shop down the block from the Regnum legislative office. Rachelle has a commanding presence. Tall and graceful, African American, with high cheekbones that give her a regal and an impervious persona. I suspect she is an enigma to her opponents. I'm not sure how well Neil had briefed her until she says, "Claire, you will do most of the talking. I won't say anything unless I feel they are straying off topic. You don't have to be here. You are here as a courtesy to them. You don't owe them anything but they do need you. Do not agree to anything. Agree only to consider and get back to them, and I advise that you don't even hint at considering a payoff."

"We have no interest—"

"You may say that now, but when they put big numbers in front of you, you will be surprised how tempting it can be."

"The only reason we gave them a heads-up is so they could pull all the contaminated lots and determine if there are any other risks we don't know about. When we go public, we want—"

"Why do you want to go public?"

"Um, because the public has a right to—"

"Not good enough. You need to be confident in the repercussions if you don't go public. Millions wasted in research dollars by those still searching for the cause, vets on a narrow margin still using the recalled vaccine, loss to the scientific community of the scientific discoveries you have made and the potential application to future problems. Not to mention your personal career loss." She looks at each of us. "For all of you. They are going offer you some big bucks and counter that with all the vaccine lots recalled and destroyed, there is no point going public. You must not waver in your position or they will pounce on any weakness."

"Got it. Okay. Yes." We talk over each other. Rachelle stands and we fall in behind. The cool air invigorates us as she leads us down the street into the building, into the battle.

"This whole meeting frosts my ass," Anna hisses as we spin through the revolving doors. "They have no interest in meeting with us except to find a way to keep us quiet."

Rachelle turns on her heel and stops dead. "Agreed. That is why you need to all react very slowly, weigh their questions carefully, and use measured responses. Show no emotion. The only thing you want from this meeting is to be able to say that you met with them to encourage them to work with you for the good of the public. Give them nothing."

I like her. I feel much better knowing that she will kick me under the table should I start to compromise our position. Although she is intimidating as hell.

We are greeted at the building security desk by an executive administrative assistant who has obviously been sent to wait for us. Clearly she reports to the Chairman of the Board, and though entrusted with escorting us to the meeting personally, she seems a bit indignant at having to lower herself to handling our motley group of scientists. She leads us to and up the elevator like a schoolmarm leading her charges on a field trip. We have to go through a second security checkpoint on the top floor where Regnum's upper echelons are well-guarded.

We are escorted to their main conference room. Large windows frame the far wall. Serious-looking 15th Street law offices fill the block. In the distance, the Washington Monument stands at attention. We are instructed to make ourselves comfortable. Austere, uncomfortable-looking leather chairs give us the eye, each with its territory delineated by a clean pad of paper, a company pen, and company-branded bottled water. Chris, Anna, Rachelle, and I sit along one side of the big mahogany table under the watchful eye of the Regnum logo on the opposite dark-paneled wall. I'm glad I wore my red frames today.

Their team enters: the CEO, COO, CFO, and CSO, the Chairman of the Board, and of course their lawyers, plural. Introductions are made, and they sit. All men. They are stoic, somber. Their corporate headquarters is in Chicago, but here they are, all together in the land of lobbyists and Congressional hearings. They grace us with their executive presence. Chris had refused to wear a tie. I'm proud of him.

The Chairman, Spencer Thorn, thanks us for coming; he is surprised that I brought the others, and there really is no need for a lawyer. He obviously does not want to acknowledge that he has faced Rachelle before. He commends us for our excellent work, and asks if we mind addressing some questions about our methods and findings. Each of them, each of us, has a copy of the notebook we prepared placed squarely above our paper pad. Rachelle points out that the original notebook had been marked Confidential and Do Not Duplicate. He assures us that these are the only copies and that they will be destroyed after the meeting. The Regnum team each reach for theirs, and turn to page one. We follow suit.

I am questioned first. Why am I the only one who signed the cover letter? Other than those in the room, who else is on the team? Did the university approve of our research? Was the work funded by the university or any other grants that would have a claim to the results?

I'm the lead investigator. The complete complement of team

members will not be disclosed at this point. And yes, my university is fully aware of all of the work we did as evidenced by the cc: on the letter. It was funded by an undisclosed donor. They press for a name. I do not cave. They ask about our samples, whether Anna withheld any from the national sample collection effort in order to give me first access, whether any of the funding we received for Addison's was used for this research, whether we had permission from the dog owners to use their samples for the study. They are on the hunt for weaknesses.

The meeting is formal, tedious, and unproductive. Rachelle, in a do I have your attention tone, tells them that we are here voluntarily; we are not here to have them make subtle innuendos regarding our ethics or the validity of our work. This is not a legal proceeding, and they are not to be questioning anything except to clarify our conclusions, again, voluntarily provided by us.

They sit stone-faced in their reactions, polite, and Stepfordish.

The COO comments, "Then why bring a lawyer?"

Rachelle stares straight at him and tells him there will be no further data provided; they have our summaries. We have an obligation to report our findings to the CDC, and we will do so on Monday. We have provided our summary simply as a courtesy.

The CEO closes his notebook, folds his hands across the top, looks directly at me and says flatly, "We are prepared to compensate you for all your work, and to establish a fund for any follow-up work that might be necessary." There is no mention of what they want in return.

They are masterful in their assigned roles. They have carefully placed Milk-Bones on the double yellows down the center of the highway, hoping to entice and then eliminate their problem. I tell them we have no interest in compensation. They look to Rachelle, suggesting that she might advise her clients of the significance of their offer, implying we may not grasp the magnitude because we are obviously naive, idealistic scientists. She closes her notebook and nods to me to respond.

"I will take your offer into consideration."

I can pee just as high on the tree.

We are silent in the elevator and as we walk two blocks following Rachelle's long strides, our pack is defiant. We enter the Caffeine Corner, a different, smaller shop from where we met this morning, and are greeted by the smell of fresh coffee.

Without stopping, Rachelle says, "Would you please grab me a plain coffee with milk and I'll meet you at the table over there?" pointing to a table away from the windows as she heads to the back of the store.

As if a corset was released, we collectively exhale and welcome the difficult decision of which combo of caffeine, milk, and sugar to order. By the time we get our order, Rachelle is back.

"Sorry, I drank way too much coffee earlier. Wow, you were great!" Rachelle says to me in a totally different personality, upbeat and friendly. "I thought they were going to choke when you said you weren't interested in compensation!" I like this Rachelle too. "Neil said you could keep your cool, but I rarely see people who don't at least flinch when faced with such a testosterone-infused wall of aggression with dollar signs in their eyes."

"It was rather amusing," Chris says, giving me a one-armed hug. "But not surprising."

We chat about the unfortunate sellout of some of the men in the room; scientists turned corporate, trading in their jeans and lab coats for neckties and business cards. Neil never quite fit in with this crowd. Rachelle says that we don't need to have any further discussions with them, we've done our duty, and it's likely that we won't need her any further, but she gives us each her card just in case. She elbows me and says that the university lawyers would probably resent her involvement, but if Anna or Chris want any counsel, she's available.

When she finishes her coffee, Rachelle turns serious. "Don't discuss, don't debate. Wait to see what Neil has to say." She obviously knows that I'm meeting with him later. She stands and commands all of our full attention. She looks directly at me. "They are going to come after you, so steel yourself," she says. "It's been a hoot! Stay strong." And she leaves.

Neil and I have agreed to meet for dinner, though out of town in Ballston, away from watchful eyes of Washington suits. Anna and Chris are staying in DC, keeping their distance; I'll head back in when Neil and I are finished and they will pick me up from the metro for the drive home.

Neil looks tired. He is already seated and has a half-finished Scotch in front of him. He rarely drinks. I take off my coat and sit, skipping my usual kiss on the cheek. We make a few comments about the coming of spring, what's good to eat here. I order a drink.

"My lawyer is insisting that I distance myself from you and them, but I have made it clear that I stand on your side if it comes down to it," he says.

"That's good to know. Why do I sense there is a *but* coming? Wait, what lawyer?"

"You have to separate yourself from me, too," he instructs. "I don't want your reputation sullied."

"What? What are you talking about? Association with you won't ruin my reputation. It may have when we were in graduate—" He is not responsive to my kidding. "You're serious. What are you implying? There's no evil plot that involves you."

He looks me dead on. His tone is, what, resigned? "Really,

Claire? You are one of the smartest people I know. Think about it. They could easily craft a scenario that pins the whole thing on me."

"What the fuck?" I say a bit too loudly. "Where is this coming from?" I can see a few people around us judging my mouth.

Spreading his hands to create a headline in the air he announces in a hushed voice, "Former CSO created CRFS for personal gain." He drops his hands and leans in. "Followed by the made–for-TV story. While at Regnum, former CSO conspired to engineer CRFS in order to create a panic in the dog world. After distributing contaminated vaccines across the country, he abruptly resigned, and subsequently funded and collaborated with a long-time friend—who was also duped by him—to identify the link to the cat in order to profit from the solution." He flashed a big fake grin, "You like it? I even purposely did not award you one of the Regnum grants so you would not be involved in collaborating with Regnum on the early research. Otherwise you may not have been so willing to work with me after I left. Pretty ingenious of me, wasn't it?"

I'm drowning. Trying to keep afloat but struggling to swim to the top. In a careful and measured delivery I say, "But there's the flaw in their story. There is no antidote, no remedy, no treatment from which to make a profit, and in fact, your investment is—Crap, I just realized you aren't going to get anything back from your investment!"

"You and I know that, but they will claim there is big profit to be made from grant money and other future financing from donors and dog-loving philanthropists who want to thank the saviors of the dog world."

"They actually said all this to you? In front of your lawyer?"

"They are way smarter than that." He shakes his head, a snide look on his face. "I got a phone call within an hour of you leaving their office, from my buddy Jon Bosto. He asked me to meet with him right away at a coffee shop—Caffeine Corner. You know it?"

My eyes are wide as I grasp the implication. "Yes, you were followed," he informs me. "Jon made sure he let me know they were in control."

"There wasn't anything we said, or, anything we did that was—"

"It was an attempt to intimidate, with more to come, I'm sure. And he was testing me to see if I would flinch when I heard the location. He suspected that I would be standing by waiting to hear from you on how the meeting went, so they were keeping tabs on both of us." I was speechless. "You apparently left just before I got there. Don't really know how they intended for this to go if he showed up and I was there with you."

"This is . . . I can't even think of a word! Outrageous? Sinister?" I looked over my shoulders. "Could they have followed me here? Should I be concerned?"

"I doubt their type likes to ride public transport, but I wouldn't put it past them to try something else to intimidate you. But they already made their big move with respect to me. Bosto was given the task to engage me. He said he might be able to help move things along."

"So you went without any witnesses."

"Without my lawyer, yes. I needed to hear the unfiltered version. Interestingly, they put him up to it to avoid involving one of the board members or their lawyers."

"Did he actually keep a straight face?"

"He was scared shitless, and I told him as much when I asked him why he would do this. Why would he agree to confront me like I'm the bad guy? He knew me well enough." Neil orders another Scotch. "Jon said that he was told about my involvement and about your threats—yes, *threats* to go public—and they asked him if he would convey their desire to put this all away quietly. I guess they think that if you know they have this hanging over me, you might stay quiet to save my skin."

"Do you think he knows the truth? That you had nothing to do with this?"

"I wasn't sure, until I asked him point blank." He closes his eyes for longer than a blink.

"And?"

"And he asked me how I could have done such a thing. Killed all those dogs."

In all the years, I have only seen Neil moved to tears one time, when his brother died. Now his watering eyes stare unfocused towards the bustle of the restaurant. I reach for his hand, he registers my touch until he looks down at our hands and moves his thumb over mine. He faintly shakes his head, let's go, and sits back, looking me in the eyes. The waiter comes, trying hard to ignore the intensity of our engagement. Tonight's special is pecan-encrusted trout with a side of grilled asparagus and garlic mashed red potatoes. We place our order, though I doubt either of us will eat much. Having successfully completed his task, the waiter turns and leaves us to restart.

"What do you want me to do? I'll do anything."

"You will not do anything—anything at all—that they ask." He is adamant. "You will however, work with your university communications office to set up a press conference, as soon as possible, as in the next day or two."

"I—"

"Listen to me. They don't have all the pieces in place, especially how I supposedly created CRFS, so the sooner you go public, the better chance we have of discrediting any story they invent, and more importantly, bringing CRFS and them to their knees."

"I like the sound of 'we.'"

"I'll be there in spirit, but I don't think it would be wise to have me standing in front of cameras with you while there is still a risk I might get nailed for this."

"But they have no proof! It would have taken coordination with a whole lab at Regnum to conspire with you. You haven't done bench work for centuries." I smile, faintly. "No offense. No one would reasonably believe that you could or would have done this."

He smirks. "Quite true, but I'm sure they can create proof. Lab techs don't make much money and I had a convenient habit of walking through the labs every few weeks to promote the all-for-one team spirit. I actually knew many of the managers and even some of the techs by name. It would be easy to craft a story that I was micromanaging through these visits for my benefit."

"I'm sure Regnum benefited from your approach, as they did from all of your other ideas. By the way, you never told me why you left."

"You never asked."

"I am now."

The waiter brings rolls, sets them on the table, refreshes our water glasses. "Will there be anything else? Your order will be out in a few minutes." He is diplomatic is the face of our disquiet.

"They were taking the company in a direction that I didn't like. Moving towards capturing the best technologies and advancements by buying small start-ups on the verge of bankruptcy, but with an innovative marketable product."

"A lot of companies do that."

"True, but they were moving away from almost any investment in in-house research. It looked more profitable just to let others do the research, buy them out cheap when they couldn't afford to take their product through the regulatory phases to get to market, and turn a bigger profit. Look at what they did with CRFS, they gave out grants in the hope that they would get the credit and profits from any solution. I felt that they needed to retain a strong core of researchers if they were to maintain their standing as a premier scientific company."

"Were they planning to let any go?"

"They did. Shortly after I left, they pushed out at least twelve Principal Investigators. They used to tout themselves as 'investors in research for the betterment of mankind.' But that is no longer true philosophically or according to their books."

"Are they doing anything illegal?"

"No, I'm not saying that. Just a lot of smoke and mirrors and tax write-offs for investments, sponsorships, and losses—almost deliberate losses—that as CSO I was not willing to endorse. So I left."

Our food comes. An extra steak knife for Neil, ever the carnivore with his order of ribeye, medium rare. "Black pepper for your salad or steak? Would there be anything else?"

"No thank you." I respect the waiter's job but am barely able to show it.

"Are they nervous that you might know too much?" I ask as he slices into meat. I am surprisingly hungry, ravenous actually.

"I don't think that is their motivation here. They have great lawyers who could run circles around anything I might know or claim. Regnum's role in CRFS, like I said the other night, could bring down the company. They are in damage control mode."

"I know. I guess I still can't wrap my mind around the lengths they might go to save their asses."

"Great lengths. You turned them down, so they go after someone close to you, see if you flinch. Next they will go directly after you. Promise me that tomorrow morning you will go straight to your Dean and President and get moving on a public announcement."

"First thing." My fear dissolves to regret. "Neil, I'm sorry for all this. I—"

He takes my hand and I feel his angst in the tightness of his grasp. He looks serious, straight at me. "I'm sorry I let this happen on my watch."

I want to say that he shouldn't blame himself, but he would not be the man who I love for his strength and commitment if he felt other than responsible for letting this out of Regnum, into the world.

We spend the rest of the meal talking about nothing in particular, avoiding anything that hints of science, dogs, and careers. I talk about the girls, he genuinely shows interest in my phone full of pictures. He's planning another vacation, this time to Thailand. Still the eternal bachelor; even George Clooney caved, but Neil is content in his solitude.

Walking to the metro, it's cold and I huddle around his arm. We haven't been this close in years, in terms of involvement in a project, or physically. "I've missed you. I've missed this," I say.

"It was so much more simple back in those days, wasn't it? Our biggest concern was keeping enough data ready at hand to feed the beast if he came looking for blood. We didn't even have to worry about funding. We had it made but didn't realize it."

"Guess we have a few things to be grateful to him for."

"Nah," we say in unison, and we laugh in the release of simpler times.

Friday, Day 5

A cry in the distance. A cross between a tormented baby and someone unscrewing the head of a cat. If you haven't heard a fox call, you will consider calling the police the first time you do. I awake to this mating ritual shriek. Normally heard late at night, I'm happy for him that a spring morning brings out his animal instincts, but not happy when I see the late hour on the clock. I hovered through the night in that place where thoughts hang in a fog, but never fully dissolve, allowing a release into deep sleep.

Heading to campus, groggy, my phone rings. Haley's number shows up. She rarely calls me unless there is something going on that she can't handle, like an incubator alarm that she can't silence or something leaking. She's been trying hard to impress us all with her independence and ability to manage the day-to-day lab needs. "What's up?"

"Hi, Dr. Winthrop. I'm at the lab, but my key won't open the door and there is a big red security tag on the door that says 'Do Not Enter, call security for further information.' So I called them, but they told me they could not speak with anyone but you. Is there something wrong? Is there some kind of problem or contamination in the lab?"

"No, I'm sure they would have called me. It's probably nothing. They do random security checks and I bet we left a door unlocked or something on that they think needs to be off."

"Oh no! I always double check, and I've been . . ."

"Haley, it's okay. Text me the number and I will call them. Why don't you just go have breakfast or head off to your class. I should be there in the next ten minutes."

"I can wait if you want."

"Thanks, I don't know how long it will take to sort this out."

I'm awake now. My mind is racing; I can't call my Dean until I can focus, one hundred percent. I arrive at our building, park, and turn off the engine. I don't believe in coincidences, I hear Anna say. This has to do with Regnum. I sit and watch the bustle of life on campus. Students walking alone connected by their ears to their personalized gadget world. A few communicating the old-fashioned way, talking, laughing. I push the number on Haley's text. Call? My phone asks. I tap again.

"Sergeant Valesco."

"Hi, this is Dr. Winthrop. My lab over in Building—"

"Yes, Dr. Winthrop, we've been given instructions to ask you to call or go to the President's office as soon as you arrive on campus."

"What? Is there something wrong in my lab?"

"No ma'am, I mean I don't know. We were just asked to keep it locked and deny access to anyone until we are notified by the administration that it's all clear."

"You can't do that! We have work that can't be interrupted. I-" This is not his doing. He is just following orders. "Sorry, I'll call right away."

"Yes ma'am. Have a good day."

I text Megan, Jamie, and Haley: *All, lab is closed for the day. Nothing to fret about. I'll let you know when it's open again. Let me know if there is anything urgent that needs to be done, as in it will waste money if we don't do it today. No questions please, I don't have any answers.*

Megan: *Got it, nothing to do*

Jamie: *ditto*

Haley: *the r46 cells need to be fed, but can probably wait a day*

Me: *Thanks all. Will keep you posted.*

I pull up the Internet on my phone to search the university directory for the President's office, and start to type, then back space, back space. Just out of curiosity I type Regnum, tap search. Their website pops to the top. I type Regnum recall, search. It takes me to a page that lists all of their recalls, of which, surprisingly, there are quite a few. I have to ask Neil if this is normal. The top one is FeLV vaccine, lot #170427. Due to suspected contamination, all vials should be returned to the manufacturer. No known risks to cats have been identified. A link to return instructions is provided. That's it. No mention of risks to dogs, link to CRFS, or urgency. Bastards.

Strange that the no one called me about shutting down my lab.

I check my recent calls, and apparently my Dean did call late last night, but I missed the notification. He left a voicemail. His message is friendly and short. "Hey Claire, can you come see me first thing in the morning before you head to the lab. No worries, just following standard protocol when a public relations issue is looming. I understand you've made some fascinating discoveries? See you in the morning!"

Yikes. Dean Austin was on travel for the week, and I figured this would all be settled by the time he got back. He's back early. How did he find out? What did he find out? Public relations issue? He is not going to be too pleased that I didn't give him a heads-up. I should have called him on his cell on Monday to fill him in, damn it. Why is the President of the University involved? I close my eyes for a few moments and try to relax. It is going to be another long and complex day.

I dial the department's main number. Mary, our department administrator, answers. "Oh, hi, Dr. Winthrop, how are you?" She is such a great asset to our department. She knows all of the staff, most of the graduate students, and a fair number of the undergrads. She's everyone's mom, loves her job, and is loved by everyone around her, as evidenced by the piles of cookies and other baked goods delivered to her desk around the holidays. Of course she leaves them out so we can all share in the sugar high.

"Actually, I don't know. My lab is closed and I have no idea why. You have any clues?"

"Really? No, I don't. But there was a message from Karen, you know, the President's assistant? She said she wanted me to set up a meeting with you, Dean Austin, and President Abrams as soon as we heard from you."

"Dean Austin? So he is back?"

"Yes, and Dean Austin asked me to put you through or send

you in to his office as soon as I heard from you. Is there something exciting about to happen?"

I hadn't even stopped to think of it that way in the last few days. It is a very exciting scientific discovery, and it's such a relief to know that CRFS will stop, literally within days of halting the use of the contaminated vaccine. "I hope so. I'll let you know as soon as I'm able."

"Please do, I would love to post something in the department newsletter!"

Unfortunately I think our department's publication will get scooped. "Absolutely. I will make sure you get all the details. Will you tell Dean Austin that I will be there in about five minutes?"

"You don't want to speak to him now?"

"No, I would rather talk to him in person. See you in a few." I turn off my phone and put it in my purse and sit back. I crack a faint smile as it occurs to me that I will be meeting with my Dean and the university President, Nathan Abrams, today, and they will know what we have accomplished. The cat is out of the bag, so to speak. It is no small feat, and regardless of what Regnum is trying to do, they cannot deny or cover up all of the work that we did, and the magnitude of the discovery. My confidence renewed, I open the door to the crisp air and head towards our Department's main building. Did I just feel a warming breeze? A few of my students pass and greet me; it's good to be back in my world.

"Go right in," Mary says, "he's waiting for you."

"Hello, Douglas. How are you today?" I ask as he gives me his usual one-armed hug and gestures for me to have a seat.

"Amused and curious. I take it what you are holding in your arms has something to do with the mysterious call I got from President Abrams last night. He said that he received a call yesterday afternoon from Regnum, the pharmaceutical company."

"Ah." I'm not sure what to say.

He joins me at the little table in his office motioning for me to take a seat. "And they said it was urgent that they meet with him, today, concerning one of his professors. You. Apparently he asked for details, but they were not forthcoming, except to say that they believe that you have research that directly relates to one of their products and that they need to discuss any release of information that may be of a proprietary nature."

I burst out laughing. Douglas looks amused but not surprised. I nod as I lay two envelopes in the center of the table. "I'm sorry I didn't call you earlier."

"No matter," he says. He has always been very matter-of-fact and unflappable. He slides one notebook out and opens it to the first page. "Want to give me the highlights?"

"Absolutely. This page summarizes all the data and findings." I skim to the bold lettering **CONCLUSIONS**. "All the data show that without a doubt the cause of CRFS is the contamination of one of Regnum's cat vaccines."

"You mean dog vaccine."

"No, cat. It's got an extra promoter in it that affects the dog GR gene. You want the Reader's Digest version or the extended books on tape?"

He is standing and putting on his jacket, then coat. "I'd love the long and detailed version, but we have to head over to the President's office right now so you can tell us both."

"Seriously. I really messed up the communication on this one, didn't I?"

"Nah. We scientists have never been the best at the administrative stuff." He's letting me off easy. "It's taken me years to master enough so I can run the department."

"You're being too kind. I should have—"

"Nonsense. Tell me what you can with the time we have as we walk over. Claire, my dear, I think your research has put us in a curious position." He picks up the notebook, I pick up the other envelope, and he extends an arm to usher me toward the door.

"Good curious or bad?"

"I'm sure it will end up good, but based on the short conversation I had with Nathan this morning, Regnum's lawyer—"

"Lawyer?" I interrupt. The elevator doors close. I'm suddenly feeling trapped.

"Yes, their lawyer was the one who called, and he said they have grave concerns about any movement forward without their consent."

My heart is racing. "What did Dr. Abrams think?"

"He chuckled and said, 'This is going to be fun!'"

We step outside and I am blinded by the bright sun. We walk quickly. I tell him what I can on our short walk to the Administrative building. I have less than two minutes on the elevator to tell him about our meeting with Regnum. I don't tell him about their threats to Neil. I apologize, again, for leaving him in the dark.

"It's okay, happens all the time that a researcher takes their results to an outsider before informing the machine grinding behind them."

"I'm so sor—"

"I did it plenty of times myself." He smirks.

Nathan's office door is open, and we half say hello to Karen as he waves us in. "There's the woman of the hour! Come in, come in. Would you like some coffee, water? I have Scotch in my drawer."

"You do?"

He shrugs. I'll never tell. "Hello, Dr. Abrams, good to see you again." He's a big guy, six-foot something, and gives me a bear hug. We've known each other for ten years, since he was Dean of my college. I've been to his house for dinner with his wife Katherine and him, I've watched his children grow up as they dashed through the dining room and through the changing photographs on his desk. But I always give him his due and shift to the formality of the university structure when the situation warrants.

"How's Chris? How are the girls?"

"Good, good. It's been forever since I've seen Katherine. Please give her my love." She had ovarian cancer a number of years ago. Caught early by a very lucky ovarian cyst that encircled the tiny tumor and then bloated itself with fluid so it couldn't be ignored. "I'm so sorry I haven't been in touch. How's she doing"?

"You have teenagers—you know your life is not your own! She is doing great. Just passed the five-year mark of clean PET scans. We will plan a dinner celebration once we clear up this mess."

"Wow, five years. I'm so happy to hear that. It would be great to see her, and you, outside of these walls." I feel sheepish. "So you see it as a mess? I was hoping you'd see the humor in it." I glance at Douglas.

"Oh, I do. This is going to be an intriguing challenge, but it is a mess right now as we have to deal with the pain in the ass lawyers from Regnum. But they tell me you have made a significant discovery. Congratulations."

"Thank you." Another demonstration of why he was chosen to be President. He is smart, thoughtful, and supportive of his staff. And he recognizes when research outcomes have the potential to become big news.

"I would like us to spend the remaining time before they get here, though, going through everything: the science, the administrative and regulatory requirements, and even the ethical considerations—Oh, hi, Laura, come on in and join the fun."

I turn to see Laura Dechaines, Lead Counsel for the university. I've met her at a few university functions, but she has no reason to know me, until now.

"Hello Nathan, Douglas, and"—turning to me with a

welcoming grin—"Claire, the woman of the hour! I'm looking forward to working closely with you in the next few days."

That's the second time I've been called that in the last five minutes. Clearly, there have been some discussions on this campus about me that I have not been privy to. I'm starting to feel very uncomfortable with Nathan's "before they get here" comment.

I hand Nathan the other envelope, and walking over to the small conference table at one end of his office, he asks us to join him. He bellows to Karen to bring in any of the paperwork that she has been able to gather. She too offers us coffee, water, and soft drinks after handing him a file folder.

"No Scotch though." Nathan winks at me. "We have to work. Besides, I think I drank it already."

We all sit, and for the next hour, go carefully over all the details. After reviewing all the data and the summary report, Nathan opens the file folder from Karen. "Now for the paperwork," he says. Laura and he want to verify that I have filed all the proper paperwork to obtain permission from the university to conduct the research. Check. Provided routine reports to my department on the progress? Check. Ensured that any funding—Neil's money—was properly recorded and fees divvied up to the appropriate university coffers? Painfully . . . check.

Laura asks why, when we were certain of our results, I contacted Regnum before contacting anyone at the university. I explain that I didn't contact them, that my funding source did the initial contact, as we felt it was critical for Regnum to immediately pull the contaminated vaccines. Why did I then meet with them a few days later, again without informing the university? She seems a bit peeved, Douglas seems to be chagrined, but Nathan is non-fazed. I apologize for blindsiding them. I didn't think it through properly, and admit that I should have brought them into the loop at the beginning.

"No big deal," Nathan says, putting his hand on my arm. "We just need to make sure we have all the answers and our script for when they get here."

There it is again. "Who constitutes they?"

"Oh sorry I didn't tell you. Regnum's legal team and Chairman are on their way from DC and scheduled to meet with us after lunch."

Laura nods, confirming my impending doom. "Yes, they are on the way, and I think that Nathan and I should meet with them first, then bring the two of you in. I think I have all the facts that I need." Seeing the anguish on my face, she looks directly at me and says, "Don't worry. We are all in your court and have your back. We just need to make sure that we are not putting the university in any danger of a lawsuit, unfounded or not, and that we are solidly in position to make a public statement." She must see me as I struggle for words. "That is where we are heading, correct?"

"Actually, that is exactly what I was intending to do this morning. I was going to contact you"—I look at Douglas—"and request that we start the ball rolling to meet with whomever to begin the process for going public. Guess I'm a day late."

Douglas stands with a broad smile, breaking the tension. "I'm starving. The University Club? My treat."

"Sorry Doug, I have to give the Governor's office a call about this, but I'll be back over at one when Regnum gets here." My eyes must have tripled in size, so Laura says, "It's a state university, so we are obliged to tell them of any potential litigation issues or discoveries worth noting, and I would say this qualifies as both."

I stand in the restroom at the club, back against the side wall of my fancy-schmancy stall that has its own sink. Large donors are obviously entertained here. In the club, not the stall. I close my eyes for a few moments, seeking calm and focus. I could use a dog right now. Even when Ania slowly invades my space, pushing her feet into my stomach, physical contact soothes me and I easily shift and find balance. Balance evades me now, even with artful granite propping me up.

Douglas and I sit in the waiting room outside of President Abrams' office. He gave it the old college try to keep our lunch conversation upbeat and focused on our achievements, but as he patted my arm offering me reassurance in physical contact, all I could feel was feet in my stomach but couldn't find balance. The Regnum folks had already arrived when we returned from lunch and were seated down the hall in the large conference room.

"That was a rather austere group," Karen says quietly.

"Were they? How many?" I ask.

"Six, all dressed in black suits. They looked like the Men in Black without the sunglasses."

"Hoping to induce memory loss, are they?" Douglas says, elbowing me, but I am rigid. "Relax, we have to trust Nathan and Laura. This is not their first rodeo. Besides this is some unbelievable stuff you've uncovered. You should be very proud. I hope you are prepared for the public attention and scrutiny you are about to face."

Karen sits up straight. "Oh! Sorry to eavesdrop, but that reminds me. Dr. Abrams asked me to set up an appointment for you late this afternoon with our public relations director. Do you know her? Sandy Jenkins? She's very sharp. She said to just give her a call, even if it is this evening or over the weekend, and she'll work with you whenever and however long you need." She hands me a blue sticky note.

I stand and take it silently, and plop back down in one of the reception chairs. Oh my God, this is really happening! My heart is pounding. Douglas gives me a big grin.

Over an hour later, having read every magazine in the waiting area, I know everything about the university, the aeronautics industry, and colleges today. I would have preferred the distraction of Hollywood gossip, and reality magazines' heroes of the day, but this is an educational institution.

Karen's phone buzzes. She answers, listens, and hangs up. "They are ready for you," she says.

Douglas and I walk silently down the long hall. It's formal in a modern sort of way. Former Presidents give us frozen grins, doors to smaller conference rooms whisper, "In here." I could easily duck in, but they would find me. We can see into the room at the end of the hall, through the glass panels that frame the door. Same guys I met with a little over twenty-four hours ago. Same ones that put the threat out to Neil.

Douglas puts his hand on the doorknob, but looks at me before he pulls. His face is kind and fatherly. "We're on your side. Remember that." And he opens the door to the wolves' den.

They all stand. I position myself in front of the empty chair between Douglas and Laura. Laura starts to introduce the Regnum team. I turn to her and say, "No need for introductions. We all met earlier this week. Nice to see all of you gentlemen again." I shake hands with each across a much smaller table than theirs. I'm falsely cordial as I sit.

Laura explains that the group has gone over my results, and she has assured Regnum that all of the science and administrative requirements are of the utmost quality and integrity. She says that Regnum agrees, and is impressed with my work.

Regnum's lead counsel interjects, "As we told you yesterday, we are very impressed with your work. We cannot thank you enough for what you have done for our company, and for all of the dog owners who will rest easy knowing that CRFS is in the past." The same coating of sickening syrup as yesterday.

I'm supposed to say something here to their false compliment, but I don't.

"As we also told you, we would like to offer to compensate you for your efforts, and we realize that it will require some follow-up research. As well, this research effort has taken time away from your main research emphasis, Addison's, so we would like to set up an endowment for you and your university to continue your great work in that area as well."

The slimy bastards. Can't get little old me to bite? Run an end-around and dangle a giant carrot in front of the university that is always hungry for endowments? I look to Dr. Abrams, Dr. Austin, and Ms. Dechaines, Esq. All look me directly in the eyes and give me . . . no reaction. Something is going on. I can't tell if they have a plan or not; if they do, I'm not privy to it. I'm on a limb, a very skinny one, and the wind is blowing hurricane force.

"Thank you. Since you made your offer yesterday, I have had time to consider it, and while it is quite generous, I'm not sure what you want in return."

"Full rights to your research results, and a non-disclosure agreement with all of those involved, including the university."

I would blow Coke out my nose if I was drinking one. I open my mouth to speak but close it. Rachelle said to choose my words carefully. Only calculated, measured responses. I need to be very careful what I say here. If my university higher-ups want to take the money, who am I to say no? But then, what university would give up the opportunity to capitalize on having solved CRFS? That has to be more valuable down the road. But then, are they concerned about a lawsuit? Would they think a bird in the hand—a several-million-dollar bird—is better than one in the bush?

"How much money are you talking about, if I don't sound to

too crass?" I ask, just to bait them. Or am I actually considering this?

"We've provided a written offer to Dr. Abrams. It is very generous."

Nathan turns to me. "It is quite substantial Dr. Winthrop."

Obviously, I don't get to see it.

"How exactly do you think I am going to get everyone to sign an agreement?" I ask.

"Everyone will be generously compensated."

I look to Nathan and ask, "Who decides?"

Laura sits forward. "Our Board of Directors has the final say."

"They decide based on our recommendation," Nathan adds.

Screaming inside my head, "So why am I here?!? How could you have sold me out?!?" I'm trying to stay calm but my face will probably betray me. Careful. Measured response. My words are modulated. "I appreciate you soliciting my opinion, even though I don't really have standing. Obviously my opinion is biased as I would like to publish the results. I also—"

"If the point of publishing is to secure future funding, we are offering an alternative solution." Regnum's lead counsel is obviously not a scientist. Clearly, it is all about saving the company's ass—and money.

Quietly, I say, "That is not the point of publishing. The public needs to know that the origin of CRFS was identified, and understand how further infection has been contained. They have to know that this can't and won't happen again."

"We will make sure of that," their Chairman says.

"And the scientific community needs to know how we discovered the cause," I add. "It's an important scientific advancement."

"Gentlemen, is there anything else?" Nathan asks. "We have your offer, your very generous offer, and will get back to you with an answer by tomorrow morning, or sooner if we can convene a quorum for our Board."

Everyone is standing, closing folders, snapping shut briefcases. I pick up my backpack. My cardigan sweater and pants brand me as a researcher. I'm no match for this room of suits. I can feel their disdain, though they won't show it outwardly. Their livelihoods depend on the talents of scientists, yet they place themselves above us. They know I have no say in this, but they were obliged to appease the university leadership in feigning due consideration. They begin to file out of the room, shaking hands down the ivory tower line. Laura follows, escorting them down the long hallway to the elevators.

We watch in silence until Nathan closes the door and faces us all. "Well, that was interesting."

I am about to lose it. I don't know if I am angry or upset, but I can feel tears welling in my eyes. I can't show my feelings but I can't believe all our work has come to this. I start to speak. My voice cracks.

"Hang on," Nathan says, putting me on hold with a cautious smile. He buzzes Karen's desk. "Hey, can you please let the Board members know we are ready?" He releases the intercom.

Nathan walks around the table and sits facing us. "Claire, I'm sorry." And here it comes. "I'm sorry that we didn't include you in some of our discussions this morning. We've been scrambling to figure out what to do. After your briefing, it was clear that we have only one choice." I am jolted out of alternate thoughts. "To release the information to the public."

"Wha . . . ?"

He cracks a smile. "It was easy to figure out the purpose of their coming to see us. Tempting as we knew their offer would be, we knew that there was no way we could ever let them buy us or one of our researchers. We are an academic institution that thrives on research innovation. If we start selling our silence to the highest bidder, that will be our undoing. The first person we would lose, one of our top researchers, would likely be you."

Feeling like the butt of the joke, I can't think of anything to say.

"So, what, just kidding?" Douglas asks, sounding slightly irritated. Apparently he wasn't in on it either.

"We needed to have them think we were honestly considering their offer or, we suspect, they will start legal action. It looked better if a few of us—well, you two—were giving genuine responses. Sorry we left you dangling for a bit."

Relenting, Douglas leans into me, as we are clearly on a separate team. "Guess these two owe us a very expensive dinner."

"Oh, I'll buy. You played your parts masterfully," Laura says.

"And without a script! But what about the Board?" I ask, trying to catch up.

Nathan stands and heads to the door to let Karen in. "Oh, they too are in on it." She hands him a note and the two conspirators whisper in code.

"Of course they are." Douglas rolls his eyes at me, getting up to pour himself some water.

Nathan returns. "We had a teleconference after you left for lunch, and the Board agreed that whatever Regnum offered would not be accepted unless it includes public disclosure, acknowledgement of the source of contamination, and full credit to our research team. This will be our only counter-offer."

"Regnum will never agree to that," Alarms were going off in my head. "That's—wait, they are still threatening to pin the whole thing on Neil, our financial sponsor, and former Regnum CSO. I'm sorry I left that part out. This doesn't change their threat. They will still try to pin the whole thing on him and ruin him. That must be why they said they would make sure the public knows the truth. Even if we make the announcement about how we discovered the cause, they will still have to explain how it started. They intend to use him as their scapegoat." Panic is rising in my voice and crawling across my skin. "I can't let them do that!" I plead, looking from Nathan to Laura.

"Unfortunately, we can't make him our concern because he doesn't work for us," says Laura, the consummate lawyer.

"But . . . I . . ."

Nathan walks over to fully face me. "They told us about 'his involvement'." Oddly, he uses air quotes.

"He didn't do—"

"We figured there's a backstory and we trust that you would not have accepted funding from someone who wasn't above-board, but there is nothing we can do to include him in our counter-offer without knowing what actually happened at Regnum when this all started. Does Neil have any ideas?"

"I don't think so. But I don't know if he has uncovered anything. We have been trying to have as little contact as possible for the last few days since Regnum has been putting the screws to him." My thoughts are hopscotching. "Wait, you already asked Karen to set me up with the public relations person—Sandy, is that her name?—so you had already started implementing your plan or strategy or whatever, before we even met with them. You must be pretty confident that they will accept this counter-offer of yours—or are you confident that we can just leave them out?"

"Well, admittedly, we are a few steps ahead of them—and you. Again, I apologize." Nathan motions for everyone to take a seat again, though he remains standing. "Laura is going to counter to them tomorrow when she informs them that we have set up a press conference for Monday morning, so they have barely the weekend to decide." He places his hands on the table and draws everyone's attention to me. "Dr. Winthrop, we have some work to do!" He nods to Laura to take over, pushes off the table, and leaves momentarily to talk to Karen, who minutes later shows up with cookies, sodas, and a bevy of other snacks she keeps on hand to feed the students.

They ask me to keep my lab closed until Monday. I can go in for an hour later today to handle any pressing needs. Not that they think Regnum will try to do something, but if there are any information leaks they don't want anyone trying to get a scoop from someone working in the lab.

We break for a bit, but I can do nothing but stare out the window trying to clear my head. The afternoon sun dances across the campus. Blotches of shade and bright reflections hypnotize and oddly calm me.

Sandy joins us, and Nathan leaves to deal with the looming crisis of rising costs and potential tuition hikes, which ironically could be addressed with a giant grant from Regnum. For almost two hours Laura, Douglas, Sandy, and I walk through the process of the press conference, and she gives us a short course in media relations. Look directly at the audience, hands on the podium. Be prepared to answer the questions that we believe they will ask. Maintain control by making it clear what is off-limits. I am to meet with Sandy again on Sunday evening, hopefully with my whole research team in tow, to go through a presentation I am supposed to prepare, and to define each of our roles and the formal written statement. I am not one for the stage. My daughters are the theater geeks.

I group text Jamie, Megan, and Haley. *Can you all meet me at the lab at 6 pm? Sorry, I know it's a Friday evening.* I have to explain everything very quickly. I won't say anything about Regnum's bribe. When it is all over, I will tell them. I doubt they will be disappointed in having missed out on a share of the hush money. They will have their name on what will likely be one of the biggest scientific publications of the year. Not too shabby for graduate students and an undergrad.

Throughout the day I have called and texted Chris with updates. Standing in an alcove on the way back from a restroom break, I confess my nausea over how this is turning out. He reminds me, repeatedly, that this is a good thing, the most exciting finding and the biggest announcement of my career. I should be excited and proud of the outcome. There will be no late night in the lab tonight. Maybe we could actually relax on a Friday night and have a quiet dinner and release the tension in our lives. This is big for him too. He's right, it deserves a Snoopy dance.

I call Anna. I didn't want to talk to her until I had the total picture. "Hey, guess whose lab was locked when she arrived this morning?"

"I suspected something was going on. After I couldn't reach you on your cell I called the lab a bunch of times and no one answered." Her voice is flat. "Claire, a lawyer from Regnum paid me a visit today. He said that they intended to file a complaint with the Virginia Board of Veterinary Medicine to have me investigated for unethical practices."

"Oh my God, they will stop at nothing! What did you say?"

"I politely asked for his card, then told him to leave as I would have my lawyer contact him. I contacted Rachelle and she said she would call me back later today, but I haven't heard from her. Why didn't you answer my texts? What's going on?"

"Anna, I'm so sorry, I was asked not to. I—"

"By who? Why?" She is genuinely alarmed.

"Anna, it's okay, everything is being worked out."

"Bullshit! It's not okay. I have lawyers threatening me in my clinic, my best friend has abandoned me, and I've got a practice that has lost most of its patients."

"Let me explain."

"Please do. But I'd rather you do it in person. I wouldn't be surprised if they are tapping our phones. I'll come to your house around nine."

Dinner with Chris is off.

"Okay."

"Bye."

"Anna?"

"What?"

"It's going to be okay." I say this, but clearly Regnum is running down parallel tracks: playing the good cop with the university, but the bad cop with those on our team they think are vulnerable. I am convinced that they still have more cards to play.

Neil. Nathan left it up to me to decide whether to include him in our press conference or not. He didn't actually do any of the work, and while he funded the research, he worked for Regnum at the time this all started. Laura, less subtle, suggested more than once that I leave him out of the press conference. But I need to talk to him first. By now I'm convinced that he is either dead or kidnapped by Regnum. I feel like a stalker with the number of texts and calls I have made in the last few hours, but he hasn't answered any of them. I know he is never without his phone. I can feel something is wrong.

He must have known the risk when he told me to meet with my president today. I call again, this time leaving a message that he will likely not listen to. He typically sees I called and just calls me back, but I have to say something. "Neil, please answer your GD phone! Regnum beat me to the President's office. He, our lawyer, and my Dean, headed Regnum off at the pass, but I think they're still going to blame you. Please call me. I'm this tiny caboose trying to slow a giant freight train that is going to crash over a cliff with you in it. Please call me, leave me a message, run away with me to the Caribbean. I'm so sorry it has come to this."

Saturday, Day 6

The morning is quiet. The couches and floors are littered with shifting piles of dog and teenaged biomass as they intertwine and support one another through homework, TV, and naps. I lose myself in housecleaning, laundry, and cooking, content to nest around them.

By the afternoon I have carpool duty. They tumble into the car, hair in sloppy buns, leggings and T-shirts askew, evidence of a solid rehearsal beginning their spring production. They plunk their lumps of backpack on the floor and slam the doors.

"Oh my God mom! You won't believe . . ." Diana explodes.

"Shut . . ." Tess stops short of using the forbidden words. "I can tell her myself, you don't have to out me." I wait. "So you know that guy I have a crush on, Peter?" I remain silent; acknowledging would stifle her openness. "He's so cute! And he came up to my table at lunch and asked if he could sit down and he was so sweet asking all kinds of questions like what colleges I'm interested in, about my dogs, even about you guys . . ." She is clearly enamored.

"That's a good sign." I say in a monotone.

"Ugh mom it was, except, I'm such an idiot!"

"Because..."

"Because I started asking about him, and when he told me his father was from Austria I said, *Oh! Do you speak Austrian*?" My eyes widen. "Mom, the moment it came out of my mouth I knew what an idiot I sounded like, but there was nothing I could say!"

"What did he say?" I cautiously ask.

"He just said he grew up speaking German at home as a child, but he's pretty much dropped it as a teenager." I try not to chuckle.

"I know you're dying mom." I don't say a word. "I know you're thinking it's a good thing apples don't fall up into the trees."

I wait a moment. "Nope not me. He sounds like a nice guy."

"He is," She threw her head back. "I'm such a dope!"

A few heartbeats passed, and we all bust out laughing. I reached over and rubbed her arm, quickly, as to linger would overstep. As I concentrate on the road, I find comfort in knowing that I must be doing something right if my teenaged daughter is able to have a sense of humor about herself.

Like microwaving popcorn, their teenage energy bursts out in punctuated excitement briefly filling the car. But by the time we stop by the grocery store, silence reigns, induced by the levity and self-professed wisdom of posts on Reddit and Twitter. "Facebook is for people *your* age, Mom," I've been informed many times.

Finally, Chris and I retreat to our bed. Lying on his chest, I feel the protection of my soul mate, and am reminded of an anonymous poem I found in high school: "Baked in an enamel shell, I am strong. But please don't scrape too hard. Porcelain cracks so easily.

Sunday, Day 7

Anna is up to speed on everything, though still adamant about releasing samples and our data through the CDC if something goes wrong and this is not settled by tomorrow, Monday COB. Rachelle fended off Regnum's attack on her over the weekend, which means they will likely have no reason to move forward with their threats.

The university is moving ahead with our press conference. Anna, Jamie, Megan, and Haley are all here at our house; so is Sandy, who briefs us all on what to say, but mostly what not to say. I practice my presentation, revised by Sandy for the public, and receive a rousing ovation from the peanut gallery. Their excitement is infectious and I can feel a renewed sense of purpose melting away all sense of trepidation. We have stopped CRFS.

We call it an early evening. It's going to be a wild and busy day for us tomorrow. Chris and the girls and I cuddle watching a taped episode of *Portlandia*. Tess claims it's based on Chris and me, with our bohemian wardrobe and his role as the recycling police. The dogs sprawl out on the floor. I'll remember this.

The girls are in bed, Chris reading in ours. Ania sits in the hallway in anticipation, watching me shut down my computer. I close the lid, she stands. We are both creatures of habit. I pick up my phone to plug it in for the night. There is a text from Neil that I somehow missed. *I'll be in touch tomorrow. You're going to love this.*

Finally. *Okay*, I respond, content that he is alive and apparently amused. We head for the bedroom. I glimpse myself in the hall mirror. The stress-induced resting bitch face has softened, replaced by a kinder, gentler me.

Sofie, snuggled in my space, moves to the floor, while Ania assumes her hierarchical spot. I crawl under the covers just as Chris is turning off his light. We cuddle goodnight, and I retreat into the dim light of my Kindle and Ania's warmth at my feet.

DOG GONE

Monday, Day 8

Somewhere between Mark's insistence that they stay for another set, and Tasha walking on the beach to clear her head, I fell asleep in the plot of a mediocre novel I will never finish. It is morning and I am swept up in the current as the day flows around me. Chris is showered, dressed, and has placed a cup on my nightstand, inches from my nose. Coffee essence lures me to the conscious world. Voices and dog feet are quiet, as sunlight slowly fills the house.

Almost ready, I step out on the screened-in porch. It is surprisingly warm. I sit down and draw in a breath of pristine air. The trees have shed their hard edges and seem relaxed in the coming of spring. Soon they will return to work filling the empty spaces with dappled green.

Chris gently breaks the spell as he joins me. "We need to get going."

The girls, still sleeping, will be picked up by our neighbor and brought to the university. They were excited last night to be included in today's events. While they seem to grasp the importance of our results, getting out of school for the day seems to be the more significant reason.

"You look ready," he says.

"You think I look too much not like me in this suit?" I ask. "Funny how I feel solid with all the technical stuff, but I'm unsettled by picking out clothes."

"You'll be facing a lot of people, including the press. Makes sense you want to influence their impression." He gives me his best smile. "You look perfect. Professional. You."

"I was going to go with the tortoise shell . . .

"I like those blue frames better, they'll look good on camera. Did I mention, you look hot?" and he offers his hand affirming why he is my life.

We are on our way to pick up Anna and then head over for a final meeting with Nathan, Douglas, Laura, and Sandy. Laura called yesterday morning and asked us to have Rachelle contact her. She too will be joining us, I guess for Anna and Chris' benefit.

Karen is there to greet us and shows us into the large conference room. "Can I get you anything this morning? You all must be so excited!" She smiles brightly. "Dr. Abrams is almost here, but the Regnum folks called and said they are stuck in traffic, so they will be a little late."

"Regnum?" we say in unison.

Before she can reply, Nathan bursts in and dumps his briefcase on the table, tossing his coat on a side chair. "Good morning all! Beautiful day for a press conference, don't you think?"

"Dr. Abrams, would you like me to take your coat to your office? I'll bring you coffee."

"The coat can stay, Karen, but coffee would be perfect, thank you. Anyone else?" He registers our deer-in–the-headlights expressions. "Please, please, sit. Get comfortable." We don't. Opening his briefcase he takes out a stack of folders and slides one across the table to each of us. "We don't have a lot of time, but—"

"Good morning, folks!" Sandy announces. Douglas, Laura, and our lawyer Rachelle follow behind.

"Good morning, all. I was just passing out the new script to everyone but haven't told them yet what transpired late last night." Great, more Nathan surprises. "You must be Rachelle; nice to meet you in person." He extends his hand for a greeting and offers her a seat. "Please take a chair."

"Well, let's get started, shall we?" Sandy beams. "We have so little time before they get here."

None in my group have uttered a word yet. Rachelle is smirking.

As Sandy and Douglas are sitting, Nathan says, "so it seems that Regnum decided if you can't beat 'em, join 'em, and they called late yesterday afternoon with an offer to do a joint press conference."

"You agreed?" Anna asked, shocked.

"Sit, sit, please." Reaching out again, Nathan says, "You are Dr. McDowell—Anna, right? We've met a few times at some of the university functions."

She shakes his hand and slowly lowers herself into her seat. "Yes, and you are Dr. Abrams."

"Nathan, please. And Chris? Good to see you again." Engaging Anna, Nathan says, "Back to your question. Yes, we agreed because it is all on our terms and more. I trust that when this is all on the table, all of you will be very pleased." He sits and puts on his glasses, pulling one of the folders in front of him. "Now, if you will open the folder I just gave you." Karen quietly places a coaster and his coffee. "Thank you." He smiles at her.

We are barely though the details; have not even begun to process, much less rehearse the revised presentation when Karen's voice comes over the intercom. "The Regnum team is here."

"Wonderful! Bring them in," Nathan says cheerily. "Be nice," he whispers to us as he stands to greet them.

We all stand as they enter. The President, CFO, CEO, CSO, Chief Counsel and two of his minions, and Neil. Neil and a woman in her sixties, elegantly dressed and poised. Nathan motions for me to do the introductions, but we don't really need any. I round out the formality with "Of course some of you know Neil, and—I'm sorry I—"

"Donna, Donna Peebles." She smiles genuinely, extending her hand. "We've never met but we've spoken many times."

Barely perceptibly, I can feel Neil laughing his ass off.

It's time. Karen is standing at the door. Nathan sees her, looks at his watch and says "Folks, it's show time!" We all stand and Karen leads our procession down the hall; two loose lines, we are careful not to mingle with the Regnum folks. Like being inches away from a growling dog with nowhere to run, the elevator ride to the auditorium is unsettling. Chris gently takes my hand and squeezes a smile out of me. Feeling like Ania having retrieved the ball from the deep weeds, I hold my head up as we take to the stage.

A pre-release from the university stating that it had news to announce on the findings and end of CRFS, resulted in a packed room, including a gallery of not just local but national press. Megan, Jamie, and Haley are seated in the front row, along with the girls, Anna's technicians, Dr. Martenson's lab group, and other members of my department. Bright stage lights blind us from above, while news media flashes give a strobe-like effect. We file onto the stage and are seated, separated from the Regnum team by the podium where Nathan takes his place, puts on his glasses, and lays open his folder. Five hundred people sit suspended in silence.

"Ladies and gentlemen, thank you for coming this morning. I

am pleased to announce the discovery of the cause of CRFS by our research team lead by Dr. Claire Winthrop. She will be giving a statement and details on the discovery in a few minutes and she will be taking questions at the end of her presentation." Indiscriminate comments rumble the room. "The cause of CRFS"—abrupt silence —"The cause of CRFS is a contaminated cat vaccine for Feline Leukemia Virus or FeLV. Dr. Winthrop will provide details on the mechanism of infection, but put briefly, in the normal process post-vaccination, cats shed the contaminated modified virus for a period —typically twenty-four to forty-eight hours. In this case, dogs who were exposed to the shed virus were affected by the contaminant, which caused a catastrophic collapse of their adrenal system."

Like rolling thunder, chatter erupts. A few brash reporters yell out questions. Nathan waits patiently for quiet that slowly comes. He's enjoying this.

"Folks, this is going to be a long morning. We have prepared slides to walk you through the science, and handouts will be available upon exit. We will make sure that we provide as much detail as you need and allow plenty of time for questions. I ask that you all give us the first ten minutes to walk you through the research and actions taken, and I promise you this will all be made very clear." The audience engine returns to idle. "Thank you. As I was saying, the cause is a contaminated cat vaccine made by the pharmaceutical company Regnum. Joining us in this announcement today is the President of Regnum, Dr. Scott Tennant, who will explain their investigation and what they have done to stop any further spread of CRFS." A few of the reporters cannot contain themselves and fire questions at the stage.

"You are lying!" A man shouts as he unfurls a Canine Crusaders banner. He is quickly shut down by security.

"Before I bring Dr. Winthrop up to the podium, I would like to tell you a little about her, and acknowledge the incredible significance of her team's findings. Over the last nine months we have all seen the tragic loss of thousands of dogs across the country. Dogs who were companions, friends, and members of families. The heartbreak that has unfolded before our eyes cannot be adequately described, but it ends now thanks to Dr. Winthrop's dedication and brilliance as a researcher." Yikes, this is uncomfortable. "Dr. Winthrop and her colleague Dr. Anna MacDowell have been working tirelessly for a number of years to find a genetic link and remedy for Addison's disease in dogs. This love of dogs is what drove her team to work diligently to help find a cure for CRFS. As she will explain, better than I can, CRFS affects dogs much the way Addison's does, and it is this parallel that provided the key to unlock the mystery of CRFS. Ladies and gentlemen, please join me in thanking Dr. Winthrop and Dr. MacDowell, and their whole team, for their hard work and significant research."

The room erupts in applause as Nathan turns to me inviting me to join him at the podium. He is beaming, crashing his hands together as if they were cymbals. Everyone is rising around me. The room is erupting in a standing ovation. I look to Chris, who stands, and offers me his hand to lift me to this new height. My heart is pounding as hundreds of flashes of light pummel me. I am propelled to the podium by some invisible force.

Nathan leans into the microphone and announces "Dr. Winthrop" and steps back. I am standing for what feels like minutes while the crowd continues to applaud and call out commendations and questions. Having never experienced this before, I am at a loss for how to quiet them so I stand, stunned.

Finally, I shift into lecture mode, comfortable in front of a class, going through slides and explaining the details. I pause several times for quick questions until I have the presence of mind to ask to hold questions until after our presentations. Control your audience, measured responses.

I would like to now ask Dr. Scott Tennant of Regnum, to join me and provide"—I have to look at my actual script—"to join me to provide his company's response to our findings and their vision for the future." I turn and give my biggest, fake smile, and offer a welcoming gesture. "Dr. Tennant."

Polite applause, if that. For the first time I really look at his face as he walks to the gallows. He is stoic and calculated. Though, I think, a bit unnerved. He adjusts the microphone higher, places and opens a folder on the podium, and grasps the podium as if preparing for a bumpy ride. I quietly take my seat.

"Ladies and gentlemen, Dr. Abrams, Dr. Winthrop, and Dr. MacDowell, thank you for all your work, and for working with us to put an immediate end to this horrific disease." He is smooth. "The spread of CRFS stopped last week when we met with Dr. Winthrop's team and learned of her research results. Even though we had not yet confirmed the results, we immediately recalled all suspected vaccine, and notified the veterinary community of the need to cease all use of the lots that contained the contaminated virus." Well, not exactly. "We have also confirmed the results, and by the end of the week, we were able to determine how the vaccine became contaminated."

The tension in the room is palpable. I can't see the audience beyond the first few rows but I could swear I hear pitchforks being readied. I shift to the edge of my seat since I haven't heard this part of the story.

"We have prepared a detailed statement which will be made available at the end of this session, but in short, a senior quality control manager became careless and negligent in his misguided attempt to prove he could increase productivity, and the FeLV product was compromised. His actions included a cover-up once he learned of the mistake, which further prevented our stringent second level of the quality assurance process to be effective. This manager has been dismissed, and criminal charges for his actions are likely."

Someone shouts out, "What about the dogs that have died?"

"You ask an excellent question. We, like so many of you, love dogs. We are dog owners, they are members of our family, and our work is dedicated to the health of dogs. We have been personally and now professionally devastated by CRFS. To learn that it was one of our own that caused it is beyond belief. We know that no words we can say, nothing we can do, will bring the dogs back. But our heartfelt condolences go out to those who have lost their dogs, and we take full responsibility." A wave of people start moving towards the microphones for questions.

"While we are still analyzing the situation to ensure that we provide the appropriate and just response, we have already established the following: A victims' compensation fund has been set up, much like in response to impacts from defective vehicles and food borne illnesses. The fund will be administered by an external board, headed by the well-known reparations lawyer Quincy Meyer, and facilitated by our former CSO, Dr. Neil Franklin, who understands the science exceptionally well. In addition to the fund, we have established an endowment here at the university, so that Dr. Winthrop and her team may continue their work on Addison's, as well as other debilitating canine diseases. We have also made generous donations to the AVMA and the AKC, which have been instrumental in coordinating the sample and information sharing between researchers like Dr. Winthrop and the CDC. And we remain committed to fund the grants we awarded last fall to support the work of other researchers who were dedicated to finding a cause and cure, so they can continue to contribute to our understanding of canine genetics. Many of them have joined us here today. I will turn the podium back over to Dr. Abrams and remain available for questions at the end of this session." He closes his folder, turns and walks to his seat.

A roar from the audience follows Dr. Tennant, but Nathan moves to the podium, quieting the room with his own silence. "Thank you everyone for your time." Nodding towards the audience, "I see that a line is rather lengthy so I ask that you keep to a single question, and if you are a member of the press, please state your affiliation prior to your question. Could I get a few extra microphones up here on stage so our folks up here don't have to play hot potato with the single one?"

"Dr. Winthrop, how long did it take you to make your discovery?"

"Dr. Tennant, how does your company think it can compensate people for such a personal loss? Why didn't Regnum discover this on their own?"

"Dr. Franklin, did this start when you were at Regnum?"

"Dr. Winthrop, has this brought you any closer to finding a cure for Addison's?"

"Dr. Tennant, how can we be sure that you have identified all the contaminated lots?"

"Dr. Winthrop—"

"Dr. Abrams—"

"Dr. Tennant—"

"Dr. Franklin—"

We eventually exhaust the crowd and ourselves, and escape from the stage through a back door, down the hall, to a set of service elevators. The elevators open to a janitorial area on Nathan's floor, and through a maze of hallways we make it to the quiet of the large conference room.

For over two hours we answered questions directed mostly at

Dr. Tennant and me. Mine were a mix of hope and curiosity. His were brutal condemnation. No matter how many ways he was asked if Regnum thought the compensation was fair, he repeated the mantra, "This is why an external committee has been established." I would feel sympathetic towards his personal hell, were it not for the overt threats Regnum had launched at Anna and Neil. I'm sure his Board collectively came up with the plan, but I suspect he gave the final go-ahead.

There is little to do now but go our separate ways. The lawyers finalized all the paperwork before the press conference since no one knew how long we would be at the mercy of the public forum. The Regnum folks, including Neil, follow us upstairs and huddle in a pack near the conference room door, then quickly bid us adieu. Neil does not engage me except for a moment when our eyes meet, and he melts away all concern with the slight smile I know so well.

Like a meerkat standing on tiptoes, Karen searches above the mob and spots me. She smiles and makes her way over.

"Excuse me Dr. Winthrop, you're wanted in Dr. Abrams' office for a few minutes."

I apologize for the leaving a conversation and welcome the excuse to escape from the crowded reception that has been thrown on our behalf. We had just half an hour to decompress before we were on again. Though the reception room is filled with university colleagues, select press, and invited friends, I still walk a tightrope careful of every step, cautious of every word.

We head down the hall to the closed office. Karen opens the door and motions for me to enter, then closes the door behind me.

Dr. Abrams' office is a comfortable blend of requisite university formality: leather chairs and dark wood desk, mixed with an eclectic collection of photographs, memorabilia, and indigenous art.

Nathan worked for a time for the Agency for International Development and his office offers a tour of the world via its encyclopedic collection. The objects are not displayed for admirers, but put to use holding pencils, offering brochures, and decorating the walls and floor.

Neil is studying the photographs on the wall opposite the large window. I am relieved to find my friend. "You're not joining the party?"

"For now I think it best that I keep my distance from you university types. I'm on the losing team, remember? Besides, I was never one for cocktail parties and large social gatherings."

"No, you never were." Though there is so much to say, I am at a loss for words. "So what now? Will I be seeing you anytime in the near future?"

"Probably. At least for a while. They're setting me up with an apartment in DC. I had to agree to spend 75% of my time on the East Coast for the next six months. After that, we will re-negotiate."

"That's a big personal sacrifice leaving your life, your dogs, not to mention having to work for Regnum again."

"As a consultant only." He hesitates but does not break his gaze. "I owe it to the other dog owners who weren't so fortunate as I and have lost their dogs."

"You don't believe you're to blame do you?"

"Not completely, but it did happen when I was in charge, so I'll never feel completely without culpability."

"You had nothing to do with it."

"Maybe I could have stopped it." He walks over to the window and stands looking out. He looks weary, so far from the young man I crashed into almost twenty-five years ago. There is so much I want to ask, but it seems cruel. He turns and smiles slightly, his soul bared.

"Can you tell me what happened?" I ask. "How did we end up here?"

"Sure." He shakes off any emotion. "Were you surprised to see me this morning?"

"Didn't you see the look on my face?"

"I told you you were going to love this." He walks to the front of Nathan's desk and faces me, propping his backside against the edge and crossing his ankles. I meet him half way and stand before him. "Remember how I told you how I knew many of the lab managers."

"Yeah"

"In particular, I knew Kevin Duncan since he first joined Regnum as a researcher in my vaccine lab. He eventually rose to being in charge of quality control for all our feline vaccines."

"So is he the one who did it? How did Regnum figure this out?"

"They didn't. As of Saturday they were still planning to throw me under the bus, especially since you guys told their lawyers there would be no stopping the press conference." He shrugs off my incredulous look. "I had already reached out to a few lab management folks with no success, but when I called Kevin he immediately broke down on the phone. I could hardly get him to calm down enough to explain to me what happened."

"Geez. Poor guy I guess."

"Poor guy my ass. He figured it all out the moment that he was told they were recalling a vaccine produced in his production line because it was connected to CRFS."

"They actually let someone outside of their inner sanctum know about a connection?"

"I think they were testing a few people."

"So he knew all along that there was a problem with the vaccine?"

"Pretty much, but not that it was connected to CRFS. He knew there was some sort of contaminant, as the quality data kept showing anomalies in the length of the vaccine virus, but he let it slide because he was trying to keep production steady and it didn't seem to him to be significant. He felt validated as the months went on and no cats turned up sick. The only good thing he did was limit the output from that run. He restarted the production process with a different cell line, as soon as he could without looking suspicious."

"So it would have gone away in time once the store of the contaminated vaccine was used up?"

"And no one would have ever known what happened."

"And everyone would live in fear of CRFS reoccurring." I sit down in one of Nathan's guest chairs and look up at Neil. "It's unimaginable to think about the long-term ramifications if we hadn't found out what happened."

"You mean you. I had nothing to do with it."

"Don't kid yourself. Without your encouragement and funding, and yes, even denying me the grant, I wouldn't have been open to looking in in this new direction."

He adds, "it was really Anna's observations that were the key."

"Judges will accept that. She deserves most of the credit. But she won't take it. That's never been her style." I sit back. "So what's the deal with Kevin Duncan? Why in the world would he let a contaminated vaccine go forward?"

"He was a promising virologist back in the early nineties and was making a name for himself in stem cell transformation. Then the Bush administration put a screeching halt to his research by banning embryonic stem cell research, and his colleagues in other parts of the world started to rocket past him in discoveries. At the same time he got married, and his wife was not about to let him move to Europe where he would have the freedom to continue his work, but at a much-reduced salary. So instead, he opted for an industry job and worked his way to the head of quality control for feline vaccines."

"Not a bad job."

"No, not bad, but rather boring for a brilliant mind after twenty-some years. In the meantime, his wife left him, and he had a heavy divorce settlement to pay, so when he discovered that there was an extra forty-three-base pair sequence in one of his vaccines, he decided to ignore it rather than risk reducing production levels in his department."

"And risk losing his bonus."

"You got it."

"For someone who doesn't like the gossipy, personal side of things, you seem to know a lot about him."

"He disgorged his life story on our call before I could get him to focus on the facts."

"But that doesn't explain how the extra promoter got there."

"Apparently by accident. He didn't actually know, but there is always a lot of turnover at the technician level, and it's not uncommon to see mistakes like transposing numbers and then pulling the wrong vial of cells that have been transformed with an endogenous virus. There is supposed to be a double verification system, but that apparently didn't happen. He said he would have noticed it but he was too distracted by his personal problems, which is fucking unbelievable."

"I guess that is better than on purpose."

"I suppose."

"So that's it?"

"That's it."

"What about Regnum. How did they find out? When did they find out?"

"That's the really fun part. They had been contacting all the lab directors and managers, and all but Kevin had responded. He was avoiding them when he got a call from me. Guess he knew sooner or later he would have to talk to someone, so he thought it would be better to talk to someone who knew him, who was also no longer up the chain of command. After he told me the whole story and cried on my shoulder about his personal life, I convinced him that it would be better for him to come forward. His career is over, but Regnum might be willing to cut him a deal if he publicly admits to what happened."

"Why would they do that?"

"Apparently he did a very good job of covering his tracks. There are no data that point to the problem with vaccine sequence length. He falsified them. It would be their word against his. The little guy in the laboratory against a giant pharmaceutical company. On Sunday, I contacted Tennant on Kevin's behalf to broker the deal, exchanging his confession for them not pursuing any criminal charges."

"But—"

"I know, they said publicly there will likely be criminal charges —'likely' being the operative word. But they are happy to let this all go away quietly without a lengthy legal action that would never do anything but make them look even more responsible and continue to remind people of their involvement. Regnum was able to confirm by Sunday afternoon that it happened just like you guys figured. A transformed cell line was used, and something went wrong in culture." He grips the desk on both sides of him, containing himself. "They settled with Duncan, and switched to Plan B, cooperating with you guys to make it look like they were part of the solution."

He laughs at the irony and stands up. "So the guy they were going to pin it on ends up being the one who saved their asses." He closes his eyes and shakes his head. "They are still going to pay big time for this, even though if you think about it, it wasn't their fault."

I kind of see his point. But it is disgusting how their first reaction was to circle the wagons and find a scapegoat. I stand and walk across the room to the sofa area where Nathan holds informal meetings. I sit and try to relax. "So, they will continue the grants, including Kendal's. Though I noticed her absence today. Why were the rest of them here?"

"Let it go. It's just a PR thing. They would look bad if they ripped the rug out from under all the recipients that they made such a big deal of just six months ago. It improved Regnum's optics to parade them out today. But her absence is your revenge. I told them as a condition of my taking the facilitator role, she would not be here today and her grant will not continue."

"I still think she—"

"Don't." He stands, facing me, "you know the drill, when they go low . . ." He cracks a smile, "besides, a cat fight is beneath you, beneath all women."

"Actually it would have been a dog fight, but Michelle is right, as are you." We are once again in sync. "Did you know it was the wrong track? Or should I be asking how did you know it was the wrong track? You did know, didn't you?"

"What makes you think I knew? It was a bit more pragmatic than that. All I knew was that it was a crowded field and in some way I guess, I figured that if anyone could find a more creative, or right track, it would be you."

"Why did you think it was the wrong track?"

"I didn't. Like I said, it was a busy track. We received seven proposals with a similar idea and it ultimately wasn't a good idea for you to get caught up in the frenzy.

"I asked you back then how you could approve the funding for her over me."

"I remember. And I answered that the board approved. I am only one vote."

"How was I supposed to read that?"

"Maybe give me the benefit of the doubt?" He comes to me and looks down. "My vote was the only dissenting vote. I came to tell you two weeks later but you weren't too thrilled to see me." His face shows no satisfaction, instead a faint trace of hurt. "I had given notice the day before I came to visit, and wanted to tell you the whole thing."

"Why didn't you—never mind, don't answer."

"You pissed me off."

"I said don't answer." I can be such a jerk. "I'm sorry by the way, for that and because I know it wasn't your office that gave her my idea, it was my technician, Kate." He looks genuinely surprised. "She didn't mean to. She thought Kendal was a collaborator."

"What would make her think that?"

"I told Kate she was an old colleague, when Kendal called to get some cat cell lines. But that was obviously not Kendal's real intention. Odd that for a split second I actually thought she had changed."

"That's amusing."

"It is now I guess. I didn't think it was prudent to openly disparage another scientist—and I use scientist loosely. Kate resigned after she overheard our conversation about Kendal's grant award."

"That's a shame. She seemed to want to be helpful when I visited your lab."

"Yes, too helpful it seems."

"That's why I like Perky, she knows how to be helpful without giving anything away."

"Touché. Wait, why is she here by the way?"

"She resigned when I did. She was asked to stay on for thirty days after I left to transition the new CSO, but packed up her stuff and walked out the door with me. She retired, but has been bored to tears, so she jumped at the chance to be my assistant for the next few months."

"Guess I misjudged her significance."

"And mine."

His brown eyes have always been so disarming and mesmerizing. Enough said. We are good. He offers his hand and lifts me to him. Sinking into his chest, I will hold him close for as long as he lets me.

"I have always loved you," he quietly says.

I close my eyes, taking in the last of this moment. "But?" I ask, not daring to look at him.

"But. You fell in love with him."

We hold close for a fleeting moment longer.

As if to shake off the emotion, he takes a step back and cracks a smile. "Despite all the feelings between us, you never looked at me the way you look at Chris."

He's right. There is no need to acknowledge. But I still love him.

He walks to the window and stands silently for a bit, releasing the past. He picks up his coat and faces me to start the future.

"Where are you going?" I ask.

"To get my soul back."

"Call me?"

"Always."

It is all I can ask of him now. I watch as he puts on his jacket and heads out the door. No reason to look back, only forward. True to form, he leaves me feeling confident and content. I sit back down on the sofa for a bit, grateful for a moment of calm. Grateful for a friend.

"You okay?" Chris asks, as he softly enters the room. "Neil texted me that you were in here."

A smile erupts from deep within me. "We are good. I feel a weight lifted."

"I'm glad. He is an important part of your life."

"As are you," I say as I wrap my arms around and merge with him. I am so blessed to share my life with two amazing men.

Morning.

The ringers on our cell phones are set on silent, our voicemail boxes are full. The reporters who were hoping to get an exclusive have mostly evaporated. The morning is newly serene. I open my eyes and there is a giant warm fuzzball six inches from my face. It's slowly breathing. It's a dog-butt morning.

I am the last out of bed. Chris is standing at the top of the hill, eyes closed, head tipped back, the spring sun warming his face. The field down the hill is barely visible through the trees. The dogs are chasing down their morning prey. He looks up and sees me and gifts me with a broad smile.

I call Anna. "You want to go out tonight and celebrate? We really haven't taken a moment to take this all in, or for me to tell you how grateful I am to have you in my life." I want her to know how I understand that without her, we would have never discovered the truth. "You know you are the one who really deserves all the credit."

"We both—we all—deserve the credit, if we were the kind to take it." She wants to move on. "I'm good. Just having my practice go back to normal is enough for me. I don't think I could have taken much more loss."

"So dinner tonight?"

"How about tomorrow or sometime during the week? I'm meeting Neil tonight to go through our paper again."

"Reeeally? Reviewing our paper over dinner. Now that's interesting."

"Yes, it is." She will not give me the satisfaction of being amused by the intrigue, but I swear there is a smirk in her voice.

He's attractive and straightforward, as is she. I hang up, content at how life sometimes just falls into place.

The house erupts in the exuberance of happy dogs, out of breath, doing a slide along the length of the couch. Chris is beaming. Set on high, metronome tails express sheer joy in saying good morning, reminding me of the human impossibility of simply living in the absolute joy of the moment.

UNEVENTFUL MOMENTS

JUST LIKE THAT it was over. Regnum pulled their vaccines.

No one made a fortune out of finding the cure.

Lawsuits are pending.

The surge of CRFS was easily traced to the episodic release of stocks of the contaminated lot; exacerbated by cat shows and holidays when vaccinations were updated, the constant stream of cats to shelters, and mouser cats versus farm dogs, the classic species rivalry.

There is still a contingent that doesn't trust the science, scientists, or a rational explanation. Having found a way to monetize their campaign, Canine Crusaders continues to promote their theory. There has to be something more, something the public is not being told. There has to be an ulterior motive, a conspiracy. Like anti-vaxxers or climate change deniers, it's an uphill battle when our own media encourages the public to pick and choose what story best fits their position, too often discarding overwhelming scientific evidence. Overwhelming evidence that is the backbone of scientific integrity.

Unremarkable at first, CRFS left an indelible scar that would never fully fade from memory. But the sadness has lifted. No longer are there daily stories about the loss of dogs to a mysterious disease.

The summer has brought a blanket of warmth and endless vignettes on social and other media of finding new dogs to love. The lazy, long days are filled with puppy breath and fuzzy feet. Hearts mend as new bonds form.

Some events in our lives are obviously memorable, like when I was a child watching the mountains recede out the back window of the car that carried me away forever from my childhood home in Colorado, or the summer I discovered I could swim when my sister and I upended our raft in the middle of the deep end, or when no longer sleep-deprived with my three-month-old in my arms I grasped the magnitude of what I held. You know when these moments are happening that they will become unforgettable, placed in that decorated box on a shelf in the brain closet, easily accessed to retrace and remind.

But there are other moments, arguably of equal value, that float in a fog, leaving not so much a memory but more of a thread that runs through the fabric, gently surfacing when you smell the season's first snowfall, you hear the opening riff of a song from your life's timeline, or as you shed the day's weight through the bond with another species. Uneventful but palpable.

Life brings the predictable and unexpected, heartbreak and contentment. We grow up, we grow old, we move on.

The one constant that I know, is that life is better with a dog.

End

REFERENCES

Please note this is not an exhaustive list of sources of information, but a list of references to credit the work of others that directly influenced this novel; to document facts that are not common knowledge; and to give interested readers the information necessary to identify and retrieve those sources. Numerous other sources provided confirmation or validation of generally accepted or known ideas and concepts, for which I am expressly grateful.

American Pets Product Association (2018). *Pet Industry Market Size and Ownership Statistics.* Retrieved from: americanpetproduct-s.org/press_industrytrends.asp

ASPCA (2018). *Shelter Intake and Surender. Pet Statistics.* Retrieved from: aspca.org/animal-homelessness/shelter-intake-and-surrender/pet-statistics

T. Bellumori, T. Famula, D. Bannasch, J. Belanger, and A. Oberbauer (2013). *Prevalence of inherited disorders among mixed-breed and purebred dogs.* AVMA 242 (11), 1549-1555.

A. Boyko, P. Quignon, L. Li, and J. Schoenebeck, …R. Wayne

(2010). *A Simple Genetic Architecture Underlies Morphological Variation in Dogs.* PLoS Biol. Aug 10;8(8)

J. Goldman (2018). *What DNA From Pet Foxes Teaches Us About Dogs—And Humans.* National Geographic, August '18.

International Monetary Fund World Economic Outlook (2018).

D. Irion, A. Schaffer, T. Famula, M. Eggleston, S. Hughes, N. Pedersen (2003). *Analysis of Genetic Variation in 28 Dog Breed Populations With 100 Microsatellite Markers.* J Hered 94(1): 81-87

L. Pray (2008) *Eukaryotic genome complexity.* Nature Education 1(1):96

B. vonHoldt, E. Shuldiner, I. Koch, R. Kartzinel, A. Hogan, L. Brubaker, S. Wanser, D. Stahler, C. Wynne, E. Ostrander, J. Sinsheimer, M. Udell. *Structural variants in genes associated with human Williams-Beuren syndrome underlie stereotypical hypersociability in domestic dogs.* Sci Adv. 2017 Jul 19;3(7)

vonHoldt, B. M., Pollinger, J. P., Lohmueller, K. E., Han, E., Parker, H. G., Quignon, P., … Wayne, R. K. (2010). *Genome-wide SNP and haplotype analyses reveal a rich history underlying dog domestication. Nature, 464*(7290).

E. Ratliff (2011) *Taming the Wild.* National Geographic Magazine March, 2011.

FROM THE AUTHOR

I want to thank all of the wonderful people who helped this book become a reality. I am especially grateful to Wayne Matten, Jane Koska, Dennis Gilbert, and Jolanda Janczewski who served as in various capacities as editors and proof readers, and challenged me on scientific accuracy. To my nephew, Chris Matten, for his amazing talent on the cover art and other illustrations. And to my daughters Andrea who graciously helped with references, and Roxanne whose wordsmithing and attention to detail is remarkable. Thank you to Lynn Franklin, author of the Jeweler's Gemstone Mystery Series, for her encouragement and guidance. Thank you to the countless individuals within the Alliance of Independent Authors for their sage advice.

As this is my first novel, I followed the age old saying, write what you know; and having had a dog by my side since the age of three, I know dogs. But, I do not claim to know everything about dogs. Anyone who has been to my home and been greeted by my unruly poodle mob, knows that I am especially deficient in knowledge of how to train them. So I did a significant amount of research to verify the science and background of the domestic dog world, in the hope that readers can be confident in and enjoy some of what I learned.

I am grateful to all of those who share their lives with dogs. To those who foster, shelter, and adopt dogs; to those who dedicate their profession to the welfare of dogs; and to those who carefully breed pure bred dogs using all the tools available – like genetic testing – to maintain the best we humans have created in these breeds. I respect that there are differing opinions on domestic animal breeding, but I believe we can all agree that no puppy should be born that is not wanted.

I am grateful to those who have helped me understand poodles and poodle breeding, especially Marion Banta, Rhonda Pacchioli, and Teresa Wellman.

I also am thankful for those in the scientific community who continue to push for better diagnoses, treatments, and cures in veterinary and human medicine—epidemiologists, virologists, pathologists, geneticists, and the myriad of other disciplines – I stand solidly in the belief that sound science is critical to a progressive and just world, and I recognize the critical need for institutions, especially those funded by tax payers, responsible for basic and applied research, including the NIH, CDC, USDA, and FDA. They need our support financially and politically.

Finally, thanks to the Ladies Pub Club of Clifton, for keeping me sane – Diane, Felecia, Kari, Laura, Lisa, and Liz – love you guys! And love to Jake, two Abbys, Sofie, Chuck, Chief, Izzy, Spencer, Harley, Cody, Luke, Quentin, Pete, Atholl, Clover, Jake, Bonnie, Wolfie, Tate, Doice, Charlie, and Keter whose faces make up the cover background.

ABOUT THE AUTHOR

As evident in her writing, Dianne is a life-long dog lover, and built the foundation of this book on that love, as well as her education and training as a scientist, and her awe of the complexity and fragility of biological systems.

Dianne has owned poodles and mutts, bred and rescued standard poodles, and is an active supporter of poodle rescue and research in canine genetic diseases. She has provided life-long care for Addison's dogs, and donates a portion of this book's profits to canine Addison's research.

Dianne has a Ph.D. in genetics, having researched the evolutionary genetics of the Canidae and Felidae families, as well as orang utans. She has worked for the past twenty plus years supporting research that underpins science-based policy and regulatory decision making.

She is the co-author of the play *Maid for Dogs*, and producer of the Clifton Dinner Theatre.

She lives in Virginia with her husband, connected almost daily to her two adult daughters, and of course, a house full of dogs.

Thank you for purchasing this book. I greatly appreciate the time you took to read my work.

I welcome reviews at on Amazon at:
https://www.amazon.com/Decoded-Dog-Canine-Disease-Mystery/dp/0578417650

To learn more about me and contact me visit:
dnjanczewski.com — Dianne Janczewski, Author (Facebook)

Dianne

75222211R00183

Made in the USA
Columbia, SC
17 September 2019